PRAISE FOR HELENA HUNTING'S NOVELS

"Hunting is quickly making her way as one of the top
voices in romance!"
—*RT Reviews* on *I Flipping Love You*

"Heartfelt, hilarious, hot, and so much sexiness!"
—*New York Times* bestselling author
Tijan on *Shacking Up*

"Helena [Hunting] is the queen of sexy Rom Coms."
—*USA Today* bestselling author Daisy Prescott

"Fun, sexy, and full of heart . . . explosive chemistry
and lovable characters."
—*USA Today* bestselling author Melanie Harlow

"The perfect combination of sexy, sweet, and hilarious.
You won't want to miss!"
—*New York Times* bestselling author K. Bromberg

"Romance that will leave you breathless."
—*New York Times* bestselling author Tara Sue Me

"Hunting [writes] a love story like no other."
—*New York Times* bestselling author Alice Clayton

"Emotional, sexy, captivating."
—*New York Times* bestselling author Emma Chase

"Sexy, funny, and deliciously naughty story!"
—*USA Today* bestselling author Liv Morris

HANDLE WITH CARE

HELENA HUNTING

St. Martin's Paperbacks

First published in the United States by St. Martin's Paperbacks, an imprint of St. Martin's Publishing Group.

HANDLE WITH CARE

Copyright © 2019 by Helena Hunting.

For information, address St. Martin's Publishing Group, 120 Broadway, New York, NY 10271.

www.stmartins.com

ISBN: 978-1-250-18399-6

Our books may be purchased in bulk for promotional, educational, or business use. Please contact your local bookseller or the Macmillan Corporate and Premium Sales Department at 1-800-221-7945, ext. 5442, or by email at MacmillanSpecialMarkets@macmillan.com.

Printed in the United States of America

St. Martin's Paperbacks edition / September 2019

10 9 8 7 6 5 4 3 2 1

CHAPTER 1

WHAT HAVE I GOTTEN MYSELF INTO?

WREN

I slip onto the empty bar stool beside the lumberjack mountain man who looks like he tried to squeeze himself into a suit two sizes too small. He's intimidatingly broad and thick, with long dark hair that's been pulled up into a haphazard man bun thing. His beard is a hipster's wet dream. His scowl, however, makes him about as approachable as a rabid porcupine. And yet, here I am, sidling up next to him.

He glances at me, eyes bleary and not really tracking. He quickly focuses on his half-empty glass again. Based on the slump of his shoulders and the uncoordinated way he picks up his glass and tips it toward his mouth, I'm guessing he's pretty hammered. I order a sparkling water with a dash of cranberry juice and a lime.

What I could really use is a cup of lavender-mint tea and my bed, but instead, I'm sitting next to a drunk man in his thirties. My life is extra glamorous, obviously. And no, I'm not an escort, but at the moment I feel like my morals are on the same kind of slippery slope.

"Rough day?" I ask, nodding to the bottle that's missing more than half its contents. It was full when he sat down at the bar an hour ago. Yes, I've been watching him the entire time, waiting for an opportunity to make my move. While he's been sitting here, he's turned down two women, one in a dress that could've doubled as a disco ball and the other in a top so low-cut, I could almost see her navel.

"You could say that," he slurs. He props his cheek on his fist, eyes almost slits. I can still make out the vibrant blue hue despite them almost being closed. They move over me, assessing. I'm wearing a conservative black dress with a high neckline and a hem that falls below my knees. Definitely not nearly as provocative as Disco Ball or Navel Lady.

"That solving your problems?" I give him a wry grin and tip my chin in the direction of his bottle of Johnnie.

His gaze swings slowly to the bottle. It gives me a chance to really look at him. Or what I can see of his face under his beard, anyway.

"Nah, but it helps quiet down all the noise up here." He taps his temple and blurts, "My dad died."

I put a hand on his forearm. It feels awkward, and creepy on my part since it's half-genuine, half-contrived comfort. "I'm so sorry."

He glances at my hand, which I quickly remove, and refocuses on his drink. "I should be sorry too, but I think he was mostly an asshole, so the world might be better off without him." He attempts to fill his glass again, but his aim is off, and he pours it on the bar instead. I rush to lift my purse and grab a handful of napkins to mop up the mess.

"I'm drunk," he mumbles.

"Well, I'm thinking that might've been the plan, considering the way you're sucking that bottle back. I'm actually surprised you didn't ask for a straw in the first place. Might be a good idea to throw a spacer in there if you want tomorrow morning to suck less." I push my drink toward him, hoping he doesn't send me packing like he did the other women who approached him earlier.

He narrows his eyes at my glass, suspicious, maybe. "What is that?"

"Cranberry and soda."

"No booze?"

"No booze. Go ahead. You'll thank me in the morning."

He picks up the glass and pauses when it's an inch from his mouth. His eyes crinkle, telling me he's smiling under that beard. "Does that mean Imma wake up with you beside me?"

I cock a brow. "Are you propositioning me?"

"Shit, sorry." He chugs the contents of my glass. "I was joking. Besides, I'm so wasted, I can barely remember my name. Pretty sure I'd be useless in bed tonight. I should stop talkin'." He scrubs a hand over his face and then motions to me. "I wouldn't proposition you."

I'm not sure how to respond. I go with semi-affronted, since it seems like somewhat of an insult. "Good to know."

"Dammit. I mean, I think you might be hot. You look hot. I mean attractive. I think you're pretty." He tips his head to the side and blinks a few times. "You have nice eyes, all four of them are lovely."

This time I laugh—for real—and point to the bottle. "I think you might want to tell your date you're done for the night."

He blows out a breath and nods. "You might be right."

He makes an attempt to stand, but as soon as his feet hit the floor, he stumbles into me and grabs my shoulders to steady himself. "Whoa. Sorry. Yup, I'm definitely drunk." His face is inches from mine, breath smelling strongly of alcohol. Beyond that, I get a whiff of fresh soap and a hint of aftershave. He lets go of my shoulders and takes an unsteady step back. "I don't usually do this." He motions sloppily to the bottle. "Mostly I'm a three drink max guy."

"I think losing your father makes this condonable." I slide off my stool. Despite me being tall for a woman, and wearing heels, he still manages to be close to a head taller than me.

"Yeah, maybe, but I still think I might regret it tomorrow." He's incredibly unsteady, swaying while standing in place. I take the opportunity for what it is and thread my arm through his, leading him away from the bar. "Come on, let's get you to the elevator before you pass out right here."

He nods, then wobbles a bit, like moving his head has set him off balance. "That's probably a good idea."

He leans into me as we weave through the bar and stumbles on the two stairs leading to the foyer. There's no way I'll be able to stop him if he goes down, but I drape one of his huge arms over my shoulder anyway, and slip my own around his waist, guiding him in a mostly straight line to the elevators.

"Which floor are you on?" I ask.

"Penthouse." He drops his arm from my shoulder and flings it out, pointing to the black doors at the end of the hall. "Jesus, I feel like I'm on a boat."

"It's probably all the alcohol sloshing around in your brain." I take his elbow again, helping him stagger the last twenty feet to the dedicated penthouse elevator.

He stares at the keypad for a few seconds, brow pulling into a furrow. "I can't remember the code. It's thumbprint activated though too." He stumbles forward and presses his forehead against the wall, then tries to line up his thumb with the sensor, but his aim is horrendous and he keeps missing.

I settle a hand on his very firm forearm. This man is built like a tank. Or a superhero. For a moment, I reconsider what I'm about to do, but he seems pretty harmless and ridiculously hammered, so he *shouldn't* pose a threat. I'm also trained in self-defense, which would fall under the *by any means necessary* umbrella. "Can I help?"

He rolls his head, eyes slits as they bounce around my face. "Please."

I take his hand between mine. The first thing I notice is how clammy it is. But beyond that, his knuckles are rough, littered with tiny scars and a few scabs, and his nails are jagged.

"Your hands are small," he observes as I line his thumb up with the sensor pad and press down.

"Maybe yours are abnormally big," I reply. They are rather large. Like basketball player hands.

"You know what they say about big hands."

I fight not to roll my eyes, but for a brief moment, I wonder if what's in his pants actually matches the rest of him. And if he's unkempt everywhere, not just on his face. I cut that visual quickly because it makes me want to gag. "And what do they say?"

His eyes crinkle again, and he slaps his own chest. "Something about big hands, big heart."

I bite back my own smile. "Pretty sure you're mixing that up with cold hands, warm heart."

His brow furrows. "There's a good chance."

The elevator doors slide open. He pushes off the wall with some effort and practically tumbles inside. He catches himself on the rail and sags against the wall as I follow him in. I honestly can't believe I'm doing this right now.

He doesn't have to press a button since the elevator only goes to the penthouse floor. As soon as we start moving, he groans and his shoulders curl in. "I don't feel so good."

Please don't let him be sick in here. If there's one thing I can't deal with, it's vomit. "You should sit."

He slides down the wall, massive shoulders rolling forward as he rests his forehead on his knees. "Tomorrow is going to suck."

I stay on the other side of the elevator, in case he tosses his cookies. "Probably."

It's the longest elevator ride in the history of the world. Or at least it feels that way, mostly because I'm terrified he's going to yak. Thankfully, we make it to the penthouse floor incident-free. On the down side, now that he's in a sitting position, getting him to stand again is a challenge. I have to press the open door button three times before I can finally coax him to his feet.

In the time between leaving the bar and making it to the penthouse floor, the effects of the alcohol seem to have compounded. He's beyond sloppy, using the wall and me for support as we make our way to his door. There are two penthouse apartments up here. One on either side of the foyer.

He leans against the doorjamb, once again fighting to find the coordination to get his thumb to the sensor pad. I don't ask if he needs my assistance this time since it's quite clear he does. Once again I take his clammy hand in mine.

"Your hands are really soft," he mumbles.

"Thanks."

The pad flashes green, and I turn the handle. "Okay, here we go. Home sweet home."

"This isn't my home," he slurs. "My cousin's family owns this building. I'm crashing here until I can get the fuck out of New York."

I scan the penthouse. It an eclectic combination of odd art and modern furniture, like two different tastes crashed together and this is the result. Aside from that, it's clean to the point of looking almost like a show home.

The only sign that someone is staying here is the lone coffee cup on the table in the living room and the blanket lolling like a tongue over the edge of the couch. I'm still standing in the doorway while he sways unsteadily.

He tries to shove his hand in his pants pocket, but all he succeeds in doing is setting himself off-balance. He nearly stumbles into the wall.

"Thanks for your help," he says.

He's back in his penthouse, which means my job is technically done. However, I'm worried he's going to hurt himself, or worse, asphyxiate on his own vomit in the middle of the night, and I'll be the one catching heat if that happens. I'll also feel bad if something happens to him. I blow out a breath, annoyed that this is how my night is ending.

I heave his arm over my shoulder and slip mine around his waist again, leading him through the living room toward what seems to be the kitchen. There's a sheet of paper on the island, but otherwise it's spotless.

"What're you doing?" he asks.

We pause when we reach the threshold. "Which way is your bedroom?"

He looks slowly from right to left. "Not that way." He points to the kitchen. It's very state of the art.

I guide him in the opposite direction down the hall, until he stumbles through a doorway, into a large but simply furnished bedroom. Once we reach the edge of the bed, he drops his arm, spins around—it's drunkenly graceful—and falls back on the bed, arms spread wide as if he's planning on making snow angels. "The room is spinning."

"Would you like me to get you a glass of water and possibly a painkiller for the headache you'll likely have in the morning?" I'm already heading for the bathroom.

"Might be a good idea," he mumbles.

I find a glass on the edge of bathroom vanity—which is clean, apart from a brand new toothbrush and tube of toothpaste. I run the tap, wishing I had a plastic tumbler, because I'm not sure he's in any state to deal with breakable objects. I check the medicine cabinet, find the pills I need, shake out two tablets, and return to the bedroom.

He's right where I left him; sprawled out faceup on a massive king-size bed, legs hanging off the end, one shoe on the floor beside him. I cross over and set the water and the pills on the nightstand.

I make a quick trip back to the bathroom and grab the empty wastebasket from beside the toilet in case his night is a lot rougher than he expects.

I tap his knee, crossing my fingers he'll be easy to rouse. "Hey, I have painkillers for you."

He makes a noise, but doesn't move otherwise.

I tap his knee again. "Lincoln, you need to wake up long enough to take these." I cringe. I called him by name, and he didn't offer it to me while we were down at the bar. Here's hoping he's too drunk to notice or re-member. His name is Lincoln Moorehead, heir to the

Moorehead Media fortune and all the crap that comes with it. And there's a lot of it.

One eye becomes a slit. "Every time I open my eyes, the room starts spinning again."

"If you drink this and take these, it might help." I hold up the glass of water and the pills.

"'Kay." It takes three tries for him to sit up. He attempts to pick the pills up out of my palm, but keeps missing my hand.

"Just open your mouth."

He lifts his head. "How do I know you're not trying to roofie me?"

I hold up the tablet in front of his face. "They don't say roofie, so you're safe."

He tries to focus on the pill and then my face. I have my doubts he's successful at either.

His tongue peeks out to drag across his bottom lip. "The cameras in the hall will catch you if you steal my wallet."

I laugh at that. "I'm not going to steal your wallet, I'm going to put you to bed."

"Hmm." He nods slowly and opens his mouth.

I drop the pills on his tongue and hand him the glass, which he drains in three long swallows. "Would you like me to refill that?"

"That'd be nice." He holds out the glass, but when I try to pull away, he covers my hands with his. His shockingly blue eyes meet mine, and for a moment they're clear and compelling. Despite how out of it he is, and how much he resembles a mountain man, or maybe because of it, I have a hard time looking away. "I really wish I wasn't this messed up. You smell nice. I bet your hair is pretty when it's not pulled up like that." He flops a hand toward my bun. "Not that it's not pretty like that, but I bet if you took it down, it would be wavy and soft. The kind of hair you want to bury your face in and run your fingers through." He exhales a long breath. "I haven't had sex in a really long time, but I feel like I would have zero finesse if I tried right now."

I smile and turn away. In the time it takes for me to refill his glass, he's managed to get one arm out of his suit jacket. He's made it most of the way onto the bed, feet still hanging off the end, but he's on his back, which is not ideal.

I set the glass on his nightstand, along with a second set of painkillers, which I'm assuming he'll need in the morning, and give him another nudge. "Hey."

This time I get nothing in the way of a response. I poke him twice more, but still nothing. He can't sleep on his back with how drunk he is. He needs to be on his side or his stomach with a wastebasket close by.

I can't in good conscience leave him like this. My options are limited. I shake my head as I kick off my shoes and climb up onto the bed with him. This is not at all what I expected to be doing when I brought him back up here.

I stare down at his sleeping form. His lips are parted, they're nice lips, full and plump, even though they're mostly obscured by his overgrown beard. His hair has started to unravel from its man bun, wisps hanging in his face. He has long lashes, really long actually, and they're thick and dark, the kind women pay a lot of money for. His nose is straight and his cheekbones— what I can see of them—are high. With a haircut, a beard trim or complete shave, and a new suit that actually fits, I can imagine how refined he'll look. More like a Moorehead than a mountain man lumberjack. I shake my head. "I need you to roll onto your side, please," I say loudly.

Nothing. Not even a grunt.

I pull on his shoulder, but he's dead weight. Leaning over him, I make a fist and give him a light jab approximately where his kidney is. "Lincoln, roll over."

And roll he does, knocking me down and turning over so he's right on top of me. We're face-to-face. Good God, he's heavy. His bones must be made of lead. He shifts, one leg coming over both of mine. I push at his knee, but his arm swings out and he wraps himself around me on a low groan, pinning my arm to my side. He's like a giant human blanket.

"How did this become my life?" I say to the ceiling, because the man lying on top of me is apparently out cold.

I try to wriggle free, I even yell his name a bunch of time before I give up and wait for him to roll off me. And while I wait for that to happen, I replay the conversation with his mother, Gwendolyn Moorehead, that took place forty-eight hours ago and put me in this awkward position underneath her drunk son.

I'd been standing in Fredrick's office, still digesting the fact that he was dead. It was shocking that a massive heart attack had taken him, since he was always so healthy and full of life.

Gwendolyn, his wife—now a widow—stood stoic behind his desk, papers stacked neatly in the center.

"I'm so very for your loss, Gwendolyn. If there's anything I can do. Whatever you need." The words poured out, typical condolences, but sincerely meant because I couldn't imagine how my mother and I would feel if we lost my father.

Gwendolyn's fingers danced at her throat as she cleared it. "Thank you," she whispered brokenly and dabbed at her eyes. "I appreciate your kindness, Wren."

"Let me know what you want me to handle, and I'll take care of it."

She took a deep breath, composing herself before she lifted her gaze to mine. "I need your help."

"Of course, what can I do?"

"My oldest son, Lincoln, will be returning to New York for the funeral, and he'll be staying to help run the company."

A hot feeling crept up my spine. I'd heard very little about Lincoln. Everything from Armstrong's mouth was scathing, Fredrick's passing references had been with fondness, and my interactions with Gwendolyn had been minimal as it was Fredrick himself who hired me, so this was first I've heard of Lincoln through her. "I see. And how can I help with that?" I could only imagine how difficult Armstrong would be if he had to share the attention with someone else, particularly his brother.

"Transitioning Lincoln." Gwendolyn rounded her desk. "You've managed to turn around Armstrong's reputation in the media during the time you've been here. I know it hasn't been easy, and Armstrong can be difficult to manage."

Difficult to manage is the understatement of the entire century where Armstrong is concerned. He's a cocksucker of epic proportions. He's also a misogynistic, narcissistic bastard that I've had to deal with for the past eight months on a nearly daily basis—sometimes even on weekends.

My job as his "handler" has been to reshape his horrendous reputation after his involvement in several scandalous events became very public. It wasn't a job I necessarily wanted, and I was prepared to politely reject the offer, but my mother asked me to take the position as a favor to her since she's a friend of Gwendolyn.

Beyond that, my relationship with my mother has been strained for the past decade. When I was a teenager, I discovered information that changed our relationship forever. Taking the job at Moorehead was in part, my way of trying to help repair our fractured bond. The financial compensation, which was ridiculously high, also didn't hurt. Besides, Gwendolyn is on nearly every single charitable foundation committee in the city, and since that's where my interests lie, it seemed like a smart career move.

"Since you're already working with Armstrong and things seem to be settled there for the most part, I felt it would make sense to keep you on here at Moorehead to work with Lincoln. He's been away from civilized society for several years. He's nothing like his brother, very altruistic and focused on his job, rather than recreational pursuits, so he should be easier to manage."

I fought a scoff at the last bit, since "recreational pursuits" was a reference to the fact that Armstrong couldn't seem to keep his pants zipped when it came to women.

Gwendolyn pushed a set of papers toward me. "It would only be for another six months. And of course, your salary would reflect the double work load, since you'll still have to maintain Armstrong in some capacity while you assist Lincoln in transitioning into his role here."

"I'm sorry, what—"

Gwendolyn pulled me into an awkward hug, holding onto my shoulders when she stepped back. Her eyes were glassy and red-rimmed. "You have no idea how much I appreciate your willingness to take this on. As soon as your contract is fulfilled, you have my word that I'll give you a glowing recommendation to whichever organization you'd like. Your mother told me you're interested in starting your own foundation. I'll certainly help you in any way I'm able if you'll stay on a little longer for me." She dabbed at the corner of her eyes and sniffed, then tapped the papers on the desk. "I already have an agreement ready and an NDA, of course. Everything is tabbed for signing."

I'm pulled back into the present when Lincoln shifts and one of his huge hands slides up my side and lands on my breast. At the same time, he pushes his nose against my neck, beard tickling my collarbone. He mutters something unintelligible against my skin.

I'm momentarily frozen in shock. Under any other circumstances, I would knee him in the balls. However, he's not conscious or even semi-aware that he's fondling me. Thankfully, now that he's moved, I have some wiggle room.

I elbow him in the ribs, which probably hurts me more than it does him. At least it gets him to move away enough that I can slip out from under him. I roll off the bed and pop back up, smoothing out my now-wrinkled dress. My stupid nipples are perky, thanks to the attention the right one just got. Probably because it's the most action I've seen since I started working for the Mooreheads eight months ago.

I hit the lights on the way out of the bedroom, pause in the kitchen to grab a glass of water and check out the sheet of paper on the counter. It's a list of important details regarding the penthouse, including the entry code. I nab my purse, snap a pic, and head for the elevators.

I have a feeling this is going to be a long six months.

CHAPTER 2

STILL SCREWING ME, EVEN FROM THE GRAVE

LINCOLN

It feels like a million tiny elves are trying to hammer their way out of my skull. Fucking scotch whiskey hybrids. Fucking stupid funeral. So much inconvenience.

That sounds assholey, even in my head.

That's what being near my family does to me; it turns me into one of them.

My alarm goes off for the hundredth time. And my phone rings. Again.

I've been hitting snooze and ignoring calls since seven.

I peek out from under my pillow to check the clock. The slice of light filtering through the curtains makes it feel like someone is trying to stab out my eyeballs with sunbeams. I'm really damn hungover.

It's approaching eight thirty, which incidentally is when I'm supposed to be at Moorehead Media for a mandatory meeting. We're reviewing my father's will and a bunch of other BS I have no interest in dealing with.

I haven't set foot in that office since I graduated from Harvard. My father wanted me to come work with him. Since the only thing he'd done for me was put me through school, I didn't feel any kind of obligation to follow in his footsteps. Especially since his footsteps were full of infidelity and absentee parenting.

Considering Moorehead is a good thirty-minute cab ride away with the rush-hour traffic, I'm already going to be half an hour late, and that's if I roll out of bed and into a cab. Based on the way my head feels, it's going to take me a while to get moving.

I groan as my phone rings again. This is the one and only time I'm going to grace the brainless drones at Moorehead with my presence. I don't get why I can't be a silent partner. I'd sell my shares if it meant getting away from my useless, bag-of-dicks family.

I'm hoping we can get through whatever paperwork is necessary quickly, so I can get on a plane and out of New York by the end of the week. I've only been here for forty-eight hours, and I already want to commit seven different kinds of murder.

Blinking away the knives in my eyeballs, I note the tumbler of water and two painkillers on the nightstand. I must've been on the ball when I dragged myself up here from the bar. Although I have zero memory of that.

It's not even my place. My cousin's family owns the building, and he's away for the next few months, so he gave me the go-ahead to stay in his penthouse. He flew in yesterday morning for the funeral and then took a flight out last night. I wish I'd had the option to go with him. It would be a lot better than being here.

I sit up and throw my legs over the edge of the bed, planting my feet on the floor. I'm still wearing one shoe.

The room spins, and my stomach twists then somer-saults. It takes several long moments for the nausea to pass. Once it does, I take the painkillers and down the water.

My phone rings for the millionth time. I stab at the screen and put it on speaker. "What?"

Silence follows—a long silence—before a woman fi-nally answers. "Your car is waiting for you, Mr. Moore-head, and has been for forty-five minutes."

"Well, it's gonna have to wait a little longer." I end the call and scrub a hand over my face. I feel like gar-bage. My mouth tastes like I ate from a sewer, and my head is full of cotton. I also need to take a leak. And possibly vomit. Hopefully not at the same time.

I drag myself to the bathroom, catching my reflection in the mirror—yeah, I've seen better days. It appears I slept fully dressed. I'm a mess. I strip out of my rumpled suit and get in the shower, where I puke. And puke some more. I manage to wash myself, sort of, and towel off.

I find a pair of discarded jeans and a T-shirt draped over the lounger thing in the corner of the bedroom and struggle into those. I have to lie down for five min-utes when the room starts spinning and the post-booze sweats hit.

Eventually I sit up, but it takes another five minutes of breathing through the waves of nausea before I can do anything else, like stand. I gather my hair up in a half-assed man bun—nope couldn't be bothered to get it cut or shave my beard for the funeral—brush my teeth and almost throw up again thanks to the strong mint flavor.

I pocket my phone and check to make sure I have my wallet on my way out the door. As an afterthought, I go back for the trashcan I had the foresight to put beside my bed and head for the elevator. I almost hurl again on the way down.

It's nine o'clock by the time I get in the car. The subway is out based on the way my stomach is rolling. We sit in traffic for what I predicted to be a half hour, and the entire time my phone rings. But I don't answer. I'm late. The world isn't going to end.

I try to piece together last night. The funeral was in the afternoon. What a shitshow. Hundreds of people showed up to pay their respects. From what I observed, it was more of an opportunity to network and figure out what was going to happen to Moorehead Media. Surprisingly, there didn't seem to be a whole pile of his mistresses in attendance.

My mother sat in the front pew, dabbing her dry eyes, possibly to make it look like she was crying. She hasn't slept in the same room as my father since I was a child, so any tears she sheds will likely result from knowing not all the money will go to her. My jackoff younger brother, Armstrong, sat beside her, probably scouting the room for his next conquest.

He got married a while back. For all of twelve hours. He was caught being blown by one of the guests, and it had been broadcast to the entire reception hall. Idiot. Thankfully I missed that event, and his ex-wife, if twelve hours of marriage even warrants that title, is now engaged to my cousin Lexington. It's a bit like a soap opera, but they seem happy together, and Armstrong seems miserable and clueless as usual, so all is right with the world there.

Except not for me, because now I have to deal with my brother for the third time in three days. Being forced to go to the funeral for a father whose only real role in my life was to foot the bill for my Ivy League education, and now this stupid meeting for a company I have no interest in, led me to the bar last night.

I remember the bottle of Walker, ignoring two flashy women who looked like they had an agenda, and then possibly getting shot down by a woman who may have been hot, or the booze goggles had been thick. Who knows? I hug the garbage can and close my eyes, breathing through the urge to hurl.

Memories return in sporadic flashes. Getting off my stool and nearly falling over. A pair of black heels, not Louboutins either since they were missing the red sole women usually favor. Long legs. A black dress. Conservative but still feminine and sexy.

Did I bring a woman up to the penthouse? My pants were already undone this morning, so it's possible. It would've been a train wreck of an experience, though. I doubt I had the coordination or the ability to string together a coherent sentence, let alone manage sex, considering how foggy everything is. I check my wallet, all my cards are in there and so is my cash, so I didn't get taken for a ride.

I put my phone on silent and close my eyes. I spend the rest of the trip half asleep. The worst of the nausea seems to have passed. At least until the stench of New York exhaust and sewers assault me as the driver opens my door.

I lose my protective hold on my garbage can as I enter the building, and it clatters to the floor. A huge clang echoes off the marble everything, bringing back the throb in my head. It also startles the receptionist behind her desk and the security guard.

"That was loud," I say to no one in particular.

The security guard takes a cautious step forward. "I'll need to see some identification, sir." He's older, probably in his seventies, well past retirement. His name-tag reads BOB. I wonder how many years he's wasted here, doing this thankless job in the pit of my family's personal merry-go-round of hell. Bob looks familiar, but his name is common, and it's probably because any-one who's spent their entire life in a place like this has the same pale, washed-out look about them, along with thinning, graying hair.

"What?"

"Your identification, sir." He looks me up and down, as if I don't belong here. Which I don't. I'm wearing a pair of wrinkled, beat-up jeans and an equally wrinkled T-shirt. My running shoes have holes where my socked toe pokes through.

I motion to my face. "Imagine me without the beard, except thirty years older." Apart from eye and hair color, I look like my father, which is the biggest genetic insult in the world. My father has the face of a cheat and a liar, because he is one. *Was* one.

At his frown, I sigh. "I'm the son of the prick who used to run this place and the brother of the one who does now."

The furrow in his eyebrows deepens and then sud-denly lifts. "Lincoln?"

"Yeah. I'm late for a meeting, pretty sure there's a state of emergency over it considering the number of times my phone has rang this morning." I wish I'd worn a baseball cap. The lights in here are making my head pound and my stomach roll again.

"I haven't seen you in more than a decade. I'm so sorry about your father."

"I'm not. He was an awful human being. The world's a better place without him."

He seems shocked for a moment, eyes darting around

to make sure no one else is listening, but every single person within earshot suddenly looks away, indicating my less-than-appropriate comment regarding my father's death has been heard by everyone.

Whatever. It's the truth, and they all know it. "Anyway, I gotta head to the seventh circle of hell, whatever floor that's on."

"I'll get your pass, Mr. Moorehead."

"It's just Linc, and thanks."

A pass magically appears, and Bob presses the button because clearly I'm incapable of managing simple tasks, either that or he's treating me like this because he believes it's necessary to keep his job. Either way, it irks me. Everything about being here does that, though.

The elevator arrives and I get in, staring at the buttons, not sure where exactly the seventh circle of hell is. Thankfully Bob reaches inside, presses the button for the twenty-seventh floor, gives me a somber nod, and steps out of the elevator.

The doors slide closed, and as soon as the elevator starts to move, I wish I still had my garbage can. Thankfully, no one gets on and the trip is blissfully quick, albeit queasy. The twenty-seventh floor of Moorehead Media is a boring, sterile office space. A blond woman with lipstick the color of death wears a fake smile as I step out of the elevator and approach her desk.

Her eyes move over me, that smile wavering, but she manages to keep it in place, which is commendable. "How can I help you, Mr. . . ." She lets the question hang.

"I'm late for a meeting."

She blinks a few times. She has to be wearing fake lashes. No one's eyelashes are that thick or long if they're not fake. "And who do you have a meeting with, Mr. . . ." Again she waits for me to introduce myself.

"I have no idea. I assume it's with whatever pompous douches sit around a conference table and circle jerk each other."

Her right eye twitches, and she blinks about fifty times in a row.

This is fun, a lot more fun than the meeting I'm going to have to sit through. Hopefully they've started without me. I'm late enough that there's a possibility it'll be over by the time I arrive and all I'll have to do is sign a few papers. Then maybe I can book a flight out of this concrete hellhole.

Her right hand moves slowly across the desk. I bet she thinks I'm some whack job who managed to get by security.

"I wouldn't do that if I were you." I nod to her hand creeping toward the phone like a five-legged spider.

She raises it in the air. "Please don't hurt me. You can have whatever money I have in my purse."

I bark out a laugh that makes me sound unhinged, although this building will do that to a person. "I'm Lincoln Moorehead, son of the guy who used to run this nightmare. If you'd be so kind as to point me in the direction of my shit stick of a brother and his team of lemmings, that'd be great."

"Oh my God. Mr. Moorehead. I didn't know you were on your way up. Security usually calls." The phone on her desk rings.

"That might be security now. Go ahead and answer it. I can wait."

I lean on the desk while she picks up the phone with her perfectly manicured nails, hand shaking. I almost feel bad, but then she's one of my father's drones, so I get over it pretty quickly.

"Moorehead Media, Lulu speaking, how may I help

you?" She's silent for a moment. "Yes. He has arrived. Thank you, Bob." She hangs up the phone and gives me a wide-eyed, terrified smile. "I'm so sorry, Mr. Moorehead."

I wave her off. "It's fine. The longer this takes, the less time I'll have to spend in my brother's presence, which means I might be able to refrain from punching him out. Again."

She seems like she's trying to figure out if I'm kidding. I'm not.

Eventually she stands and comes out from behind the safety of her desk. "I'll show you to the conference room, then."

"If you must." I study the art on the wall behind her desk. It's a picture of a tree without any leaves. Kind of depressing, like this office. She walks briskly down the hall, and I fall into step beside her, rather than follow along behind. We pass glass-walled offices with pristine desks on our way to the conference room. I wonder if working here feels a lot like an upscale version of prison.

I spot my brother's blond hair and tailored suit. He's pacing while a woman stands with her arms crossed over her chest about ten feet away from him, gesturing stiffly.

The clip of Lulu's heels on the hardwood draws their attention. My brother spins around, throwing his hands in the air and shouts, "It's about time! Where the hell have you been?"

"Sleeping off a hangover and avoiding you."

"Must be nice to have no responsibilities and no one to answer to. There's a room full of people waiting in there for your sorry ass to show up." Armstrong flails dramatically and wrinkles his nose. "What are you wearing?"

"Clothes. Need me to go home and change into something that costs more than most people's monthly rent so I can fit in better?"

I glance at the woman beside him. Her left cheek tics the tiniest bit, but otherwise her expression remains placid.

Armstrong ignores the comment and runs a hand down his tie, his attention shifting to Lulu. His eyes rake over her. "Lulu, you lo—"

The woman behind him clears her throat, and Armstrong jumps, almost as if he's been tasered.

I give Lulu what I hope is a polite, non-leery smile. "Thank you for your assistance, Lulu."

"You're welcome, Mr. Moorehead." She nods at me and then at Armstrong, repeating herself. "Mr. Moorehead." She does an about-face and strides down the hall like her shoes are on fire.

Armstrong watches her as if she's a steak he'd like to stab with a fork. Or his needle dick.

"You're a creepy bastard, you know that, right?" I tell him.

He frowns. I'm fairly certain he's been getting Botox injections based on the lack of movement in his forehead. Must be one of his mother-son bonding experiences. "You look like you're homeless."

"That's all you've got?" Making fun of him won't even be enjoyable if this is the best he can do.

He opens his mouth to speak, but is cut off by the woman still hovering behind him. "Is it possible to put the sibling squabble on hold until after the meeting is over? We've already waited more than an hour and a half for your arrival, Mr. Moorehead."

I finally give her my attention because it's clearly

me she's addressing. Her voice is familiar for some reason—soft and smoky, but firm and authoritative. My lippy response gets stuck somewhere between my brain and my mouth as I finally take her in.

Her skin is creamy and pale for mid-July in New York, possibly because she spends every waking moment trapped in this human fishbowl. Her eyes are a striking shade of gray, ringed with navy, contrasting beautifully with her chestnut hair, which seems a little dark for her complexion. Her gray dress should be boring, but the way it complements her eyes and hugs every luscious curve takes it from simple to exquisite. Her heels are a vibrant blue and pointy enough that she could take out an eye with one if she were so inclined, and judging from the look on her face, she might be very inclined right about now.

"You must be—"

I'm cut off mid-sentence by my grandmother, which is probably a good thing considering I was about to say something regrettable. "Lincoln! Where in the name of all that is holy have you been? And what are you wearing?"

"I was sleeping off the scotch. And these are called blue jeans and this is called a T-shirt, G-mom." I motion to my attire.

Penelope Moorehead narrows her eyes, grabs me by the ear, and drags me across the hall into an empty office, slamming the door behind me.

As soon as she lets go, I rub my ear. "You know that's considered workplace harassment."

She crosses her arms. "Do not sass me, Lincoln Alexander Moorehead. And do not call me G-mom in front of the goddamn staff. How am I going to keep my battle-axe reputation with you shouting nicknames that make me sound like a second-rate rap star?"

"Remember when you cross-stitched me a hoodie for my tenth birthday?" I bite back a grin, because getting G-mom riled up has always one of my favorite pastimes, and that hasn't changed at all, even if a lot of other things have.

"This is not the time for jokes, Lincoln. And this is definitely not the time to show everyone how uninvested you are in this company. Your father passed away, show some decorum. Despite your tumultuous relationship with your parents, you need to put aside your grudges today and act like the Harvard MBA graduate that you are. Not some know-it-all who makes everyone around them feel like crap because you think what you do is better than what everyone else does."

And just like that, my g-mom takes me down a peg or five. She lost her son. I need to remember that just because I didn't have a relationship with him or my mother, it doesn't mean it was the same for everyone else. G-mom has always been more of a parent to me than either of the people who brought me into this world. And because of that, she's one of the few people in my family that I genuinely love and respect. So I dial back the douche.

I drop my head, the ache behind my temples flaring again, and rub the back of my neck. "I'm sorry. I know this is hard for you."

"No one ever expects their children to go before them." She sighs and paces the room, then comes to a stop in front of me, her spine straight, shoulders rolled back, expression stoic.

She's barely five feet tall, but she's a force of nature.

She was the brain behind this entire network. My grandfather might've had the name, but the woman in front of me has always pulled everyone's puppet strings. And I love her for it.

"Look, Linc, I know this is the last place you want be. I get it. I understand that you love helping people and that being a project manager for building homes and helping communities in developing countries, while not the best for your financial well-being, is certainly noble. I'm also aware it's a big f-you to your parents and all the money they shelled out for your education, and I applaud your moral standing." She taps her lips and shakes her head. "I can only imagine how being here makes you feel. I realize your relationship with your father was strained, but he was not a bad man. I don't know what kind of karmic bomb your parents managed to set off when they created your brother." She paces around the room, coming to stop in front of me. "But Armstrong cannot handle this company on his own. He will sink it inside of six months."

She has a point. Armstrong has never been good at following directions, although neither have I. The difference is, Armstrong is a narcissistic egomaniac who abuses any shred of power he has. I just don't like bending over for the man. "So what does that mean?"

"I need your help."

This time when my stomach flips, it's not because of the nausea. "Help how? What's the plan if you're not putting Armstrong in charge?"

"I need you to stay in New York for a while and help manage things." It's less request and more order.

"I don't know anything about this company."

She leans on the edge of the desk, fingers tapping

restlessly. "You have a Master's in Business Adminis-
tration from the best school in the country. You understand economics and the bottom line. The rest you can
be taught."

"I don't want to be here. I can't stay here. I'll go nuts."
Panic hits. It feels like the walls are closing in.

"I didn't expect your father to go so soon. I thought I
had time to prepare for this. Years to train someone else
to takeover. I had hoped Armstrong would eventually
come around, but he lacks any kind of moral compass or
ability to take direction. He's not capable of managing
his own damn grocery list, let alone this company. It's
temporary, Lincoln."

I run a hand through my hair, and then remember it's
in a bun. "This isn't making my hangover any better,
G-mom."

She rubs her own temples. "It's not making mine
any better either. I need your help, Lincoln. We can't
have your misogynistic, self-absorbed, sycophant of
a brother running this company without someone to
keep him from going off the rails. He can't have that
much power." She crosses the room, pulls out a bottle
of scotch and pours two glasses. "Give me six months."

She passes me the glass. It'll either ease the shakes or
make me puke. I feel both light-headed and nauseous.
Likely because my grandmother, who I love dearly and
cannot say no to, is asking me to do the one thing I des-
perately don't want to. Also, she just lost her son, and I'd
be a seriously horrible grandson if I said no.

"Three months."

"That's not enough time."

"New York makes me miserable, and I'm in the middle
of a project in Guatemala. I can't abandon my team."

"You have an amazing staff who can handle it for a few months without you. Send your cousin Griffin to stand in for you for a few weeks if you need to. I know he loves these kinds of projects like you do."

"I don't know if he's available." Although I can pretty much guarantee he'd jump at the chance if he's able. He and I worked on a project together last year in a small village in China.

"I lost my only child, Linc. I know Fredrick made some poor decisions, but he also made you. Give this old lady something to keep going for. Don't let this company and our family's legacy go down in the hands of your brother."

I close my eyes because I can't see that look on her face. It's her sweet grandma look. It's such crap, she's pulling on my heartstrings on purpose. I crack a lid. "You're hitting below the belt."

"I know." She nods, then raises a brow. "Is it working?"

I sigh. Resigned. I can rearrange the Guatemala schedule and get someone to help with project management. It's not ideal, but it's possible. "Fine. But six months and that is it. I'm on a plane out of here as soon as the time comes."

"Deal." She clinks her glass against mine, and we both swallow the scotch in one gulp.

I don't vomit right away, so that's a plus.

She takes both glasses and sets them in the sink. "Are you ready to deal with Armstrong now?"

"Is anyone ever?"

She pats me on the cheek. "It's as if you were gifted with every single good trait your parents have combined, and all the leftover crap went to your brother. Even with this Fabio business you have going on with your hair, and this hippie attire, you still manage to be handsome. It's good he didn't have to grow up in your shadow." She opens the door. "Get ready for the temper tantrum of the century."

CHAPTER 3
G-MOM ATTACK

LINCOLN

I haven't been paying attention to the meeting. Mostly it's my father's lawyer blathering on about division of assets and company BS while my mother, grandmother, and brother ask questions I don't care about. Instead of listening, I've been staring at the woman across the table—the only non-family member apart from my father's lawyer—seated next to my mouthbreather brother, trying to figure out what her deal is.

I was drunk out of my mind last night, but I still remember her. Vaguely. At least I'm pretty sure I do. I just can't piece together how she fits into my night. Or what exactly her role is here. As I openly stare—I don't even look away when she lifts those mesmerizing gray eyes and catches me—fragments of last night filter through my brain in a disjointed, foggy mess.

I recall the woman passing me a pale pink drink, and later she was in the elevator with me? Did she drug me? Was I so drunk I can't remember? My hangover is pretty damn bad this morning, so it's possible. I have a hazy recollection of her bringing me a glass of water and some painkillers, which means she was in the penthouse with me.

I don't think there's any way I could've had sex with her. But I remember a boob and being pressed against a soft body, or maybe that was a dream. I'm unsure.

What I am sure of is that this woman, whom I don't know, may be familiar with my brother in ways I find offensive. He's extra jumpy around her, which could mean a variety of things; she could be fondling his balls under the table—which is unlikely since I can see both of her hands, although feet are a thing. Conversely, maybe he's had sex with her and she regrets it, as most women would tend to, or it's possible he's made a pass at her and she's rejected him, aggressively.

All options irritate me for very different reasons.

I'm startled out of my thoughts when my brother jumps up and shouts a bunch of profane nonsense, hands flailing like he's trying to swim on land, or approximate the chicken dance while on an LSD trip. He knocks over a cup of coffee, which spills into my fixation's lap.

"You can't do this! It's absolutely ludicrous!" Armstrong yells, apparently unconcerned that he's potentially burned his most recent sexual harassment case.

I look around the table, trying to piece together what I missed.

"I'm sorry, Armstrong. I know this is a shock, but we feel it's in the company's best interest to put Lincoln at the helm during this transitional stage," G-mom says firmly.

At the helm? I look to G-mom, who's busy not looking at me.

Armstrong jabs at finger at himself. "But I'm the one who's put in all the time here! I deserve to run the company! Lincoln doesn't know the first thing about Moore-head. All he knows how to do is dig wells and forage for food in the wilderness. How are those valuable assets here?" He turns his attention to our mother. "Did you know about this? How can you let this happen? Look at him. How can *that* be the face of our company? He looks like he crawled out of a gutter and mugged a twenty-year-old college kid while on a bender. How is this better for our bottom line?"

My mother clasps her hands in front of her. "I'm sorry, Armstrong, but this decision wasn't mine to make. I know this is hard for you, but your grandmother and fath—"

Armstrong stomps his foot, exactly as a toddler would. "The company is mine! Lincoln can't have it!"

I raise a hand, half to quiet my brother and also to find out what the freaking deal is. "Whoa, let's back this bus up. Can someone explain what's going on?"

"You've been appointed as the CEO of Moore-head Media, according to the will," Christophe—no *R*, because that would make it far too pedestrian a name—my father's lawyer says.

I'm working on trying to remain calm as I address my grandmother. "You didn't say anything about me be-ing CEO. You said you needed my help."

"Running the company, yes," she says through a practiced, stiff smile.

It's her warning face, but seriously, when she said she needed my help for a few months, I figured it meant I'd be keeping Armstrong in line while she sorted out who was going to take over the company, which I realize now was a stupid assumption.

"I didn't think that meant CEO. How am I going to run a company with this useless twit on staff?" I motion to my brother.

"The name-calling is unnecessary," G-mom replies.

"Lincoln's not even part of this family! He hasn't attended one event in the past five years except for Dad's funeral. He couldn't be bothered to come to my wedding, and now he's going to run the company? How is that fair?"

I snort. "Your wedding was an expensive joke."

He crosses his arms. "I was set up. Amalie had cold feet and made me out to look like the bad guy."

The woman beside him shoots him a disgusted look.

Armstrong clears his throat and tugs at his collar. "My wedding is not the real issue. The point is that you've never involved yourself in any part of this family, and now you think you can come in and take over. I will not stand by and let this happen!" He keeps jabbing his finger at me, as if he's engaged in a finger sword fight.

I lean back in my chair and lace my hands behind my neck. Armstrong has always been reactive. And egotistical. For a while it seemed like he finally had it together—back when he was engaged. But ever since that fiasco of a wedding, he seems to have come completely unglued. Again. But worse this time. "Someone needs a time-out."

"Screw you, you . . . you . . . homeless-looking bastard."

"You need some new material because that's getting real old." I sit forward and rest my elbows on the table. "Look, Armstrong, I get that you're not happy about this, and if you can't tell, neither am I. But let's be real, the only thing you've done for this company is drag its reputation down the drain. How many millions of dollars have gone into paying off the women unfortunate enough to have been subjected to you? Are there reports on that, or have we paid someone to get rid of those as well?"

Armstrong waves his hand around dismissively. "There's no proof any of that is true. It's all hearsay."

"Really? So it was hearsay when everyone heard you getting blown by someone who wasn't your bride at your wedding? And was it also hearsay that you slept with our cousin's fiancée and got her pregnant?" I'm grateful Griffin gave me the CliffsNotes play-by-play on my brother's antics over the past year, since it provides ammunition for this fight.

Armstrong sneers. "It's not my fault; she came onto me."

I've had it with his mouth. I push out of my chair and stalk around the table.

"Boys! That's enough!" G-mom slaps a palm on a table. "Lincoln! Sit down right now!"

"Don't worry, G-mom, I'm not going to break anything important."

Armstrong grabs the woman in the coffee-stained gray dress by the shoulders and moves her so she's in front of him, acting like a human shield.

"You are literally the biggest pussy in the world. Don't think I can't knock you out even with your pretty little shield."

I realize half a second too late that I've very much said the wrong thing. That my words are no less offensive than Armstrong's by objectifying and demeaning said shield.

Before I can issue some kind of apology and retract that statement, the woman in question snarls at me. Then she proceeds to pull some kind of self-defense maneuver. In less than three seconds, she has Armstrong on his knees in a headlock.

"In accordance with clause six-nine-six, appendix D of my contract, I'm invoking the right to use self-defense in the event of unwarranted physical contact."

Who is this woman?

Armstrong raises his arm as much as he can, considering his position. "I'm sorry, I'm sorry! I thought he was going to punch me."

"I'm waiting for her to let you go, and then I will," I say with a smile.

"Armstrong, you know better than to make physical contact with Wren!" my mother says. "And Lincoln! This is not how we conduct ourselves!"

"Should I give you a few minutes to sort this out before we continue?" Christophe asks.

"Are you kidding me with this?" Gray Dress woman—whose name is apparently Wren—shoots me an angry glare and motions to my mother, grandmother, and Christophe. "We're in the middle of reading your deceased father's will. Have some decorum and stop acting like toddlers fighting over a damn cookie." She releases Armstrong from the headlock and points a finger at my face. "Sit down, both of you. This isn't a playground, and you're not challenging each other to a thumb war behind the slide."

I glance around the conference room and realize everyone, including my g-mom, is looking at me like I've lost my damn mind. That's what being around this family does to me.

I don't argue with Wren. I may not like this situation, but the last thing I want is to give my g-mom a heart attack or make a bad situation worse, which is exactly what's going to happen if I keep pushing. So I back down, for now.

But I will most definitely be dealing with my brother later, when I can get him alone and remind him that his mouth and my presence will be the least of his problems if he keeps up the tantrums.

CHAPTER 4
BROTHER'S GRIM

WREN

Lincoln rounds the table and takes the seat next to his grandmother, who's glaring at him. Gwendolyn's expression is slightly pinched—which is saying something because most of her face usually doesn't move. Christophe seems shaken, whether by my actions or the sibling squabble, I can't be certain.

"I want cookies." Armstrong drops back down in his seat.

I exhale slowly through my nose. My underwear are sticking to my crotch since they're covered in my one-sugar, one-cream coffee. Armstrong has not apologized for spilling it on me, so I'm done being nice. I turn to look at him. I'm sure my annoyance is obvious.

"What? You mentioned cookies and now I want some. Do we have any? Gluten-free and sugar-free, preferably. Also, low-carb. I don't spend all that time playing squash to mess it all up with too much sugar." He motions to his lean physique.

"Can't we duct tape his mouth shut until we're done here?" Lincoln says.

Penelope elbows him. "Enough, I won't say it again."

"Sorry," he says. "But it would sure speed things along if we did."

I ignore their low-level bickering and Lincoln's snide remarks while I stare at Armstrong. I wish I had some kind of superpower that would allow me to mute him. "Are you done?" I ask through gritted teeth.

"Yes. I believe I am. Is someone going to get me cookies now?" He swallows thickly and taps on the arm of his chair a few times when all I do is blink at him.

Someone sighs loudly on my left. I think it might be Gwendolyn.

"No, Armstrong. No one is going to get you cookies. Please refrain from speaking for the rest of the meeting unless you're asked for a direct response or you have something of value to contribute. I'd like to avoid black eyes as they're difficult to cover up for press conferences."

A scoff comes from across the table, which I ignore. I am currently experiencing some serious regret over signing that contract prior to meeting Lincoln.

Christophe resumes the reading of the will as if the almost-brawl never happened, and once they're finished, Penelope reviews a number of pressing Moorehead matters that will require Lincoln's immediate attention. Nothing like going from death to business without so much as a rest in peace.

I hope Lincoln will be able to manage the demands. I can create a pleasing public image, but I can't control his mouth when he's speaking in front of thousands. His reference to me as a pretty little shield does nothing to instill confidence. Nor do his threats to beat down his brother.

It's noon by the time the meeting finally wraps up, and thankfully it's outburst-free. Christophe packs up his things, and Penelope follows him out, leaving Gwendolyn, Lincoln, Armstrong—who's still muttering about cookies—and myself in the room.

Gwendolyn gives me a tired smile. "Wren, I'd like you to arrange a suit fitting for Lincoln, and brief him on upcoming events, press conferences, speaking engagements, whatever is happening over the next week or two."

"Of cour—"

"I have plenty of suits, and I don't need my brother's babysitter, or Dominatrix, or whatever she is, briefing me on anything." Lincoln shifts his disapproving gaze my way, his fingers curled around the back of the executive chair he's now standing behind.

Clearing my throat, I meet that vivid blue glare of his. And just like last night, it feels like I'm being pulled right in, which doesn't make any sense since he insulted me. "First of all, my name is Wren, so you can address me by something other than *she* or *her*. Also, I'm not Armstrong's babysitter, and I'm definitely not a Dominatrix, or a *whatever*. I'm an independent PR consultant, and I'm in charge of overhauling your public image."

"Says who?" His eyes dart to his mother. Dear Lord, this man's brow is probably permanently furrowed. I might condone Botox if he looks this angry all the time.

"Fredrick, initially." I nod to his mother. "And I was asked to stay on to handle you."

"Handle me?" He crosses his thick arms over his broad chest. It's inconveniently distracting. "By putting me in a suit and being my personal calendar? That's cushy. What else do you handle, Wren?"

I don't miss the hint of innuendo. I fight to keep my expression neutral and my voice even as I motion to him as a whole. "My job is to clean up your appearance and make sure you don't screw up interviews with offensive comments."

Gwendolyn makes an odd noise and motions to Lincoln. "While I'm sure your current attire worked for your previous position abroad, as the face of Moorehead, you need to dress and look the part. Miss Sterling has an impeccable reputation in her field, and I expect that you'll treat her with the same courtesy as you would treat me."

Lincoln purses his lips and sighs. "Fine. Suit fitting it is. If there are reports or a schedule you need me to look at, hand them over and I'll ask questions if I have any."

I pass him the stack of folders, the bottom one wet with coffee, and follow him out into the hall, leaving Gwendolyn to deal with Armstrong. I'm sure his temper tantrum is far from over. Lincoln stands there, looking lost, not to mention rough from last night's alcohol binge. "Your office is at the end of the hall." I point to the one without a nameplate. I'm sure it will be up by the end of the day.

"Thanks," he grumbles and stalks away.

I wish my office were in the other direction, but it's not, so I'm forced to follow him. He has something white stuck in his man bun, a string, or a fluff or something. I take in the shirt stretched tight across his back. Does this man even own clothing that fits, or are they all two sizes too small?

I can actually see the muscles in his back flex with each swing of his arm. He wrenches open the door to his office, his lovely, cushy corner office with the wall of windows overlooking the city.

I continue down the hall to the office I've been provided while I'm on contract here. The lone, small window boasts a view of the building across the street. It's also beside the photocopy room, so it smells constantly of ink, and the ceaseless drone of paper cycling can be maddening. I immediately put on some music to drown out the sound and turn on both of the ancient box fans set up in opposing corners of the room.

Inhaling a deep breath of inky-smelling air, I cross over to the small closet and retrieve my spare dress. I'd like to say this is the first time Armstrong has spilled coffee on me, but it's not. He's a hand talker, particularly when he's annoyed about something, which is pretty much every moment of every waking day, so it happens more than one would think. Normally I drink from a thermal mug to avoid this issue, but I was in a rush this morning and forgot it. It's likely sitting on my kitchen counter.

Ensuring my office door is locked, I quickly slip out of my gray pencil dress and into the maroon dress with the high neckline and full skirt. I never wear dresses that show even a hint of cleavage because I hate having to remind Armstrong to speak to my face, not my chest.

I seal my coffee-stained dress in a plastic bag and toss it in my purse. The dress doesn't match my shoes, so I change those too, and then set an alert on my phone as a reminder to bring a new spare dress tomorrow.

My panties are still damp and sticky, and I don't think I can deal with wearing these all day. It's too distracting. I step out of them and drape them over the vent under my desk, hoping to dry them. I suppose I can always run out at lunch and pick up a new pair, which I'll bill to petty cash since it's Armstrong's fault they're in the state they are.

It feels odd to be without panties, but I should be able to rectify it in the next hour or so.

I sit at my desk and take a deep breath. The pungent aroma of ink seeps through the vents and into my nostrils. I'm not allowed to burn candles in here because it's a scent-free building, so I'm forced to keep the giant box fans going all the time. They're loud, but they're somewhat effective. I crack my office door to help pull the air through, but not enough that it's an invitation for people to come in and socialize.

Lulu, who is . . . nice enough, has a tendency to stop and chat every time she uses the copier, which is at least half a dozen times a day.

My first order of business is to review the calendar of coming events and arrange Lincoln's suit fitting.

I've just gotten off the phone with a Saks representative and arranged the suit fitting and scheduled a haircut and manicure at the spa close by when Lincoln bursts into my office, the door slamming against the wall. The cross breeze sends the papers on my desk fluttering to the floor. Goddamn it. I hadn't paper clipped them yet.

"Do you know how to knock?" I snap.

He stalks across the room, his long legs eating up the distance in two strides—it's not a big room, but still, he's tall and his strides are aggressive.

He drops a folder in front of me, causing the remaining pieces of paper to fall to the floor.

I gesture to the mess he's made. "Thanks so much for that."

He slaps one hand on my desk and leans in, his eyes narrowed with anger and mistrust, neither of which I've earned.

He stabs a jagged-nailed finger at a piece of paper. When he speaks it sounds like his vocal cords have gone

a round with a cheese grater. "An average PR consultant in Manhattan makes between sixty and seventy-five
thousand dollars a year and that's on the high end, and
you make close to four times that. Explain to me exactly
how you managed to wrangle that kind of salary out of
my father."

I glance at the contract I signed eight months ago.
Just wait until he sees the new one. "First of all, I'm not
an average PR consultant. I work with people in situations that are particularly unsavory and handle them."

"Handle them how?"

"I find a way to smooth things over in the public eye."

"So you're trying to tell me your ability to *handle*
my brother is worth a quarter of a million dollars? Were
you sleeping with my father?" His nostrils flare and his
cheeks tics. "Or was it Armstrong?"

I push out of my chair and round my desk, so I'm
standing in front of him. It frustrates me that I have to
look up to meet his gaze, but there's no way he's getting away with such heinous accusations. "I don't care
if this is your company now. I am not your employee,
and you have absolutely no right to barge into my office
and make unwarranted assumptions based on my salary.
Secondly, I have no idea what your relationship was like
with Fredrick, or how you've framed your opinion of
him, but at no time during my contract did he ever make
a pass at me—God rest his troubled soul."

He's the king of squinty eyes with all the narrowing he does at me. "What does that mean, 'God rest his
troubled soul?'"

"Have you met your brother? He's a goddamn human
parasite."

If I had to guess, his lips are pursed, but I can't tell
through the lumberjack beard. The only version of him I

like remotely so far is the drunk one. Although, my job isn't to like him, it's to make him presentable.

"Is it really a surprise that I'm being paid this much money to sort out Armstrong's shitstorm? While you've been off saving the world, I've been trying to clean up his messes. And let me tell you, I earn every damn dollar because there are a lot of messes, and I hope you're not going to be the same kind of problem, because if that's the case, I'll be renegotiating for more money."

"You're trying to tell me you make this kind of money for babysitting my brother?"

That's it in a nutshell, but that makes me feel . . . like I'm falling short on my potential. This job as a whole makes me feel that way. I imagine it's what it would be like to get a degree in journalism with the hope that I'd be writing stories for *Time* magazine or a reputable paper and end up writing clickbait articles on things like giant cocks or tattoo regrets instead.

"I make that money for ensuring his previous bad behavior isn't splashed all over the media and whatever else that entails."

"It's the 'whatever else that entails' that I want to know more about."

I mirror his crossed-arm pose. "Not that I need to defend myself to you, but I would rather sleep with an angry grizzly bear than allow your brother to touch me."

Lincoln arches a brow. "He put his hands on you today."

"And as you witnessed, I handled him. I have authorization to restrain or subdue him if the situation calls for it. It's written into my contract. Are there any other family members you'd like to accuse me of sleeping with to validate my salary? Your mother or grandmother perhaps?"

His eyes flare, and he makes a gagging sound. He straightens and runs his palm over his scraggly beard.

I want to take a brush to it. And to his hair. The unruliness is driving me nuts.

He's still staring at me, and I'm still staring at his mess of hair. I doubt he even bothered to brush it this morning. Thank God I don't have to wait long before it's taken care of. "Well?"

"That's just . . ."

"Horrifying to consider? Which is exactly how I feel about the possibility of sleeping with any member of your family in exchange for money. I may handle a lot of unpleasant things, but your brother's penis is certainly not one of them and never will be. Are we quite done here?"

"Uh, I guess." He has the decency to appear chagrined. He makes a move toward the door but stops and pinches the bridge of his nose. "Wait, no. You were at the funeral. And then you were at the bar last night."

"I was." I nod and fold my hands behind my back so as to appear composed rather than nervous. I sincerely didn't believe he'd remember me. Now I have to question exactly how much he recalls.

"You took me to my cousin's penthouse. Where I'm staying. You were in my personal space. Why did you do that?"

There really isn't a point in lying. If he doesn't trust me, it's going to complicate my role here. "Because I was asked to ensure you made it home safely. You were drinking heavily and your presence was needed here today."

"You gave me painkillers."

"And water, yes."

"Was that part of your job as well?"

"To help nurse your hangover? No. But it was meant to make my job easier today, although I'm not sure it's had the impact I would've liked. You're rather surly despite my efforts to make your hangover less of an issue." A thank-you would be nice, though I doubt I'll get one.

For a split second it almost looks like there's a smile under all that beard. "So, just doing your job?"

I nod. "Just doing my job."

"Right." He collects the folder and turns to leave.

"You have a suit fitting tomorrow morning."

"Tomorrow morning? I have lots of suits; I'll make one of those work."

"Are they like the ones you wore to the funeral?" I ask.

"Yeah, why?"

"Well, they may have fit you five years ago, but they certainly don't fit you now. I'll text you the details and add them to your personal calendar."

"You can't do that without my cell number." His smugness would be grating if I wasn't two steps ahead of him.

I flash a fake smile. "I already have all of your personal details, Lincoln. Right down to your shoe size. And you can't be late like you were this morning, so it might be a good idea to avoid the scotch tonight so you're less bear and more human. You'll need to use these things called manners. I can email you a refresher on what those are, should you need it."

"Sarcasm is a weapon of the weak."

My ears are on fire as he heads for the door. *Jerk*. I was being witty, not sarcastic. "Thanks so much for offering to help clean up the mess you made." I turn to address the crinkled papers scattered on the floor.

It's common courtesy to offer assistance if you're the

one who made the damn mess. Even Armstrong, who is the most epic of douches, has some manners. Usually he'll try to look up a skirt or down a shirt while he's being polite, but it's better than this.

I turn to retrieve the papers when two things happen, a power surge ramps up the box fans—it happens at least twice a day, and at the same time Lincoln pulls the door open again. The simultaneous actions create a vortex of air inside my office, and my skirt flutters into the air. Like I'm Marilyn Monroe and I've stepped onto one of those subway grates. The fabric rises quickly, and a breeze hits me right between the legs, which is the exact moment I remember that I'm not wearing panties.

I drop the papers and battle the fabric back down. It's fruitless, though, the wind tunnel whirls through the room like Dorothy's freaking tornado, and the back of my dress goes up. I meet Lincoln's gaze from across the small room. All it takes is a second of eye contact before those ridiculously blue eyes pull me in, and weird, inappropriate things start happening to my body. It's irritating as hell. I don't even like this guy, but my body seems as if it hasn't gotten the same memo as the rest of me. Even more aggravating is the realization that based on his expression, he totally caught an eyeful of cooch.

Lincoln stands frozen at the door, eyes wide and fixed on my crotch, mouth hanging open.

"Close the damn door!" My voice is siren high. And loud.

"Right. Yes. I'm going. Now." He steps out of my office, pulling the door closed behind him.

My dress settles around my knees. "Dammit." I drop into my chair, which is probably what I should've done as soon as the wind tunnel started, but clearly I'd been too panicked to think straight.

On the upside, I went to see my waxer last week, so he's seen my girl bits when they're looking their finest.

On the downside, my project for the next six months has seen my naked girl bits.

CHAPTER 5
MAKEOVER MORNING

LINCOLN

I head for the balcony with my coffee in hand. While I'm not a fan of the city, I can still appreciate the view from the penthouse floor.

It's early, before seven, but I'm used to rising with the sun. In Guatemala, we'd get up at the crack of dawn and put in as many hours of labor as we could before the sun made it impossible to do anything but hide.

Here I wake up to air-conditioning and stainless steel appliances. My coffee is freshly ground and there's a breakfast menu on the kitchen counter—in case I need to order something from the condo's twenty-four-hour restaurant instead of putting bread in a toaster. It's excessive luxury.

The air is cool, but even this high up, I can still smell the exhaust and pollution. I miss the freshness of trees and sunshine on grass.

"How'd the meeting go yesterday?" Griffin's voice breaks up as I switch to speakerphone so I can have my hands free.

"It wasn't the best."

"Armstrong being a pain in your ass?" The question comes out with bite, which isn't a surprise considering he knocked up Griffin's ex-fiancée, before she became his ex.

"When isn't he?" I gather my hair up so it's not blowing in my coffee and secure it with an elastic. "He's not my biggest problem, surprisingly enough."

"What else is going on?"

"They've made me the CEO of Moorehead."

The pause is so long, I wonder if the call dropped until Griffin speaks. "Are you serious?"

"As a heart attack." I cringe, considering that's exactly how my father went. "Okay, that was bad, but yeah, I'm serious."

"I'm sorry, Linc. Is this permanent? What're you going to do about the Guatemala project?"

"G-mom said it would only be for six months, but we'll still have to find someone to take over when I leave. I can leave Carlos in charge of the project for the short-term, but I'm going to need to hire someone to manage it eventually if it really takes more than a couple of months to sort this all out. You interested in taking it on?" I'm only half joking.

Griffin blows out a breath. "You know I would if I could. We've got another month in Panama, and then we're supposed to head to Costa Rica after that. I can see if I can shift some things around—"

"It's all right, don't worry about it. I have people I can call, but I'd still really appreciate it if you'd stop there before you head to Costa Rica like we planned."

"Of course I'll do that. I wish I could drop everything here and go now, but we're right in the middle of a hotel reno, so we have to stay put."

"I get it. I'm disappointed we aren't crossing paths. I'm hoping this is going to take a lot less than six months, but I have no idea what's been going on here apart from the Armstrong drama you've updated me on."

Griffin grunts. He may have moved on after everything with his ex, but I doubt he'll ever get over what my brother did to him. "I guess you can't really blame them for wanting your help. Armstrong can't handle Moorehead on his own. But, man, you haven't had any part in managing that gong show. What exactly do they expect from you? Is this some kind of payback for taking off and leaving your dad to run the company with your brother?"

"Hell if I know." Although I suppose I can see what Griffin means about payback. I didn't know my father well enough to be able to say with any kind of certainty what his motives were.

"So, six months in the city? How are you going to survive that?" It's a serious question, not a joke. I haven't lived in the city in years. Any time I pass through it's only to see Griffin if he's here, and I typically stay for a couple of days before I'm off again.

I scrub a hand over my face. "I have no idea." I'd say take up drinking, but I'm still feeling the effects of yesterday's hangover, so I don't think that's a solution for me.

"I'm so sorry, Linc. I know this is the last place you want to be. Is Armstrong losing his mind?"

"What's left of it, yes." I pinch the bridge of my nose. Dealing with him is going to be a challenge. A beep filters through the penthouse signaling someone has entered. "Do you have a housekeeper I should be aware of?"

"Yeah, she comes on Mondays, but you can change the day if that doesn't work for you."

I strain for the sound of movement in the penthouse. "Is there anyone else who has the code to this place?"

"My brothers, but they know you're there, so they wouldn't stop by without calling. What's up?"

"I think I have company." I leave my coffee on the balcony and grab the closest heavy object—which happens to be a weird piece of art, likely belonging to Griffin's girlfriend—and head for the hallway.

"Lincoln?" a familiar female voice calls out.

It takes me a few seconds to place it. "I gotta go. My handler's here."

"Your what?"

"I'll explain later. Enjoy the beach and your girl. I hope you packed Viagra."

I end the call with a smile and set the phone on the cradle—he's one of the few people I know who still has a landline. I nearly slam into my handler when I round the corner.

"Oh!" She stumbles back a step, and her hand goes to her chest.

"You're letting yourself in now?"

"I knocked several times. And texted. And called. You didn't answer."

"Maybe I didn't want to be disturbed. What are you doing here so early, and how'd you manage to get in?" I also haven't so much as looked at my phone since leaving Moorehead yesterday, mostly because I'm not the least bit interested in dealing with any of this.

"I took down the code the last time I was here, in case you proved to be difficult to get in touch with. Better get used to me, Lincoln. I'm going to be like your shadow for the next several months."

She strides through the living room, head held high like she owns the place. She's wearing a pantsuit today.

Probably safer than a dress if she routinely runs around without panties on. I fight off the memory of what I saw yesterday, irked by the spark of excitement that comes with it. She's also wearing bright purple heels. They clip irritatingly on the hardwood.

She drops her bag on the kitchen table and spins to face me. A pair of dark-rimmed glasses frame her eyes, making the gray pop. Her too-red lipstick sets everything off balance. I want to hand her a tissue and tell her to wipe it off so it's not a distraction, but I might end up in a headlock for that.

Instead, I go with something snarky and only somewhat improper. "You decided on breeze-appropriate attire today, huh?"

The only sign that I've gotten to her is the slight tic in her cheek. She blinks once and drags her pink tongue across her red lips before she smiles. "Watch yourself, Lincoln. You're sounding a lot like your brother, and we both know how I deal with him. Next time you'll know to knock before barging into my office and throwing out asinine accusations."

"First of all, they weren't asinine accusations. You should know that, considering you're the one cleaning up all my brother's messes. Secondly, who the hell wears a dress without panties?" Okay, that last question should have stayed inside my head instead of coming out of my mouth; however, I'm curious as to the answer. Also, I say this kind of stuff to be funny, where my brother would say it expecting to get lucky, which is not the same.

Being panty-less in an office with my brother seems dangerous.

"My panties were wet," Wren snaps.

I arch a brow, and her eyes flare.

"Because of the coffee that Armstrong spilled on me. And sticky. They were wet and sticky and uncomfortable from the coffee."

I fight to keep from smiling while I nod. "Makes perfect sense."

"Speaking of panties, it would probably be a good idea for you to put something else on to cover yours, considering we need to leave sooner rather than later." She spins on her heel and stalks down the hall in the direction of my bedroom.

"What are you even doing here?" I rearrange my cock, because for whatever reason, it seems to be responding to the female company. Clearly it doesn't realize she's an annoyance yet.

"You have a suit fitting this morning and an appointment at the spa to clean this up." She makes a circle motion around her face. "If you'd bother to check the messages I sent you, or your calendar, or your voicemails, you would've known that. Also, I told you yesterday when you were in my office accusing me of being paid for sexual favors."

She throws open the closet doors and steps inside. Despite this being the spare bedroom, the right side is filled with my cousin's suits. It's his winter wardrobe, so he rotates with the seasons. He's particular about his clothes. I try not to be too judgmental about it.

Wren lifts one from the rack and frowns. "This is a great suit, although a little heavy for the season." She checks the tag on the inside then holds it up in my direction, mouth turning down even more. "Why is it so big?"

"Everything in here belongs to my cousin."

"Is he a descendant of the Hulk?"

I lean against the doorjamb as she combs through the suits. "He's actually the smallest of his brothers."

She waves in my general direction. "You're already more than enough man; anything beyond this is ridiculous."

"Is that right?"

Her head turns in my direction. "I didn't mean it like that."

"Like what?"

She brushes past me. "Nothing, never mind. We have to be at Saks in forty-five minutes. You need to get dressed so we're not late. Where are your clothes?"

I motion to the worn, oversize backpack on the lounger in the corner of the room. "Most of it's still in there." I hadn't planned to stay, so I never bothered to unpack. Now that it looks like I'm sticking around, I'm going to have to find alternate living arrangements and clothes that aren't meant for hard labor in warm climates.

She rummages around in my bag and pulls out a pair of faded black jeans and a shirt with a hedgehog that reads WHY CAN'T YOU JUST SHARE THE HEDGE?

She arches an eyebrow. "I guess these will do. We'll need to update your casual wardrobe while we're at it."

"The kids in Guatemala love my T-shirts." There aren't a lot of shopping opportunities, at least not where I was, and the ridiculous shirts made the kids laugh, which is the reason I wore them.

"I bet they do." She graces me with a smile that seems almost genuine. "Okay, time to cover up all the prime real estate unless you'd like to give all the women at Saks heart palpitations." Her eyes flutter shut, and she grimaces. "Stupid mouth." She slaps the clothes against my bare chest. With that, she strides quickly through the bedroom and disappears down the hall.

I'm not sure how to take her, but at least she's interesting. I throw on the jeans and T-shirt and meet her in the kitchen. She's typing away on her laptop, having made herself at home. As soon as she sees me, she slams it closed and slips it back inside her bag. It's huge, almost the size of my backpack.

"Ready?"

"No, but I don't think you're going to leave me alone unless I do this, so let's get it over with."

My moderately okay mood takes a swift turn into Fuck-This-Ville when we get stuck in New York morning traffic. The car crawls along, horns honking, the semi-fresh air from the penthouse floor is replaced by exhaust, subway fumes, and sewer grates.

"I hate this city," I gripe as we pass yet another double-parked Lamborghini. "The people here are DBs."

"DBs?" Wren asks.

"Douchebags."

"Oh. Not all of them."

"All the people I know are, with the exception of my cousin," I grumble. "It's just a bunch of self-centered narcissists who need to show each other who's got the biggest balls with their environmentally irresponsible cars. None of this is natural. It's not normal to be surrounded by concrete all the time." I motion out the windows at the endless buildings and complete lack of trees.

"There are green spaces everywhere in the city," Wren argues.

"As if that makes it better. I don't get the point of this. I have plenty of suits stored away at my mother's. Maybe there's something in Griffin's closet that will fit me."

Wren levels me with an unimpressed look. "The suit you wore to the funeral is five years out of date and looked like something that fit you back in high school. You'll swim in Griffin's suits."

She's right, but I really hate this. "Fine. But we can cut out the spa treatments. I can take the electric trimmer to this and be done with it." I motion to my hair.

She looks up from her phone, horrorstricken. "Absolutely not. You are not shaving your head. I forbid it!"

"Pardon me?"

"Your hair is thick and full and fantastic. Shaving your head would be a disservice to men around the world. And women. You're getting a professional haircut. End of conversation."

"You can't tell me I can't shave my head or force me to get a haircut."

She arches a perfect eyebrow. Even her eyebrows irritate me. "I have ten years of self-defense classes under my belt. I can bring you to your knees before you even blink. If you try to give me a hard time about the haircut, I have authorization from Gwendolyn to use whatever persuasion methods necessary."

"I'm guessing that means you're not planning to sweet talk me into it, huh?"

"I'm pretty sure that won't work with you, so I should warn you that my persuasion tactics may include duct tape and rope."

"Sounds kinky."

She turns her attention back to her phone and clicks away furiously while her cheeks flush pink. "Wouldn't you love that. You're getting a haircut. You can do it the easy way or the hard way. That's your only choice in the matter."

"Whatever you say, Wren." I'm almost tempted to find out what the hard way is with this woman. I have a feeling it might be the fun part of an otherwise craptastic day.

CHAPTER 6

FLIRT LIKE YOU MEAN IT

WREN

As unpolished and infuriating as he may be, Lincoln Moorehead smells fantastic, and being trapped in this car with him is making it impossible to think. Also, now the image of him in nothing but a pair of tighty-whities seems to be stuck in my head.

Lincoln's body is ridiculous. He's all sculpted muscle and tanned skin—likely from his time spent in the sun working in Guatemala, digging wells, and building orphanages. It's clear the photos I've stumbled across online aren't staged, and he truly is involved in the projects. It's one checkmark against all the *X*s he's racked up with his behavior so far.

And while his attitude still sucks a lot, I can understand better where it comes from. If Armstrong were my brother, and I was under (what I believe may be a misguided) impression my father was a serial cheater, I'd probably have the same reaction. Also, I don't mind the city, but I can see how it can be overwhelming.

"So, how'd you end up as my brother's babysitter?" Lincoln asks.

I glance up from my phone. I'm in the process of setting up new social media accounts for Lincoln since he has none. "Please don't call me that. It's demeaning and undermines what I do."

"Fine, how'd you end up as my brother's *handler*?"

"My mother is friends with your mother. She asked me to do this as a favor. It looks good on my resume and pays extremely well. And your family needed someone who could handle the situation discreetly, which is something I'm good at, so I took the job." It's the abridged version, but he doesn't need all the gritty details.

Lincoln tips his head to the side. "Is your mother a nice person?"

That's an odd question. "Yes. Most of the time."

"Hmm." He glances out the window, stroking his beard thoughtfully.

"What does 'hmm' mean?"

"What does 'most of the time' mean?" he fires back.

"She's human; no one is nice all of the time. You're a case in point, aren't you, with your accusations yesterday and your current surly mood? However, when you're drunk out of your mind, you're quite entertaining, if not mildly inappropriate."

He regards me for a few seconds, and his expression is somewhere between chagrined and defensive. "I don't like the city. Or my immediate family, apart from my grandmother. I don't want to be here, but I don't want to make my grandmother's life difficult, so I have to stay."

"You've made the not-wanting-to-be-here part rather clear." I set my phone in my lap, abandoning the social media account setup for the time being. "What does 'hmm' mean?" I ask again.

"It means hmm. I haven't quite figured you out yet. Other than a hefty salary, I'm not sure why you'd put up with my brother for as long as you have. And my mother is a shrew, so it makes me wonder if yours is too."

I look away, unable to handle his intensity. I love my mother, but she's made some poor choices in her life, ones that have had an impact on who I am and how I view honesty and trust. As for his mother, until recently, I haven't had to deal with Gwendolyn much during my time at Moorehead. She's cold, but then lots of women in business present that way. I certainly don't come across as warm and fuzzy, and for good reason; show Armstrong an iota of warmth, and he sees it as a green light for sexual advances.

"Having the Moorehead name on my resume will give me opportunities in the future. Your family donates to all the major charities, so I'm hoping after this I'll be able to secure a PR position at one of them." Then I'll be able to do something meaningful.

"So, you want to work for a charity organization?"

"Yes."

"Those positions don't come with the kind of salary my family is paying you," Lincoln says.

"It's not about the money. My current salary will help me build a nest egg so I can eventually set up my own foundation. It's about making a difference, not adding to my bank account, something I thought you might understand."

He nods and taps his lip. "My family doesn't donate because they're altruistic. They do it because it helps the bottom line and gives them a tax break."

As much as I don't love Moorehead Media's news

slant, I at least thought they were genuinely invested in the charities they support. And maybe they are, maybe Lincoln's wrong and he's saying it to get a rise out of me.

"How can you say that? Your mother's on the board of almost every notable charitable committee there is in the city."

"She doesn't do it because she cares; she does it because it gives her connections and makes my family look good."

"And what about you?"

Lincoln drags his attention away from the window. "What about me?"

I've done all the research the internet will allow on Lincoln. What's out there makes him look like a golden boy. "You've spent the past year in Guatemala working with foundations that support sustainable communities, and before that you were in China. Is that to make your family look good?"

Lincoln snorts derisively. "My whole family is a bunch of assholes. Except my cousin Griffin. And his brothers, they're all good people." He taps irritably on his leg.

"Griffin Mills, of Mills Hotels?" That family is richer than God.

"Yeah. I'm sure you're familiar with the name, given what happened between my brother and him."

I'm definitely familiar with Griffin since it was his ex-fiancée—who wasn't an ex at the time—that ended up pregnant with Armstrong's baby. It was the reason Fredrick hired me, actually, but I don't bother to tell Lincoln that. "You're close with Griffin?" That's what Fredrick intimated last year, anyway, and the few pictures of them together in China seemed to confirm that.

"Yeah. He's more like a brother than a cousin. We've worked on a few projects together over the years, but he's heavy into the family business, so it's harder for him to find the time."

I probe a little more, trying to understand who this man is and what makes him tick, because it's certainly not a suit fitting or the city. "Did you all grow up in New York together?"

Lincoln nods. "Yeah. We're the same age, so we spent a lot of time together when we were young. If you haven't noticed, Gwendolyn isn't exactly maternal, so Armstrong and I were dealt with by nannies, and the other half of the time we were at our cousins' house. At least until I was ten, and they shipped me off to boarding school."

"Why boarding school?"

"To get me out of Gwendolyn's hair? Who knows? My parents were fighting a lot at the time over my father's inability to honor his marriage vows. Anyway, they put me in some program for the academic elite, or whatever. The tuition was probably absurd. It was better for me in the long run, since it got me out of that house and away from my family. Apart from holidays, I never really went back, until now, anyway."

I want to ask more questions, but his phone rings. He feels around in his pocket for it, frowning as he checks the screen and answers the call. "Lincoln here."

He's silent for a few seconds. "Yeah, thanks, Carlos, it's a shocker all right. I appreciate that, we weren't particularly close, though, no . . . no." He pauses again tapping on the armrest as he listens. "Uh, yeah, that's what I wanted to talk to you about. It looks like I'm going to have to spend some time in New York cleaning things up with the family business. Not ideal considering where we are in the project, but I'm hoping you can manage without me for a while."

He's quiet for a bit. "I'd like to say it's only going to take a few weeks, but my grandmother pulled a guilt trip on me, so it's probably going to be longer than that. We can talk about bringing in someone to oversee the project if you think it's going to be too much for you to deal with on your own."

The car pulls up in front of Saks. "Can I call you back later? You gonna be around in a few hours?" He tugs at his beard and chuckles. "Nah, they have me hooked up with some kind of baby—handler whose job is to clean me up. Apparently my T-shirts aren't considered appropriate attire, so instead of doing something valuable with my time, I get to try on suits. Seems like a waste of resources and money that could be used to bring fresh water to the disadvantaged, but I guess I'm the one with skewed priorities here." He glances my way. "He's actually a *she*."

I swallow back my irritation at the way he's talking about me while looking directly at me. Not to mention the way he demeans my job.

"I can't comment on that. She's sitting right beside me. Yeah, I'll call you when they're done messing with me." He ends the call and pockets his phone. "Let's get this torture over with." He throws open the door, and several people nearly slam into it and him as he steps out onto the busy sidewalk.

Lincoln shoves his hands in his pockets, his mood souring further as we approach the store. "They don't open until ten." He nods to the hours posted on the door.

"It's a private fitting. They scheduled you outside regular hours."

That scowl of his grows scowlier. "I hope these poor bastards are getting paid overtime for this."

A saleswoman with the body of a model and the face of an angel opens the door for us. If I were with Armstrong, I'd have to threaten castration to prevent him from hitting on her within the first three seconds. Lincoln, on the other hand, barely grunts out a greeting and doesn't so much as give her a once-over.

We follow her into the fitting area where a selection of suits are hung beside matching, headless mannequins. A team of people await our arrival. An entire breakfast spread is laid out, and the second we enter the room, the team flock over, offering refreshments and coffee.

Lincoln looks to me, his expression almost panicked.

"Would you like something to drink?" I ask. "Or eat?"

He rubs the back of his neck. "Uh, I can get it myself, thanks." He grabs a croissant and shoves it into his mouth—the entire thing, all at once—and motions to the bottles of water. "Can I get tap water instead of this?" His mouth is still full and he's chewing, so none of the sales team understand his garbled speech.

"He'd like tap water," I explain to the confused saleswoman. It looks like we'll need a refresher on table etiquette before the next public dinner function.

She blinks a few times, the request clearly throwing her. "Oh, of course. I'll be right back."

The angel model smiles widely and claps her hands together. "Mr. Moorehead, we're honored to have you here today. Let me introduce you to our team. I'm Bianca, and I'll be attending to all of your needs today. Anything you want, you ask and I'll provide it." Of course she punctuates this with a wink. Way to keep the innuendos subtle, Bianca.

"You all right? You got something in your eye?" Lincoln motions to her face and then slips his hand in his pocket, possibly feigning innocence, or maybe that went completely over his head.

Bianca's cheeks flush, but she recovers quickly. "Probably an eyelash."

I cough to cover a snicker, and Bianca moves on down the line, introducing the rest of the team. "This is Bradley, your tailor, he'll be taking your measurements and fitting your suits. They'll be custom-made to your exact specifications."

"Once we're done here, we'll head over to the spa where you'll meet with the barber and the aesthetician."

Lincoln throws me a narrow-eyed glare. "What do I need an aesthetician for?"

"Just for a little polishing, nails and such," I say breezily.

"My nails?" He looks down at his jagged nails and callused palms. "Who cares about my nails?"

"You'd be surprised." I put on a bright smile and add, "Personal grooming says a lot about a person in the eyes of the media, Lincoln."

His eyes crinkle at the corner as they dip down and pause at my crotch. His cheek tics, which I take to mean he's smiling. Or maybe smirking is more like it. "Mmm." His gaze is slow to return to mine. "Yes, I suppose it does."

This time my cheeks flush, aware he's referencing my own personal grooming habits and the up-close-and-personal view he got yesterday in my office. Stupid fan-inspired wind vortex.

Bianca claps her hands again; it must be her thing. "Shall we get started with the suit fitting? Which styles are you most fond of?"

The crinkles disappear from the corner of Lincoln's eyes, and he lazily flicks a hand in my direction, back to being grumpy. "Might as well ask Wren. She's the one who has to approve everything, anyway."

I decide the best option is to have him try on every style, so I can determine which complement his build best. He seems annoyed by the level of attention, and the way people manhandle him—the opposite of his brother.

He pulls at the collar of a dress shirt while Bradley adjusts the lapels of his jacket. "This is too tight. I feel like I'm being choked to death."

I can't decide if he's being overdramatic, or if he's tired of being prodded. I get it. He's been living in jeans and T-shirts for a long time, a suit, even if it's made of silk, is going to take some getting used to.

"Can you stop poking at me for a minute?" he snaps at Bradley.

"Yes, sir. I'm so sorry, sir. Can I get you something to drink? A mimosa or a Bloody Mary perhaps?"

"You might wanna just bring me a bottle of vodka," he grumbles.

"He's fine, just give us a moment," I tell Bradley, then give my attention to Lincoln. "Let me see if I can help."

"How are you gonna make this better?" He rolls his shoulders and tugs at the lapels again.

I ignore his theatrics and adjust the collar, so it's not all bunched up. Then I attempt to slip two fingers between the collar and his skin. He stills, and his warm breath caresses my cheek.

It's not the shirt that's the problem. When I drag my fingers across his neck, goose bumps rise along his throat.

"It's your tie." I loosen and adjust it, smoothing it out with my palm. "How's that? Better now?"

Lincoln swallows a couple of times, eyes bouncing around my face. "Yeah. Better."

"Excellent." My voice is pitchy, which is ridiculous, as there's nothing going on here that should make it sound like I'm huffing helium. I drop my hands and step back, giving Bradley space to work again.

While Lincoln complains about being tortured, I ignore him and continue to set up his social media accounts. It's another hour before the suit fitting is finally done. Thankfully one of the suits needed only the most minor of alterations, so we're able to take it with us. The rest I'll pick up sometime next week.

He seems to relax somewhat when he's back in his jeans and his juvenile, ill-fitting shirt. We leave Saks, and for about five minutes, he's not grumpy, at least until we enter the spa, at which point his mood sours once again. We're introduced to our team, which consists of Ulrich and Belinda, who will deal with his hair and his hands.

Ulrich guides him to one of the chairs, and Lincoln pulls the tie from his hair. His sloppy bun uncoils, long hair cascading over his shoulder, falling halfway down his back.

I step up beside Ulrich and give in to the urge to finger comb it. I've never been a fan of long hair on men, or ponytails, or man buns, but even I can appreciate how incredible Lincoln's hair is. It's thick and dark and shiny and fairly healthy apart from the split ends.

I comb it with my fingers again as if I'm trying to get rid of knots. "Women would kill to have hair like this."

"It's so soft," Ulrich replies.

"And luxurious," I add.

"Such a shame to cut it," Ulrich sighs.

"Maybe we could leave some length?" I suggest. It's almost a travesty to get rid of it.

"What if I donate it? You know, for wigs for cancer patients?" Lincolns suggests.

"The length is certainly there. We'll have a good twelve inches if we cut it off at the nape."

I rest a hand on Lincoln's shoulder and finger a lock of silky, shiny hair. "That would be incredible."

He shrugs. "It's just hair. It's not like it won't grow back."

"Bald men all over the world must loathe you," Ulrich murmurs. He's still running his fingers through Lincoln's hair, almost like he's petting him. He moves around to stand in front of him, and I follow. "And what about the beard? Are we shaping? Trimming? Getting rid of it?"

"Too bad we can't donate it as well." Against my better judgment, I run my fingers through it too, which seems to shock Lincoln.

He recovers quickly, though. "Who says we can't? We could make merkins out of it."

I drop my hands and bark out an incredulous laugh. Ulrich doesn't seem to get the joke.

I'm almost positive Lincoln's smirking. "We could have one made for you, in case you wanted to change things up every once in a while." He glances briefly at my crotch. If he were Armstrong, he'd get a warning, but Lincoln's comment isn't accompanied by any kind of smarminess, and it's actually kind of funny, even if it's also embarrassing.

"You're unbelievable." I give him a cautioning glare.

"I thought it was a good idea."

"Right, well, whatever you want to do with the beard

is up to you. Let's clean this up and make it camera-ready." I motion to his face in general and grab my purse. "I'll be back in a bit."

Lincoln's thick, warm fingers wrap around my wrist, but he releases me just as quickly, possibly because he hasn't seen the contract I signed and doesn't know whether or not his includes the same self-defense clause as Armstrong. "Wait! Where are you going?"

"I have a quick meeting. I won't be long."

"With who? I thought your job was to babysit me today."

"I'm not a babysitter, Lincoln." I pat his cheek; it's condescending, as it's meant to be. "And while my job might often feel very much like babysitting, I do have other things to take care of. Don't worry; you're in good hands. Oh, and be nice. I've authorized back waxing should you prove to be unpleasant with the staff, so be on your best behavior."

I leave him with Ulrich and head down the street to the café to meet up with my friend Dani. Beyond being my bestie, she's also a PI, and I've asked her to look into Lincoln and see if she can dig any skeletons out of his closet. Everyone has them, and I want to find out if Lincoln's are ones we need to worry about.

"I ordered your usual," she says as I slip into the booth beside her.

Her short, blond bob is tucked up in her customary baseball cap. While I wear dresses most of the time, Dani lives in black jeans, sports jerseys, and combat boots or Chucks. Her face is pixie sweet, and her tongue is sharp.

"Thanks. Sorry I'm late."

"Everything okay?"

I wave off her worry. "Just a busy morning." Because

of the nature of my contract with Moorehead Media, we don't discuss my job, and since she's a PI, we can't really discuss much about hers either.

"So you'd be jealous if I told you I rolled out of bed half an hour ago?"

"I might be, except I'm pretty sure you went to bed around the time I got out of mine."

"If you got up at six in the morning, you'd be correct in that assumption." She rubs her hands together. "So, I did some preliminary recon while I was waiting. You want to get right down to the dirty?"

"Might as well."

She turns her laptop, so I can see what she's pulled up so far. "So, I have the usual, school, family, yadda, yadda. While there's lots of drama there, it seems to revolve mostly around his brother. Anyway, he got into some trouble at Harvard, but other than that, I haven't found anything else."

I perk up at that. "What'd he get in trouble for at Harvard?"

"You're going to love this. Protesting the sanitation products in student bathrooms. They're manufactured in a plant that was known for ignoring child labor laws."

Well, that's commendable but disappointing. "He can't really be that squeaky clean. I mean, he has to have done something bad at some point that someone will use against him. What about his relationship history? Ex-girlfriends, that kind of thing?"

Dani shrugs. "I haven't found much apart from a grainy prom pic and a few college photos, but as far as I can tell, he either hasn't had much in the way of relationships, or he's extra careful about not being public about them. It's possible his family has paid to keep him off the web, but aside from a few pictures of him working on projects in various countries over the past few years, there's a whole lot of nothing. It's tough when there's no social media to work with. And he doesn't appear in family photos. Obviously I'll dig deeper and see what else I can find, but so far he's coming up roses. Nothing like the brother."

She clicks on an image from the funeral. "Dude is giving off some serious Aquaman hotness vibes. What's he like? Please don't tell me the altruism is a front, and he's an actual jerk-off like Prince Charmless."

"The jury's still out on that. I'll have to spend more time with him to get a better sense of what he's like. So far, he's grumpy and difficult, but then he's related to Armstrong, so I'm not sure if it's a genetic trait, or what."

"At least he's nice to look at. You won't have to deal with him much, anyway, right? Since you'll be done with that circus soon?"

"Uh, well . . ." I stir my coffee. "I'll be working PR with Moorehead longer than I expected."

"Oh my God, what fresh hell did you fall into now?"

"They extended my contract. Lots of transitions with Fredrick having passed. It'll be fine." I'm grateful that our food arrives, since I can't really say much else on account of the NDA I signed.

"If you say so." Dani closes her laptop and slips it back into her messenger bag. She's aware of Armstrong's reputation in the media, and she knows how tough this year has been at times, so her wariness is understandable.

"So, what about you? Working any exciting cases?"

Dani rolls her eyes. "Hardly. It's more of the same: cheating spouses, employees stealing from work, the occasional suspected murder, which usually ends up being paranoia. People are ridiculous."

I point a strip of bacon at her. I love all-day breakfast places. I could eat breakfast food three meals a day and be happy for life. "And that's a fact. I was kind of hoping for something scandalous."

"I recently worked on a case where the wife thought her husband was cheating on her, but it turned out he was a cross-dresser."

"Was the wife relieved?"

"Seemed that way. Would've saved them both a lot of money and worry if they'd been honest with each other in the first place, but I'm not going to complain, since their lack of communication pays my bills."

I raise my coffee cup. "Here's to communication-less marriages." It comes out with bite, mostly because my own parents went through a phase early on in their marriage where communication fell apart and the result was less than desirable.

Dani grimaces. "Sorry."

I wave her off. "You don't need to apologize."

"How's Senator Sterling doing these days? I saw him and your mom on TV the other day talking about the new hospital initiative." She tips her head, waiting.

My heart squeezes. "He's good, busy but good. I saw him last week for lunch. He keeps trying to get me to take up golf, so we can spend more time together." Yoga and jogging are more my speed than golf, but I'm willing to swing a club for a few hours if it means I get time with him.

"And what about your mom?" she presses.

I know what she's getting at. Things have been better since I started at Moorehead, but it'll never be like it was. Still, it's a start. "She's good. She's been putting a lot of time in at the neonatal unit."

"Oh, is that abnormal for her?"

I poke at the center of my egg, watching the yolk pool and then drip down the side.

"Wren?"

"No. I think it gives her peace to be there." When I was three, my mother gave birth to my baby sister, Robyn. She was severely premature; on top of that she had a rare genetic disorder that compromised her immune system. She only survived a few days. "She asked if I wanted to volunteer with her."

Dani's expression remains placid. "It might be good for you, for both of you," she says gently.

"Maybe. I told her I'd think about it." Like my mother, I've spent a lot of time volunteering in hospitals, but until now, it's been a solitary thing for me. Going with my mom would mean facing down a lot of demons, so it's something I have to psyche myself up for emotionally, but I know Dani's right. It would probably go a long way toward making things better between us.

"Families are complicated, aren't they?" Dani smiles sadly.

"They sure are." I flick a hash brown at her. "Okay, enough of this sad BS. Tell me something good. Oh! Wait. What about that guy you met at the coffee shop the other week, did you ever see him again?"

Dani rolls her eyes. "Sure did."

"Uh oh. What happened?"

"I ran into him a week later in the grocery store. With his wife."

My excitement deflates like a popped balloon. "No."

"Oh yeah. Nice, right?" Dani makes a face. "Honestly, I don't even have time for dating since most of my evenings are spent staking out people who are screwing around on their significant others."

"At least we have each other, right?"

"BFF's forever." She makes a heart with her hands and grins cheekily.

We finish lunch and make a plan to eat pizza and binge-watch TV later in the week.

I'm gone nearly two hours by the time I return to the spa to finish my afternoon of glorified babysitting. I assume they'll be done with the whole beautifying routine. I requested they give him a facial if the whole beard disappears. I chuckle to myself at his potential irritation.

The first thing I notice when I enter the spa is a man checking himself out in the three-way mirror. His suit hugs every muscle of his incredible body perfectly. His hair is cut short, but the top is longer, almost like that mobster style that's made a comeback recently. He's clean-shaven, and even from across the room, I'm pretty sure he's a delicious specimen of man. I sure hope Lincoln cleans up half as well.

As I pass him, his gaze shifts, snagging on me. I add extra sway to my hips and throw a smile his way. I might not have time for dating, but I can still be flirty from a distance. He turns, a smirk pulling up one corner of his mouth.

"Like what you see?" he calls out.

The cocky comment gives me pause, and then I realize I recognize the voice. "Lincoln?" I try to keep my jaw from hitting the floor.

"I can't tell if that shocked look on your face is a good or a bad thing." His grin tugs nervously upward.

"Holy hell." I cross over to him. "Oh my God. I can't . . . This is . . ." I'm full-on gawking, but seriously, he looks like a totally different person. "Dear sweet baby Jesus riding a unicorn."

"Uhh . . ." Lincoln's brow furrows. It's a very different expression now that I can actually see his face. And what a face it is.

I can't seem to put words together in a sentence. I'm too busy being blown away. I reach up and run my fingers over his smooth cheeks. Good God. His jaw is made of all things magic, square and strong and just . . . bitable. His lips are full, and they look incredibly soft. I have the restraint necessary not to touch them, although I suddenly have the irrational urge to find out how they'd feel against mine.

I follow the contour of his jaw with my fingertips and sigh—or possibly moan—when I reach his chin. He has a dimple. A sweet little dimple that softens all of the hard masculine angles of his gorgeous face. I cover it with my fingertip. Chin dimples are my kryptonite. *I'm not sure why I bothered with panties today since I'm pretty sure they've just incinerated.*

"Want me to check for you?"

I look up from where my finger is still pressed against his chin dimple. "Huh?"

Lincoln is full-on smiling. And it's beautiful. His eyes light up with mirth. The right side of his mouth tips slightly higher than the left, making his grin lopsided. His front tooth is turned ever so slightly, a tiny endearing imperfection. He's magnificent. "Your panties, Wren. I'm happy to check the state of them for you, if you'd like."

Dammit. I said that out loud.

CHAPTER 7

IT'S NOT ALL BAD

LINCOLN

My phone—which I've taken to leaving in the kitchen at night so my sleep isn't disrupted by the constant emails and messages that come in at all hours—is currently buzzing away. I can hear it from down the hall, but I have zero desire to get my ass out of bed to find out who's calling.

I glance at clock on the nightstand. It's 7:02 a.m., which means it's probably Wren. As trying as it is having someone tell me how to dress, I will say that being around her is entertaining.

While I haven't seen her in person since the suit fitting, she's been messaging me constantly over the weekend about upcoming events and things I need to be briefed on this week.

She may not like my attitude, but based on her comment at the spa, she likes what she sees. She also told me I'm not allowed to grow a beard ever again. In fact, she threatened to set up a laser hair-removal appointment if I allow it to go past two days of growth.

So, of course, that means I haven't shaved all weekend.

My phone goes off three more times before the alarm to the penthouse beeps. Several seconds later, it's followed by the echo of heels clicking down the hall and a knock on my bedroom door.

"Lincoln, are you awake?"

"Yeah." It comes out heavy and thick with sleep and gravel. And maybe a hint of excitement. Wren is quickly becoming the highlight of being in New York. She's witty, snarky, and no BS. So far, she's the only person here apart from G-mom who doesn't pander to me. It makes me feel less shitty about my circumstances.

"I'm opening the door," she warns.

I grin at her lack of request and kick off the sheets so the fabric only covers the space below my navel to just below where my balls would hang out. I've taken to sleeping naked now that the sheets don't feel like sandpaper and there's no risk of ending up with bug bites on my junk. As much as I dislike New York, it's nice to sleep in a real bed for a while.

Wren shoulders the door open. She's carrying a stack of clothes so high, she can barely see over it, and I can barely see her.

She crosses the room and dumps the pile on the edge of the bed. Her dress is navy and fitted, showing off her curves, despite the high neckline and the hem that falls below her knees. It's classy, yet sexy without being provocative. Or maybe it's provocative without being classless. I don't know. Either way, both my eyes and all the important parts below my waist appreciate the dress. Which is unexpected since generally we're annoyed with Wren. This new development is inconvenient.

She opens her mouth to speak, but it clamps shut as her eyes lift and flare. She blinks a couple of times, and her tongue drags across her too-red bottom lip. I don't know what the deal is with the red lipstick, but I wish she'd go with gloss or something. Too bad I can't tell her what to do like she does with me.

Her gaze moves over me in a slow sweep, catching on the strategically placed sheet before moving over my chest, all the way to my face. Her brows pull down and her eyes narrow. "You need to shave unless you want me to call my laser girl."

"Good morning to you too. Is this going to become a regular thing? You busting in my bedroom unannounced all the time?" I tuck my hand behind my head, causing the sheet to shift lower.

She turns her attention to the pile of clothes on the bed. "I tried to call. Three times. You didn't answer."

"Maybe I was busy."

Wren snorts. "Busy worshiping your abs. I brought you some new clothes. It's not quite office attire, but it'll get us through until the rest of your suits are ready for pick up, which should be in a few days."

"When did you have time to go shopping for this stuff?" I motion to the pile of boring tan and white with some striped crap thrown in.

"Over the weekend."

I'm displeased that she's working outside office hours for some stupid reason. "I can buy my own clothes."

"I'm sure you can. However, in the interest of presenting a positive image to the public, it's part of my job to make sure you're dressed the part. The quirky shirts need to stay in your weekend wardrobe. Actually, I highly recommend you wear them outside of office hours because some of them are quite witty and they show a fun side to your personality, but you cannot wear them to the office anymore. Or the ripped jeans."

"Sir, yes, sir!" I salute her.

She purses her lips, far from amused, which entertains me. "I'll need you to try everything on to see if it fits."

"Now?"

"Yes. Now. We have a meeting this morning at nine thirty."

I sit up, throw my legs over the edge of the bed and stand, giving her a view of my bare ass.

"Oh my God. You're naked!" Wren covers her eyes with her hands. Except her fingers are parted, which means she's checking me out.

I cover my junk with my hand—what I can mask anyway—and turn to face her. "I sleep naked."

"I'll just step outside. And wait." She stumbles back a step. "For you to contain your business."

"Probably a good idea. I'd tell you to make yourself at home, but seeing as you let yourself in, that's a given."

Her cheeks flush, and she rushes for the door, pulling it closed with a slam. Just to aggravate her, I make her wait several minutes before I come out of the bedroom wearing a pair of khaki pants and a black golf shirt. Talk about boring. I feel like I'm becoming a drone, and I've barely been here a week.

I find Wren in the kitchen, trying to figure out the coffee press. Griffin has some high-tech coffee machine, but I discovered the single-cup press years ago, and it comes with me everywhere. I lean against the counter and watch while she struggles to assemble the parts. It's not complicated, which is probably part of the issue. It looks like it should be more difficult than it is.

"Need some help?"

"Oh!" Wren fumbles the pieces, and they bounce

across the counter and fall to the floor. "You surprised me!"

"We're almost even, then. You've showed up here un- announced twice, now."

"I tried to call. Both times. And the suit fitting was scheduled, if you'd bother to check your calendar every once in a while. How does this thing even work?" She turns to face me. "Hmm." She taps her red lips with a fingertip.

"Hmm, what?" I reach for the base and the filter. She's missing the paper component, which is essential if she wants to avoid a cup full of grounds. I open the cupboard, grab a filter, slide it in place, and screw it to the base.

Wren watches as I add grounds and boiling water be- fore I press the coffee through. "Would you like a cup?"

Her nose crinkles. "Is it any good?"

"I think so." I push the fresh cup toward her and tap the cupboard beside her head. "There's sugar in here and cream or milk in the fridge if you need it."

I empty the grounds into the compost and repeat the process while she adds a sprinkle of sugar and two drops of cream to her coffee. It doesn't even change the color in the remotest way. She brings the cup to her lips and blows before she tips it up and takes a tentative sip.

"Oh, wow, this is really good." She takes another, more robust sip and makes a face. "And extremely hot."

"Yeah, careful you don't burn your tongue off, there." I add a full spoon of sugar and a healthy dose of cream. It's an indulgence I haven't had much of in the past couple of years. Cream isn't something I often had ac- cess to, and I'm not a fan of powdered milk in my coffee so I switched to mostly black, but now that I'm in New York and I can buy cream at every corner store, I plan to capitalize on the luxury.

"You never answered my question," I prompt.

"What question?" Wren regards me from over the lip of her cup.

"You hmmed me and never explained what it means."

"Oh! Right. Yes." She sets her coffee on the counter. I notice the complete lack of lipstick mark on the cup, which should be impossible considering the color and the white mug. "Let's take a look."

"A look at what?"

"How everything fits." Her tone implies I'm ridiculous for even asking. She takes my coffee cup and sets it beside hers, then arranges my arms at my sides. "Roll your shoulders back for me, please."

I stand up straighter and flex. "I feel a lot like a prize cow right now."

She snickers. "Prize cow? That's cute." Wren adjusts my collar and runs her hands over my shoulders and down my biceps, slipping a thumb under the cuff of the sleeve. "Is this comfortable?" She smooths her hands over my pecs. I get that this is supposed to be a professional assessment, or whatever, but my body seems unaware.

"Lincoln?" Wren blinks up at me, her wide gray eyes fixed on my chin again.

"Huh?"

She goes back to feeling up my pecs. "The shirt, is it comfortable? It's tighter across the chest than I anticipated. We may want to go up a size. I'm worried about it shrinking in the wash since you don't seem like the dry cleaning type."

"Uh, it's okay, I guess."

"We'll see how the others fit." She moves around to stand behind me and makes another noise, fingertips skipping along my traps. "This is good. The pants are a nice fit. I think we should tuck the shirt in, though, and add a belt. It'll look more professional." She grabs me by the belt loop and starts jamming the fabric down the back of my pants. Which means she's sort of touching my ass. I'm wearing briefs, but it's still contact. She keeps tucking, moving to the right and then to the left before she comes around front.

For a second, I think she's going to go ahead and shove her hand down the front of my pants. Just before that happens, though, she seems to realize she's been manhandling me, or treating me like a toddler who doesn't know how to dress himself.

Her cheeks flush, and she steps back. "You can get that part."

"You sure? You're doing such a good job. I wouldn't want to mess it up."

"I won't be here every morning to help you out. This is good practice." She grabs her coffee from the counter and takes a sip, possibly to hide her embarrassment. Or a smile. I'm not sure which is more likely.

I stuff the shirt down the front of my pants and do some rearranging to hide my body's unexpected reaction. All the while, Wren's gaze stays locked on my chin.

"How's this?" I hold my arms out.

She taps her lip, eyes moving over me in an assessing sweep. "You need a belt. And shoes. Come." She motions for me to follow her down the hall.

I spend the next half hour striping down to my briefs—I don't bother going to the bathroom since I get a kick out of how she pretends to look away, but really she's watching me from the mirror.

Not everything she picked out is beige and white or black. There are a few shirts with color that she felt would go well with my skin tone, and a selection of button-downs. I have to admit, she has good taste in clothes, and nothing is outrageously expensive. In fact, a few of the shirts have sale tags on them; something I appreciate. I wonder if she did that intentionally since I know my mother and Armstrong would never buy anything on sale.

Before we leave for the office, Wren sends me into the bathroom to shave. I come out with only the hint of a stash. I think it's pretty damn funny, but apparently she doesn't. She forces me back in, makes me sit on the closed lid of the toilet, and finishes the job for me.

It's hot and maybe a little scary to have an irritated woman wielding a razor close to my mouth. But she manages to do it without nicking me.

And as much I don't want to admit it, I kind of appreciate that she's pushy and doesn't bow to me. So far, all anyone's done at the office is kiss my ass, but not Wren. She happily dishes out the snark. I may not like my new job, or this city, or my family, but at least my handler is keeping me entertained.

CHAPTER 8
ADF EMERGENCY

LINCOLN

Two weeks post-funeral, I'm beginning to settle into my new role. I'm not necessarily getting used to it or comfortable, but I'm starting to figure things out. I've done two very brief, very public news conferences. It wasn't what I would consider fun, but I made it through without messing up. Wren seemed pleased with my ability to speak in public without saying something inappropriate, which is definitely a plus since it means she's less up my ass about every single damn thing.

The learning curve is steep, though, and the volume of files I have to review is astronomical. Moorehead is a massive company that covers every conceivable type of media. The numbers I've been over so far tell me we've been paying out a lot of money for things that don't appear to be remotely business-related. It's not a surprise, but it means I have to figure out where all the money went and explain what appears to be hundreds of thousands in non-business related expenses to the board.

I'm reviewing files for one of our magazines prior to

a meeting this afternoon to discuss moving from print to digital only—print sales are down by 50 percent, incidentally; the decrease in sales seems to correspond with the timeframe in which my brother screwed over his ex-wife at their wedding. Since the competition smartly scooped her up, the content has suffered and the sales have disintegrated while the competitors have quadrupled their online readership and doubled their print sales. Doesn't seem like much of a coincidence. Obviously his ex's replacement isn't nearly as good at the job as she was. That and all the great content has shifted to our competition, where she now works.

I blow out a frustrated breath, resentful of the sunshine streaming through my office window. What I wouldn't give for a little fresh air right about now. I loathe that I'm stuck twenty-seven floors in the air and that I can see the park from my window, taunting me. I'm also frustrated at the sheer amount of money that's been spent protecting my brother's disturbingly entitled, misogynistic ass.

I throw down my pen at the knock on my office door. I swear to God, if my assistant asks me one more time if I need another coffee, I'm going ban her from speaking to me directly. Or I can have Wren do it.

"What?" I snap.

Wren pops her head in my office. Speak of the devil. Or the angel. I'm on the fence. "Really?"

I lean back in my extremely comfortable chair, which cost five thousand dollars—I know because I looked it up in the expense budget—and fight a smile, ready for the tongue-lashing I'm about to get. Somewhere along the way, it's turned into my favorite part of the day. "Really what?"

She closes the door and props her fist on her hip.

"We've talked about this, Lincoln. You had no idea it was me behind that door. What if it had been a client?"

"All my client meetings are scheduled in my calendar, and they all have four million alerts set by you. I knew it wasn't a client."

She purses her red lips. That lipstick drives me up the wall. It's always on. Always perfect. Always a distraction. And today, her dress is covered in huge flowers. A rainbow of colors. She's like the sunshine cutting a bright line across my desk, melting the chocolate bar sitting on the corner. I should move that.

"Lincoln?"

Dammit. She was talking and I missed it. Probably chewing me out about something. "Huh?"

Her nostrils flare, and those impeccably shaped brows draw together. "Did you hear a thing I said, or did you tune me out like you do everyone else?"

"I don't tune everyone out." That's not entirely true. I tune a lot of people out. I'm not used to having to pretend I care about someone's five-million-dollar campaign for lace underwear that costs more for a single pair than my monthly grocery budget, and how we can help them advertise. There are more important things in this world than panties. I think even Wren would agree with me on that.

"What the hell are you smiling about?"

I rub my chin because that's where her is gaze is currently fixed, as usual. Half the time I think I have food on my face. "Nothing. I was thinking about something."

"This isn't a joke, Lincoln. You can't use that tone with staff."

I motion toward the closed door. "Do you know how many times a day Marjorie stops by my office to see if I need coffee?"

"She's trying to be helpful. It's her job."

"I don't think twelve coffees a day is helpful to anyone. I'm worried one of these times she's going to roofie me, and I'll end up hog-tied in a closet."

"Is that a fantasy of yours?"

I give her some of her own sass back. "This isn't a joke, Wren. I can't have my staff trying to kidnap me and keep me in their basement as a pet or a trophy."

"That's a little high on the drama, there, Lincoln. Maybe you've been spending too much time with your brother."

I push out of my chair and plant my fists on my desk. "You did not compare me to that asshole."

"We can get a drama-queen crown. You two can take turns wearing it." She bites her bottom lip, her smile making her eyes twinkle with mischief.

"I'm not being dramatic. I need Marjorie to cut down on the office visits, and I don't want to hurt her feelings. I already have a shadow. I don't need another one."

Wren's smile drops, and her expression goes blank. At first I can't make sense of the sudden shift.

"I see. I'll speak with Marjorie. I only stopped by to remind you that we have a meeting shortly. I'll see you in the boardroom." She spins on her heel, the skirt of her dress flaring, and stalks toward the door.

It's then I realize how she's taken that comment. I'm around my desk and blocking the exit. I'm fast when I want to be.

She stumbles back a step, and I see, for the first time, a hint of vulnerability. She lifts her chin and twists her head away, eyeing me from the side.

"I wasn't referring to you, Wren. I meant—"

She holds up her hand and cuts me off. "You don't need to explain."

"Uh, I think I do, because you look pissed, and while I incite that reaction in you frequently, generally you aren't under the impression that I'm insulting you. I was being quite literal." I motion to the floor where my shadow bleeds into hers. "I know I suck to deal with, but I hate this place and you're pretty much the only decent thing there is about working here. Aside from G-mom. She's awesome, but she's not here every day like you are. Interestingly enough, I piss her off a lot too. You're the only person here who isn't constantly bending over to kiss my ass. So please, Wren, don't take what I said the wrong way." I don't know why I'm saying all of this, or why I sound like I'm imploring her to believe me.

Maybe because I have to sit beside her in a meeting, and I don't want the angry glare she usually directs at my brother aimed at me. Or maybe it's because what I've said is true. At some point in the weeks since I agreed to take on this godforsaken role, I've started to . . . rely on her? Get used to her? Which I guess is the damn point. Despite how aggravated we always seem to be with each other, I don't want to hurt her feelings. If she even has any of those.

She looks in my direction, but still not at me. Her gaze is on my tie, or my chin, or my eyebrows. I don't fucking know. "I'm trying to help you acclimate. If you need space, all you have to do is say so."

What I do next might flirt with workplace harassment, but she's not listening, and it's infuriating. Now I guess I understand her frustration with me. I grab her by the shoulders, gently, of course. Her dress has cap sleeves and a wide, high neckline. It's modest—as are all her dresses—but still sexy. She almost looks like someone out of the fifties. Especially with her hair pulled in a ponytail that does this twist thing at the end.

She glances at my hand, cupping her shoulder. She's shorter than me by a lot, even with heels. She's curvy, but she feels almost delicate. I need to stop making these observations.

"You're not listening to me."

"I'm just saying—"

"Wren, look at me." I'm snippy, but for fuck's sake, she's not listening.

She purses her lips and stares at my neck. I duck down, getting right in her space. This is probably really bad. I've blocked the exit to my office, and I'm physically preventing her from leaving. Although, she's adept at self-defense. If she wanted me to stop touching her, I'm pretty sure I'd be on the floor with her heel against my jugular.

"Look at me. Not my chin or cheeks or my forehead—my eyes, meet them, please."

She exhales slowly. Her breath smells sweet, like something fruity, citrus maybe. Those gray eyes finally lock on mine. Some kind of weird energy seems to pass between us. Wren rarely, if ever, makes direct eye contact with me. I don't know why. But now that I have her full attention, I don't want to let it go. God, she's beautiful. *Why am I focusing on this now?*

"I've spent a lot of time in fairly isolated environments over the past five years. Interacting with people on a daily basis who need me to fix problems I didn't create is new and difficult. I don't love this job. I don't think I even like it, if I'm going to be honest, but you, your presence makes it bearable, even if it seems the opposite." As I tell her this, I realize it's not a load of BS meant to make her feel better and prevent her from being pissed at me for the rest of the day. I don't know when it happened, or how it happened, but it's not just that I'm used to her. I think I actually might like her. I drop my hands and step away from the door. "I'm sorry I touched you. Please don't put me in a headlock."

Wren chuckles. "Don't worry. I won't invoke my self-defense clause."

"It's kind of messed up that you have one at all." I motion between us. "Are we okay?"

"We're fine. You're fine."

"Are you fine? I mean, look at you, obviously you're *fine*." It would be fantastic if I could stop digging myself into a verbal hole. I've been out of the game for far too long. "I mean, in the emotional sense of the word. I really can't have you pissed off at me for like, longer than an hour max, otherwise shit goes downhill fast around here."

The last time I really made her angry, which was two days ago when I showed up at the office in jeans and a suit jacket—I figured if I was sitting down, no one would see the jeans, so it wouldn't matter—she rescheduled all my meetings and made me sit with Armstrong to review paperwork as punishment. At least it felt a lot like a punishment.

"I'm fine." She picks some lint off her skirt. "Is there anything you need to review before the meeting? It's pretty straightforward. You'll have to listen to Easton Davidson talk about how big his balls are for a good hour, but you're adept at tuning people out. I'll sit beside you and give you a nudge whenever you need to respond."

"Wait, are you serious?"

"About?" Wren's still picking at imaginary lint.

"He's really going to talk about . . ." I motion to my crotch, which isn't a great idea since for some reason, today my body's response to bickering with Wren is to get excited about it. Thankfully, she doesn't look where I'm pointing.

"Oh!" She laughs and waves a hand in the air, embarrassed maybe. "That was a figure of speech. All of these men do the same thing every time we have a meeting. It's like a measuring contest. Half the time I expect them all to whip their pant pencils out and set them on the table so we can see whose is the biggest. He's going to talk about how amazing he is, and you have to pretend to care. It'll be fine."

Her phone buzzes from somewhere in her dress, and she slips her hand into the skirt to retrieve it. "It's ten to; we should head to the boardroom unless you have any other questions."

She slips the phone back into her pocket and straightens my tie, as is her habit. She moves on to my hair, fingertips grazing the shell of my ears before her palms glide along the sides of my neck so she can adjust my collar. And then she's back to my hair. Her nose wrinkles, and she licks her thumb then reaches up.

I catch her by the wrist before she can make contact.

"Your left eyebrow is wonky," she explains.

"You can't lick your thumb and touch my face. I'm not a toddler, Wren. How would you like it if I did that to you?" I lick my own thumb and swipe it across her eyebrow before she has a chance to duck out of the way. The pad comes away with a brown streak.

I hold up my thumb. "What the hell is this?"

Her cheeks flush an even deeper pink, and she smacks my hand away. "It's eyebrow pencil; something you wouldn't know anything about since you're a man and you don't have to manage this kind of thing." She gestures to her face and then to mine. "You style your hair and shave your face, and you're good to go. It's a lot more work for me."

"That's a choice, though, isn't it?"

"Not if I don't want to look like a hag in a pretty dress every day."

I don't know if I believe that. I think it's more likely that women have been conditioned to believe they need makeup to look good by some of the magazines this company owns and endorses. I bet she's equally gorgeous without the makeup, but I don't say that because I'm unsure how the compliment will be taken.

Under that brown pencil her eyebrow is significantly lighter. I tug on the end of her ponytail. "Is this your natural hair color?" I'd like to say I already know, since she flashed me that first memorable day, but there was nothing but smooth skin to compare it to, so I'm at a loss.

"It's lighter than this." She motions to her head.

"How much lighter?"

"Why does it matter?"

I shrug. "It didn't until you started getting defensive about it."

"I'm not defensive."

"Yes, you are."

Wren huffs out a breath. "I'm naturally fair. My hair is dark blond. I dye it so people will take me seriously and not stereotype me as some kind of brainless ditz."

"Do you honestly believe people make those kinds of ridiculous assumptions?"

"In my personal experience, yes."

"That's terrible."

Wren shrugs. "That's life."

"Dark hair or light hair, it doesn't change the fact that you're gorgeous, or that you're incredibly proficient at your job." I'm still fingering the end of her ponytail. Being this close to her, I get a hit of floral shampoo, or maybe it's lotion. Whatever it is, I like it.

"Thank you." She adjusts my collar for the second time, fingertips grazing my throat.

Normally this kind of attention would bother me, but for some reason I don't mind when Wren does it. Possibly because I enjoy it when she's all up in my personal space. It also allows me to stare at her without her noticing, since she's so absorbed in making sure nothing is out of place.

Now that I know she dyes her hair, I detect the hint of roots at her hairline. This close, I can also make out the blond in her mascara-coated eyelashes. She has a tiny beauty mark under her right eye and another on her left cheek.

Her gray gaze shifts and meets mine, there are flecks of blue and green near the pupil that I haven't noticed until now. She's utterly captivating.

I expect her to look away, but she doesn't, and the attraction we've been masking with the constant bickering flares. Her tongue sweeps out to wet her bottom lip. *If I kiss her, that red lipstick will disappear and stop being such a distraction.*

Holy shit. I've been so wrapped up in hating my family and this job that I failed to recognize I have a serious hard-on over my handler. Quite literally.

Even though I know it's a very bad idea, I tilt my head down, an infinitesimal shift that speaks louder than words ever could. Those lips of hers part, and she tips her chin up, eyes still locked on mine. We've been dancing around each other since she brought me up to the penthouse the night of the funeral. Half the time, my irritation and her snark seem a lot like flirting.

I'm not her boss, not really. She's not my employee.

There aren't any restrictions here. Complications, yes. She's contracted to deal with me for several more months. But this attraction is becoming difficult to ignore, especially when she's this close to me and it seems mutual.

I'm almost past the internal argument when a knock on the door startles us. Wren sucks in an unsteady breath and takes two quick steps away from me. I mutter a curse and wrench the door open.

Standing in the hall, nervously wringing her hands, is Marjorie.

"I don't need a coffee." Dammit. I'm snappy, so I tack on, "But thanks for checking."

She blinks a bunch of times, like a strobe light. "Um, okay. I'm actually looking for Wren. She's not in her office. Have you seen her?"

"I'm right here." Wren steps up beside me, looking a hell of a lot more composed than I feel. "What's going on?"

Marjorie blows out a relieved breath. "We have an ADF emergency."

Wren rolls her eyes. "Of course we do, and right before a meeting. How shocking."

"What's an ADF?" I ask.

Marjorie makes a cringy face.

"Armstrong Douche Fuckery emergency," Wren explains. She turns back to Marjorie. "Is he having a meltdown?"

Marjorie nods vigorously. "It was a code yellow before I came to find you, but it's been a few minutes."

"That means it's probably escalated to a code red by now. Where is he?"

"He was in his office."

"Okay. Let's go." Wren slips out of my office and

strides quickly down the hall in the direction of Armstrong's, Marjorie rushing to keep up. I follow along because I'm interested to see what exactly a code red ADF emergency looks like and how she plans to handle it, since it's her job and all. "Do you know what exactly it's pertaining to?" Wren asks Marjorie.

"Something about being removed from a project. I'm not one hundred percent sure."

"Has he broken anything yet?"

"Not that I—" A huge crash cuts Marjorie off.

Wren sighs. "Okay, thank you, Marjorie." She turns to the guy positioned outside Armstrong's office door. He looks halfway between a bodyguard and techie. "Hi, Carter, thank you for keeping him contained. Have you notified Lulu at the front desk?"

He nods somberly. "She knows to prevent clients from making their way down this end of the hall. I'll call her when you give me the all clear."

"Great, thank you."

"Need any help in there?"

"I think we'll be okay. Thank you, though." Wren pushes open the door to Armstrong's office. He's currently in the middle of a temper tantrum. His desktop monitor is on the floor, the screen spiderwebbed.

I follow Wren inside and close the door. Armstrong has always been on the dramatic side. As a kid if he didn't get his way, he'd fly off the handle and break things. It appears this hasn't changed at all in the past twenty years. If I had to guess, I'd say it's gotten worse. I wonder if the strain of trying to keep it together in public is making it even more challenging. And my presence probably isn't helping.

Wren crosses her arms over her chest. "What seems to be the problem?"

Armstrong spins around and stalks toward her, but as soon as she puts a hand up, he freezes, almost like a dog obeying.

"You did this!" He points at Wren, and then me. "Both of you."

Wren looks over her shoulder. "I can handle this."

"I'm sure you can. I'm here as an observer." I motion for her to go on.

Armstrong is livid, nostrils flared, face red, hands clenched into fists, hair a mess.

Wren inspects her fingernails. "You'll need to elaborate, Armstrong. What exactly did I do?"

Armstrong paces the room while flailing. "The McKenzie account was mine, and you took it away. It isn't enough that Lincoln gets to come in here and take all the glory, and now he's stealing my biggest clients!"

"Well, Armstrong, we wouldn't have to take those accounts away from you if you would stop sexually harassing the daughter of the client in question."

"I did no—"

"Three weeks ago, you sent their youngest daughter, who incidentally happens to be eighteen, a dick pic."

"That's ludicrous," Armstrong spits.

Wren's voice softens, almost as if she's chastising a child. "We both know that's untrue."

"She said she was twenty-one."

Of course, this is my brother's go-to defense.

Wren tips her head to the side, expression passive and unimpressed. "So, you felt it was reasonable to send inappropriate photographs to one of the models contracted to shoot a spread in one of Moorehead's teen publications because she told you she was twenty-one?"

Armstrong throws his hands in the air. "Well, how

was I supposed to know she was related to the McKenzies?"

"Possibly because her last name happens to be McKenzie?"

"I only got her first name, so that's not my fault."

It's unreal the way my brother shifts the blame, no matter how heinous his actions are.

Wren's tongue peeks out for a second before it disappears, and she clamps her mouth shut in annoyance. She takes a deep breath through her nose, and when she speaks again, her voice is scary low. "I am going to ask you to stop speaking because everything that's coming out of your mouth is pissing me off. I have a meeting that your temper tantrum is making me late for. One that you're no longer invited to attend."

"You can't do that!"

"I can and I will. Your behavior this morning is not fitting of senior management at Moorehead Media, and it will not go unpunished. If you act like a spoiled child, you'll be treated like one."

Wren takes one small step forward, causing Armstrong to scramble behind his desk. It's exactly the kind of move he would have pulled when we were kids. "But I—"

Wren raises a hand, and he stops talking. "I have several women who can attest to the fact that the picture you sent is unequivocally your penis."

"Maybe someone else sent it. Ever think of that? Maybe someone stole my phone."

Wren pinches the bridge of her nose. "That you were texting an eighteen-year-old girl is questionable to begin with. Armstrong, stop digging yourself into a deeper hole."

"She baited me! She was flirting with me and asked for my number! She started texting me, not the other way around."

That he's thirty and sending inappropriate pics to barely legal women is just . . . vile. I really don't understand how he's managed to get away with this for so long, or how anyone has been able to tolerate his asinine behavior.

Wren raises her hand again, and Armstrong's mouth clamps shut. "In order to avoid losing the contract entirely, you've been removed from the account. You're very fortunate that I was able to keep you from being forced to take a mandatory leave of absence. However, if it happens again, you *will* be taking some time off. Am I understood?"

His frustration is clear, but he doesn't snap like I expect him to. "Yes. Understood."

"I'd like you to take the rest of the day off. You're not in any state to manage yourself around other people, and no one should be subjected to you when you're like this." She turns to me. "Do you have anything you'd like to add?"

I've gone from wanting to kiss her to wanting to strip her naked and screw her on the closest surface after that takedown, but considering sexual harassment is the reason she's chewed out Armstrong, I figure it's better to keep that to myself. "Uh, nope, I'm good."

"Okay, well, we're late for our meeting, so we should be on our way." Wren slips past me and opens the office door.

Armstrong shoots her the double bird behind her back.

"Real mature there, brother." I follow her into the hall, leaving him to stew. "How often do you have to do that?"

Wren shrugs. "Depends on the week."

"You were incredible; you know that, right? Watching you level him verbally like that was sexy as hell." I hold open the conference room door and brace for the potential headlock, except that's not what happens.

Instead, surprise crosses her face and she smiles, her eyes meeting mine for the second time today. "Thank you."

If I thought I liked her before, I'm crushing on her hard now.

CHAPTER 9

G-MOM OBSERVATIONS

LINCOLN

After the meeting in which I had to fight the entire team on cutting not one but two magazine publications that would result in the loss of twenty Moorehead staff members, I go for lunch with G-mom. I asked for time to come up with an alternative plan that would salvage those jobs. Not just for the sake of my conscience, but also to keep disgruntled employees from defecting to the competition.

My mother was invited to join us for lunch, but thankfully she had a prior engagement and couldn't reschedule. I'm assuming she has some kind of "procedure." Also, my mother and G-mom don't often see eye-to-eye on anything, so I'm happy not to referee them for the next hour.

G-mom waits until we've placed our orders before she finally speaks candidly. "You managed that meeting well."

"I don't know about that. There still isn't a solution, so don't go patting me on the back yet. We might have to let those people go if I can't figure out a decent alternative."

"If it comes down to that, I can always do the letting go," she offers.

I scrub a hand over my face. Armstrong would derive so much joy from telling all these people they no longer have a job. All I can think about is their families and the long road of applications and job interviews ahead. "I hope it doesn't, but I don't think it sends the right message if I can't take that on myself. At least while I'm in this role."

She gives me a piteous smile. "I'm so sorry, Lincoln. I know this is hard for you. They'll all have a severance package and a letter of reference if you can't find a creative way to handle that division."

It makes me feel marginally better, but not great. "I don't want to send them to the competition and drag our bottom line down even further. This company is in enough trouble as it is, thanks to Armstrong. I don't understand why he's been allowed to get away with this for so long. I get growing up in that house messed him up, but there's something seriously wrong with him. What would prompt my father to spend all that money covering up his mistakes? This family is a mess. I mean, apart from us." I motion between us. "Well, apart from you anyway."

"You're not a mess, Lincoln. You're handling this with grace, especially under the circumstances." She sighs. "I see now that I should've paid more attention to what Fredrick was dealing with, and how he was dealing with it where Armstrong was concerned, but I assumed he had it handled."

"Apparently he handled it with a lot of money."

G-mom straightens her silverware. "Sometimes I

regret not trying harder to get Armstrong out of there like I did with you. Maybe he would've turned out differently."

"Maybe working so closely with Dad was half the problem."

"Your father wasn't a bad man, Lincoln."

I snort my disbelief. "I get that as his mother you're obligated to wear rose-colored glasses when it comes to him, but he was a shit father and you know it. He was never there, never made an effort to get to know me, didn't go to any of my sports competitions. He missed my high school graduation because of a damn meeting."

"He put too much focus on work. And his flight was delayed on your graduation. He tried to be there."

I give her a look. "Too little too late. And you and I both know it wasn't all work. He wasn't faithful to my mother, and maybe I can understand that, since she has the warmth of a corpse, but why not get a divorce, then? Why subject us all to their miserable relationship? Why not move on?"

"I really don't understand his reasons for staying, and now that he's gone, I doubt either of us ever will." G-mom gives me a small, pained smile. "I think your father probably made mistakes along the way, and how he dealt with your mother and Armstrong may have been his penance. What I know about Fredrick is that he was an honest and fair businessman, except when it came to your brother. Maybe he was trying to make up for his mistakes with you, but he allowed Armstrong to run free until he couldn't ignore it anymore."

"Well, that plan backfired, didn't it? He's left behind a hell of a mess to clean up."

"I'm only beginning to see that now that I'm so immersed in the company." She taps on the edge of the table. "Maybe I should postpone my trip. I don't want to leave you with this whole mess to deal with on your own."

I wave that idea away. "Don't do that. I can handle things here. Besides, I'm not alone. Wren will be here, and Armstrong is terrified of her." My grandmother has taken a trip every year on the anniversary of my grandfather's death. She and a few of her friends, who are also widowers, go on a month-long cruise. It's cathartic, and she deserves it now more than ever.

The server drops off our lunches, and my grandmother daintily cuts into her salmon filet while I take a huge bite of my burger. I hate to admit it, but I've missed good food like this.

My phone buzzes on the table, and I glance at the screen. "It's Wren. I'm going to check the message in case it's important."

I don't think I have a meeting until later this afternoon, at least not that I saw on my calendar. Although, I'm not the best at checking it. Normally I wait for Wren to message me about whatever I'm supposed to be doing next, which I realize is probably pretty assholey. She's not my assistant; it shouldn't be her job to tell me what my schedule for the day is.

Her message is brief and professional, informing me that my afternoon meetings have been rescheduled, so I'm not expected back at the office until tomorrow.

"Huh, that's odd."

"What is?" G-mom sits up straighter.

"Wren rescheduled all my afternoon meetings."

"Oh. That was kind of her." G-mom relaxes back into her chair.

"Why do you say that?"

"I'm sure she realized this morning was difficult for

you, so she took it upon herself to give you the time you need to think through what to do next, instead of bombarding you with things that could obviously wait."

"Oh. Yeah. That makes sense." I fire a thank-you back and flip my phone facedown. While G-mom might be right, that Wren cancelled my afternoon meetings as a courtesy, I worry the almost-kiss from this morning is going to mess up the dynamic between us. I like her, and I like that she doesn't feed me BS. I don't want to screw with that by making things awkward.

"You and Wren are spending a lot of time together lately." Her tone is conversational, but I know better.

"She doesn't really have a choice, does she? She's paid to handle me." Which is very much the truth, but it's been feeling a lot less like a working relationship and more like something else lately. Or maybe that's just my perception. Still, today it seemed like she wanted me to kiss her. Or maybe I've been off the dating circuit so long, I don't know how to tell when a woman wants to be kissed versus when she's irritated with me.

"Well, it doesn't seem like she's minding her job very much these days. She's a lot . . . happier working with you than she ever was with Armstrong."

"That's probably because I don't throw temper tantrums." Not big ones, anyway.

"Or maybe it's because she likes you. When you're not busy being pissed off, you're actually quite pleasant to be around."

"You're family. You have to like me. It's different," I counter.

"I have to disagree with that. Your brother is an insufferable brat and your mother is trying on a good day. I tolerate them only because I have to. I spend time with you because you're my favorite." She winks and I grin, but I have to wonder how much I'm projecting and how much of the attraction between Wren and me is real, and what, if anything I should do about it.

CHAPTER 10
PLUS-ONE

WREN

My father pulls me for a hug. "How's my baby girl?"

I accept the affection and don't balk at the baby-girl comment. I'll always be his baby, and I'm very okay with that. When I was twelve, not so much, but now I'm grateful for his warmth and the nickname. "I'm good. How are you?"

"I'm well." He holds me at arm's length. "You look . . . happier than the last time I saw you." He lowers his voice. "Are things okay over at the Moorehead circus?"

I laugh. "As okay as they can be, I suppose."

My father is well aware of some of Armstrong's antics. While the Mooreheads have paid an exorbitant amount of money to keep their youngest son's scandalous behavior from becoming public fodder—for the most part—not all of it has managed to stay under the radar.

"Where's Mom?" My stomach twists at the possibility that she's going to cancel.

My dad gives my hand a reassuring pat. "She'll be joining us shortly."

"Okay. That's good." Last week, she and I volunteered at the hospital together. It was emotional, but cathartic to have that experience. It's only taken me more than a decade to realize that healing happens a lot faster when you stop placing blame and start putting in an effort to make a change.

We're led to a table, and I take the seat across from my dad.

"She really enjoyed volunteering with you," he says.

"I think it was good too." I focus on smoothing out my napkin in my lap. I'd expected it to be awkward, or maybe even painful, but more than anything, it had felt like the beginning of closure for me. "Is she doing okay?" The anniversary of Robyn's birth and death is quickly approaching, and it's a hard time of year for my mother. For all of us.

"She's keeping busy, which I think is helpful."

I nod. "That's good. And what about you?"

"I'm always busy."

I smile, aware that he's trying to diffuse the sudden sadness.

He leans in, dropping his voice. "I've been watching the media feeds; you've done a great job setting things up for the older Moorehead boy."

I chuckle. "He's hardly a boy, Dad, but thanks. It's amazing what a haircut and a new suit will do for someone's image."

"Mmm . . . He's done good things based on what I've seen; all his work in developing countries will definitely appeal to the public. Lord knows Moorehead needs some positive publicity after the last couple of years."

It's my turn to *mmm* since I can't really comment either way.

My father reaches across the table and gives my hand a squeeze. "You know, Wren, I can help you get the kind of position you want if this ends up being too much for you."

"I know, Dad, and I really appreciate it, but going about it this way feels less like nepotism. Besides, the challenge is good for me." I don't have to agree with or accept other people's bad decisions. I just have to find ways to help reframe them in the public eye. And thankfully, Lincoln doesn't have a terrible reputation in the media to clean up, so it's much easier this time around.

My father gives me a knowing, sad smile. "I think you've had enough challenges thrown at you, but I know you want to make your own way. Just know that I'm here to help if you want me to."

I nod, but I can't quite meet his gaze. "I appreciate that, but Mom already helped me get this position, so I feel like halfway to favoritism is better than all the way, you know?"

"I understand, and I'm aware your mother's heart was in the right place when she suggested working for the Mooreheads, and that you took this position as a means to make things better between you, but it shouldn't be torture either. Your mother thinks the best of all people, which is a noble trait, but you and I both know that's not always the way things really are."

"I promise it's better this time around." And leaving the Moorehead position would feel a lot like abandoning my attempt to repair my relationship with my mother. "I'm a big girl. You don't have to worry about me."

He squeezes my hand again. "You will always be

my baby girl, even when you're forty and you have your own child to love."

I know he means it. And I believe his sincerity, but I also remember how devastated my parents were when they lost Robyn only days after she was born. I shoot him a wry grin, swiftly moving the subject away from painful memories. "I'd need a boyfriend in order for that to happen. Anyway, let's talk about the fundraiser this weekend. I think it's going to be great for the subsidized hospital daycare program."

"If everything goes well, we'll be able to get that project under way, which will be wonderful. As much as the Moorehead family seems to struggle with drama, they certainly know how to pull on heartstrings with their charity fundraisers."

"That they do."

"I'm so sorry I'm late!" my mother says, startling us both.

"Abigail. You made it." My father smiles broadly and pushes out of his chair. Despite having been together for more than three decades, and all the ups and downs they've been through, including the loss of a child, his face still lights up whenever she enters the room. It's a testament to his love for her.

They embrace, and my father places a gentle kiss on her cheek.

My mom turns to me, her smile slightly apprehensive, as is the way with us. But she's here, so that means something. I'm her biggest mistake, and there's nothing I can do to erase that because I can't undo my own existence.

I stand and accept her hug, already feeling emotional. She holds me at arm's length, then fingers the ends of my hair. "You did something different."

"I added a few highlights." After the eyebrow incident

in Lincoln's office, I decided it wouldn't hurt to lighten up the color a little, so I went ahead and made an appointment with my stylist. I've dyed it since I was a teenager, mostly so it's closer to my dad's hair color, at least before he started graying at the temples.

"Well, I like it. It's fresh and summery." My mother takes the seat next to my father and props her chin on her fist, eyes lighting up. "It'll look lovely for the fundraiser. Are you planning to bring a date? There's a doctor who works in the neonatal unit at Saint Margaret's Hospital who's single. I believe he's planning to attend. I could introduce you."

"Oh, I don't know about that." I can feel my cheeks flush. "I assume I'll be working that event, so I won't have a lot of time for mingling."

My mother frowns. "You're almost thirty, sweetie. I know your career is important to you, but when was the last time you went on a date?"

"Mom, please."

"What? I can't worry about my little girl? All you do is work and spend time with Dani." Her eyes flare, and she puts her hand on mine, dropping her voice. "You know your father and I would be completely okay with it if you were to tell us you're gay."

I burst out in laughter. "Thanks, Mom, but I'm not gay and neither is Dani. It's good to know you'd be accepting if I were, though."

"You never know." She pats my hand and winks. "I'll still introduce you to the doctor at the event, in case there are sparks."

"Abigail, let her be."

"Really, Kieran? Weren't you just saying how you were worried Wren is working too much and not spending enough time being young and enjoying life?"

I put up a hand. "I love you both, but really, you don't need to worry. I'm more than capable of finding dates all on my own."

"Well, if the fundraising event isn't a good place to stage an introduction, I could always orchestrate one the next time we volunteer at the neonatal unit." She pauses as if uncertain, but quickly continues. "Only if you want go with me again, though. And I don't have to introduce you to the doctor either, if it will make you uncomfortable."

I fight back the sudden swell of relief. "Okay. I mean, okay, I'd loved to volunteer with you again."

"Really? Well, that's wonderful. Maybe we could make it a weekly thing, if you want."

"We could do that, sure. But let's put a pin in the doctor introduction for now."

She smiles and blinks a few times, maybe working to control her own emotions. "Of course, we could plan for next week?"

"That would be great, Mom."

Her smile makes my heart ache, because the one thing that's always felt like the rift between us is also the thing that seems to bind us together.

"Wren, just the person I'm looking for!" Gwendolyn catches me as I return from lunch. Prior to Fredrick passing, I rarely saw her, but now she's here more frequently, which makes sense, I suppose.

I force a polite smile. I'm feeling emotional after my lunch with my parents, and all I want to do is disappear into my office and be alone so I can process. "What can I do for you, Gwendolyn?"

She threads her arm through mine. "I wanted to speak with you about the fundraising event this weekend."

"Of course. I have notes for Lincoln, and we'll be reviewing his speech and what he should expect at the event. I have a tux fitting set up for tomorrow to make sure everything is as it should be." Which I need to remind him of.

"You're always so on top of things, Wren." She pats my hand. "I'm sure everything will be in order." We slip inside Fredrick's office, which she's taken over, and she drops into the executive chair behind the massive desk, motioning for me to do the same on the other side.

Fredrick was always so much less formal, never using his desk as a barrier. Although with Fredrick, it was always he and I against whatever idiocy Armstrong had pulled. Lincoln isn't nearly as difficult to manage, which is good, considering I still have to deal with Armstrong. Although he's been less demanding and not quite the pain in the ass he usually is now that Lincoln is around. Small blessings.

Gwendolyn leans back in her chair and smiles. "Now about the event, I'm aware all invitations include a plus-one, but since you're technically working, I'll assume you'll be attending alone." The way she says it indicates that's the expectation.

"I hadn't planned to bring a date." It seems pointless when I'll be spending my time trying to keep Armstrong from hitting on everything with a pulse.

"Good, good. That's wonderful news. With this being Lincoln's first charity event, I need you focused on him, not on entertaining someone else." Her nose wrinkles, sort of. "Besides, you and Lincoln have been spending a lot of time together. We wouldn't want people to make inappropriate assumptions."

"Inappropriate assumptions?" I fight with my fingers to keep from tapping the arm of my chair.

"You know how people speculate. There have been some pictures of you and Lincoln recently, very helpful in building his popularity in the media, especially with the makeover. He looks very much a part of this family again, so job well done there." She taps on her keyboard and turns her monitor so I can see what she's talking about. There are several pictures of Lincoln and me together over the past couple of weeks. Most of them are taken as we're leaving his penthouse or entering the Moorehead Media building, but there are a few of me adjusting his tie or his lapels and they're almost . . . intimate. And the look on Lincoln's face is quite riveting.

She turns the screen away and inspects the image, and then me. It makes me nervous. Have I been lusting after him in my dreams lately? Maybe a little. Okay, maybe a lot. But they're just dreams, they don't mean anything. We spend a lot of time together, and he's attractive. It's not really much of a surprise that he's weaseled his way into my subconscious.

Ever since the incident in his office, I've been trying to convince myself that him telling me I was the only good thing about working here was purely to assuage my ego. That he didn't almost kiss me. That I didn't fully invite him to—thankfully not with actual words.

I swallow down my embarrassment. I need to have a closer look at the pictures that have gone up lately, specifically the ones *not* posted by me. "Does that mean Lincoln won't be bringing a plus-one either?"

"I haven't had a chance to discuss it with him. I can't tell you the number of women who have expressed interest in him since his return to New York. I'm sure he'll be making the most eligible bachelor's list at some point. He really is such a handsome man."

Her expression flattens, and she gets a faraway look in her eyes. "Just like his father was."

I wonder if I've misread Gwendolyn, and she really did love Fredrick. She almost looks sad.

She turns her smile back on me. "You'll need to check with Lincoln regarding his plus-one situation and do a background check on whoever he's bringing. I'd hate for his date to undo all the good this charity event will do for his image by having a questionable past."

"Of course. I can check with him now. Would you like me to do the same with Armstrong?"

"Oh! No, that will be unnecessary. Armstrong has been sorted out already. However, if Lincoln doesn't have a date lined up yet, I have a few prospective women who would be a good fit." She pushes a folder toward me.

"I'm sorry, but does this mean you'd like him to have a date? Won't he be busy with networking?" I'm confused about this whole thing, frankly.

"Mmm. I think so, yes. He will be busy, but it would be a good idea for him to have someone respectable on his arm. It will help dispel any potential speculation about the two of you. Regardless of whether he chooses one from this list or a date of his own, I'd like you to ensure whoever he'd like to bring doesn't have any demons to uncover." She steeples her hands and smiles. "You're doing a fabulous job, Wren. I'm sure with a bit more time and energy, I'll be able to put in that recommendation for the position with the charity of your choice. I believe you're interested in the Pediatric Foundation, is that correct?"

"Yes, that's right, thank you. I truly appreciate your support, Gwendolyn." I take the folder, displeased that I have to deal with this now. "Will there be anything else?"

"That's it for now." She turns back to her computer, effectively dismissing me.

Once I'm out of her office, I flip open the folder. There are at least half a dozen profiles of women in their mid-to-late twenties. All from exceedingly rich families. My stomach twists at the thought that Lincoln might actually have a date lined up for this event, and if he doesn't, Gwendolyn wants me to set him up with one of these women.

He spends the majority of his days in the office, but I have no clue what he does with his evenings. On the few occasions I've busted into his temporary penthouse, he's been alone, thank God, but I'm honestly unaware if he's actively dating. The only thing I can be certain of is that when he first returned, he said he hadn't had sex in a long time. Is that still the case? Why does it actually feel like there's a giant green-eyed monster taking over my entire body?

It's in this highly negative, territorial frame of mind that I knock on his office door.

"What?" he barks out.

I throw the door open, ready to give him hell for the less than pleasant greeting, but I'm momentarily thrown off by his huge grin. Aside from his gorgeously disarming smile, he's rolled up his shirt sleeves so his muscular forearms are on display. Why does he have to be so ridiculously attractive on all levels? Maybe I should suggest he grow the beard again. At least the chin dimple would be covered, and less of a weakness.

"We've talked about this, Lincoln," I scold.

His smile growing wider. "I knew it was you."

"How? I didn't announce myself."

"I know your knock. You rap three times quickly, pause, and rap twice more."

"I do not." At least I don't think I do.

"Yes, you do. Every time. And Marjorie has a timid knock. My g-mom only ever knocks once, and Armstrong usually pounds on the door like he's slamming his head against it, so I knew it was you." He folds his arms behind his head and leans back in his chair. His biceps pop and stretch the white fabric. I wonder what he looks like when he's working out. I've seen him in his underwear enough times that I'm sure I can accurately imagine all those muscles flexing.

"Wren?"

Dammit. I've been daydreaming. "Hmm?"

"Did you do something different with your hair?"

"What?" I touch it. Maybe I should've stopped in the restroom before I came in here and checked my appearance.

"Your hair looks different. Is it lighter?"

"Oh. I had some highlights put in earlier in the week. It's nothing." It's also the first time I've worn it down since I had it done.

"I like it."

"Thank you." My cheeks feel hot. Why am I so flustered over a compliment?

"Sorry. You came in here for something, didn't you?" Lincoln leans forward and rests his forearms on his desk.

"Oh. Right. Yes. The fundraiser event is this weekend." His smile drops, but I power on. "I have a tux fitting arranged—"

He holds up a hand. "Didn't we already do enough fittings with the damn suits?"

"Yes, but you need a tux for special events. They already have your measurements; this is to make sure it fits properly. It won't take very long."

"I hope not." He tosses his pen on his desk. "Anything else?"

"We'll need to review your speech, but that can wait until tomorrow if you'd prefer. The draft is already in your email."

"Of course I don't get to write my own speech," he mutters.

"You can give your input if you'd like."

He brushes off the offer. "Why bother? It's not like I'm going to be here in a few months, anyway."

I let it go for now. "I also need to know if you're bringing a plus-one to the event."

"What?"

"A plus-one. Do you have a date lined up for the event?" I can't look at him, so I consult the file folder of women's profiles. Potential dates for the event. I'm sure every single one of them would offer to make it a happy ending too.

"Why does it matter?" he asks.

I look up, but focus on his chin. It's better than looking him in the eye because that reminds me of the almost-kiss, and then my heart starts racing. That damn dimple winks, taunting me. I want to bite his chin. Suck that pouty bottom lip. Dammit. I focus on his forehead. That should be safe. I clear my throat and try to sound unaffected. "If you have a plus-one lined up, I'll need to perform a background check to ensure there aren't any potential issues."

"Potential issues?" he parrots.

"We'll need to know if your date has a history of unsavory behavior."

"I don't have a date lined up, so I guess there's nothing to worry about it."

I nod woodenly. "Your mother has intimated that a

date would look good for optics. I have a list of profiles you can browse."

"A list of profiles?"

I wish he would stop repeating things back to me. This could not be any more awkward than it already is. I set the file folder on his desk and flip it open. "These women have already been vetted and approved."

Lincoln looks up at me with an expression I can't quite read. I don't know if it's disbelief, or possibly anger, or maybe even disgust. "You've vetted potential dates for me?"

I swallow thickly as he flips through the profiles. "Not me personally, no, but they've all been cleared as good potential plus-ones."

He pauses at an attractive brunette. "Five-eight, blue eyes, brown hair, breasts are natural. Well, that's a real bonus, isn't it? Oh, and look at this, she was a cheerleader in college, and she has a degree in interior design. Looks like her dad owns some big company and has a giant bankroll. She sounds perfect for me, don't you think?"

"Sounds like an excellent fit," I grind out. "Her contact information is right there." I stab at the phone number.

Lincoln regards me with narrowed eyes. "Do you have a plus-one?"

"I'm sorry?"

"A plus-one? Are you bringing someone?"

"I don't see how—"

"Has he been vetted? Maybe I need to do my own background check. Make sure you're not bringing some douchebag to my family's fundraiser."

Great. For some reason he's pissed off, and now so am I. It's bad enough that I've been told it won't look good for me to bring a date, but the way he's acting is full-on jerk. "My dates are none of your business."

He slams the folder shut and pushes it toward me. "I don't need help getting a date."

"I'll still need to vet whoever you're bringing." I nearly choke on the words.

Lincoln scoffs. "Don't you worry your pretty little head, Wren. I won't screw up this precious fundraiser and ruin all your hard work making me look like the perfect CEO. I have shit to do. Close the door on your way out."

I don't know how to respond to his abrupt dismissal, so I stand there for a few more seconds and stare. My throat feels tight, and my eyes burn.

"You can go now, Wren," he barks, eyes still on his monitor.

So I leave, because for some reason I'm at risk of shedding tears over Lincoln having a date. Which tells me something important. He's not just my job anymore. If I can't have a date, I don't want Lincoln to have one either.

And more than that, if he's going to have one at all, I want it to be me.

CHAPTER 11

SOMETIMES IGNORANCE
IS BLISS

LINCOLN

I'm in a foul mood. Like the worst. I'm Oscar the Grouch and Scrooge's angry hate child rolled into one. I've been like this ever since Wren came into my office and offered me a list of prospective plus-ones.

And now I'm in the middle of a meeting, absent of Wren—she's been scarce since yesterday's conversation—and all Armstrong can talk about is letting go of the employees of the two digital publications to free up more funds.

I rub my temples, trying to stay calm and not bark at my brother every time he throws out the phrase *the bottom line*.

"What about Williams Media?" I ask.

"What about them? They're our competition," Armstrong sneers, as if I'm stupid.

What I wouldn't give to go a round with him strapped to the side of a punching bag. "Yes. And their magazines with similar content are selling four times what ours are. According to our records, there was a proposed merger in this particular division a while back, but it fell through. Would you happen to be able to shed some light on that?"

Armstrong adjusts his tie and looks anywhere but at me. "I guess it didn't work out."

"Hmm. Well, it looks like there's talk about hiring more staff over there to facilitate expanding that division, so it seems like it wasn't a bad decision for them, and it sure as hell didn't work out well for us." I've done the research. I'm aware Amalie confronted Armstrong in the middle of a meeting with Wentworth, which is the reason they have her and we have tanking sales. "I've arranged a meeting with Wentworth to renegotiate."

It doesn't take long for what I've said to sink it. "What? You can't get in bed with the competition."

"Don't you get in bed with everyone?" I wave him off before he can open his mouth and spew more nonsense. "Dad was more than willing to make a deal with them before you screwed it up, and now that I'm here, and in charge, I get to make the decisions, regardless of whether you like them or not."

"Our division is failing because Amalie sabotaged it!" Armstrong shouts.

I really wish Wren were here to put him in a headlock. "Our division is failing because you cheated on your wife at your wedding, and multiple times prior to that, and then you went and demoted her. Williams was right to snatch her up because she's an incredible business asset, and you screwed that up. So if anyone's to blame for the failure of anything, it's you, brother."

He throws his hands up in the air. "Of course you're going to blame me."

I slam my hand on the table, rattling the glasses, and likely the board members who are bearing witness to this family drama. "Can you get your head out of your own ass for five seconds and look at the bigger picture, here, which is not a mirrored reflection of your face, Armstrong? Firing twenty employees is not in our best interests, not fiscally, and certainly not when it comes to drawing negative media attention. Merging this division with Williams means we don't have to let them go. It will save money and bad press down the line."

"Lincoln's right," G-mom says from over the speakerphone. I didn't want to interrupt her vacation, but I felt like her input on this would be helpful, so we conferenced her in. "A merger is the most cost-effective, financially responsible move."

"My meeting with Wentworth is next week. That gives us enough time to run the numbers and see what we can offer as a buy-in."

"What about me?" Armstrong gripes.

"Your last meeting with Wentworth resulted in Moorehead losing the potential merger, so you'll get to sit this one out. I have a phone conference in twenty minutes, so if we're done here, I'll thank all of you for attending and we can reconvene next week after the meeting. Nash, I'd like those numbers before the end of the day tomorrow, is that possible?"

"I'll make it happen."

"Thank you. Enjoy the rest of your trip, G-mom."

"I'll call you later, Lincoln." I smile as she ends the call, aware the G-mom slip is probably the reason for her annoyed, but amused tone. I gather up my things and head down the hall, feeling a little lighter, knowing that we have a potential solution, as long as I can get Wentworth to agree.

I pass Wren's office on the way back to mine—I took the long way, but she's still not there, which is frustrating, because all I want to do is share the possible good news with someone who will actually care.

When I get back to my office, I drop into my chair and start organizing my desk, my bad mood returning when I shuffle the folder with my prospective dates aside. Having her hand me the folder in the first place was a pisser, but worse is that she never answered my question, so I don't know if she has a date for this thing or not.

I should make someone tell her she can't bring a date. I mean, she's supposed to be dealing with me, and probably Armstrong, at the event. She can't have a date and do her job. *Wren is mine.*

As that thought comes barreling into my brain like a shotgun blast, I realize it's a problem. The very idea is problematic. As is the jealousy I'm currently feeling over a date I can't even be sure exists.

But now that I'm thinking about it, I can't stop— again. I don't know what she does in her spare time, not that she has much of it with the hours she pulls. But still, she could be dating. I know she doesn't have a boyfriend. At least, I assume she doesn't. She'd have mentioned a boyfriend if there were one. I think, anyway.

I pull up her social media accounts and comb her posts. Mostly it's pictures of flowers or parks, or her with her parents at various events. It's all a bunch of staged photo ops from what I can see, but there are no boyfriend pics. She has a fish tank, but no other pets. She likes to make salad and take pictures of that, which is ironic since her favorite snack is Cheez-Its. She always has a bag of them in her desk. I'm pretty sure she uses it as a salad topping.

I give up after another fifteen minutes of searching with no luck. The last time she posted a picture of her with a guy who wasn't a family member was more than a year ago—yes, I went back that far. I still kind of want to punch the guy out, even though it's not rational.

I also need to get a grip, because clearly, she and I are not on the same page if she's bringing me a portfolio full of potential dates for this event. I'll be able to get a clear answer out of her about the date situation when we do the tux fitting. Whenever that is. She didn't even give me a time. I'm sure it'll magically appear in my calendar, and there will be seven hundred alerts to go with it. I can make it clear I need her attention on me, not some guy who probably wants to go out with her so he can climb ladders and get into her panties. If she's even wearing any.

My phone rings, pulling me out of my head and back into reality. Carlos's name flashes across the screen, so I answer the call and put it on speakerphone. "Hey, my man, how are things going without me there?"

"Good, great even. We're on schedule with the wells and building materials showed yesterday. The crew is going to break ground in the morning."

I cross over to the window and look down at the sprawling park, wishing I were out there, or better yet, in Guatemala. Breaking ground has always been one of my favorite parts, and I'm sad I'm missing it, but glad they're managing without me. "Anything I can do to help from my end?" I ask.

"Nope, I just wanted to call and let you know things are going well, and you don't have anything to worry about. How's New York treating you?"

"Eh, I'd rather be where you are, but I'm surviving."

We chat for a few more minutes, discussing the plans for construction, and I ask about funds and food supplies, but Carlos knows what he's doing, so he's on top of everything.

I end the call feeling ambivalent. It's good to know Carlos has it under control, but I miss being involved in projects that matter.

I focus on the folders on my desk. To the right are the ones I pulled from the filing cabinet in my dad's office that no one could seem to find a key for. I picked the lock and emptied the entire cabinet into a banker's box when my mother was out for lunch the other day.

I assume I'm going to find some things in there I shouldn't, considering how hard it was to get into. I open one of the hidden files. At this point, I'm used to coming across bank records for money spent on things that don't pertain to anything Moorehead Media-related.

But this time, I find something more inexplicable than usual. My first inclination is to seek out Wren, since typically she's the one who won't BS me, but she's not here, so I can't ask her.

I take the file with me down the hall to the office I least want to visit, especially after this morning's meeting, with the person I like less than a pervasive flu virus, but who will potentially have an answer.

I pass Carter, my brother's assistant, who looks like he wants to stop me, but doesn't. I enter without knocking. Armstrong flails and shouts, slamming his laptop closed, but not before I get an eyeful of some chick screwing herself with a giant purple dildo in the reflection in the window.

"Seriously?"

"Don't you know how to knock?" My brother has to tuck himself back in his pants, because, yes, he was jacking off at his desk.

"Don't you fuck the dog enough at work, now you have to choke your chicken here too?"

"I was releasing some tension after that useless meeting. What do you want?"

I ignore the comment about the meeting, slap the folder on the desk, and flip it open.

"What is that?" Armstrong squints and reaches for the paper, but I pick up the closest pen and rap his knuckles. "Ow! Why'd you do that?"

"Wash your hands, you disgusting prick."

He rolls his eyes, but washes his hands in the sink by his minibar. Of course there's a bar in his office, and a putt strip, and a couch. If it wasn't for the ban on female employees working directly with him, he'd probably have a bed set up in here too.

I wait until he's rinsed the dick off his hands before I allow him to touch the documents.

"It looks like a deed," he says.

"I know it's a deed. What I want to know is, who does the penthouse belong to?"

Armstrong frowns. Or tries to. "How should I know?"

"So it's not yours?"

"Nope." He flips his pen between his fingers. "Maybe Dad invested in some property and never got around to doing anything with it."

"Don't you find it odd that there's this deed for a condo unit tucked into his business files?"

He lifts a shoulder. "Maybe he was using it for storage."

"Storage for what? It's in Lower Manhattan. It doesn't make sense." Obviously my brother won't be any help. "I'm going to go check this place out."

"I'll come with you. Might be good to see what it's worth, and I need a lunch break."

"Don't you have meetings?"

"Nope. I was planning on doing paperwork this afternoon."

I want to tell him to screw off, but at the same time, if he's lying about not knowing about the property, I'll be able to tell once we're there. Armstrong is a good liar—he always has been—but he has a tic under his right eye that he can't control when he gets caught embellishing stories. He also does this tapping thing with his foot.

I want to take the subway, but Armstrong balks at the idea of public transit. I'd force him, but I have a feeling he'll do something embarrassing and end up on social media as a result, which will make more work for Wren that doesn't have to do with me, so we take a car instead.

We have to stop at three different places for takeout on the way. By the time we finally arrive, I've already thought of a hundred ways to murder Armstrong and just as many places to bury his body.

The building is an upscale condo on the water in Lower Manhattan facing New Jersey. It's not a Mills building either, which is unusual. My father always invests in Mills real estate because they're the best, and they're family. It sends up a lot of red flags. I have a few guesses as to why my father would have a piece of property this far away from the office.

I was smart enough to bring the deed with me, so we're able to obtain clearance to enter the apartment, but it takes a while. Of course, Armstrong bitches the entire time—until I threaten to knock out his teeth.

The sinking feeling that's taken over since I found this particular file dominates as we enter the penthouse. It's two thousand square feet of modern space. The eat-in kitchen has a small table. I run my finger across the wood surface, and they come away dust-free, which indicates someone has either been here or cleaned recently. Either way, it means this place is being taken care of. The living room boasts a wide couch and a flat-screen TV, but not much else in terms of furniture or décor. It doesn't look very lived in, at least at first glance.

I check the fridge and find three bottles of high-end white wine, two very expensive bottles of champagne, and a jug of fresh-squeezed organic orange juice. It's the brand my father favored, and it's past its expiration date. Fresh orange juice has a short shelf life, so it couldn't have been here that long, which means someone has definitely been here in the last few weeks, possibly right before my father died.

Armstrong appears behind me with an empty bin meant for groceries.

"Where'd you find that?"

He thumbs over his shoulder. "In the pantry."

"Is there anything else in there?"

"Just some canned stuff, I think." He shoulders his way past me and starts emptying the bottles of wine and champagne into the bin.

"What're you doing?"

He glances over his shoulder. His expression indicates he thinks I'm an idiot for asking. "It's good wine. I'm taking it home."

"Sometimes I'm honestly baffled we share the same DNA." I leave him to his scavenging and check out the pantry.

I have a feeling my suspicions about this place are right. The wine and champagne seem to fit my theory; this is where my dad brought his mistresses. I have to assume it's a plural and there wasn't just one.

I step inside the large room, and as soon as I get a load of the contents, I have a hell of a lot more questions. Lining the floor-to-ceiling shelves are several rows of cereal boxes. Sure there are a few other items, such as preserves, peanut butter, noodles and canned sauces, but the majority of the shelf space is taken up by sugary treat cereal we were never allowed to eat as kids.

I pick up a box of Cocoa Pebbles. It's good for another six months. My dad was always such a healthy eater, mostly because Gwendolyn would bitch at him if he so much as looked at sugar the wrong way. Holy fuck. What if my dad had an entire second family? One where the kids got to eat whatever fucking cereal they felt like. It's the thing soap operas are based on. And those bad afternoon talk shows.

Shelving the box, I cross through the living room and peek into the master bedroom. It looks normal. The huge four-poster bed is decorated in feminine colors. The comforter is gray and pink. The room looks a lot more lived in than the rest of the place, which again leads me to believe this is definitely where he would take his mistress. I check the closet and find both men's and women's clothing. Based on the sizing and the style, none of it belonged to my mother either. Beyond that, the cereal brings up a whole new set of concerns. Like maybe he knocked one of his mistresses up, and this was where he hid her. And if that's the case, where was she now?

I leave the master bedroom and head down the hall, terrified I'm going to find a second bedroom outfitted for a kid. Instead, I stumble on something incredibly weird.

I don't find a kid's bedroom, but what I do find leaves me with a lot more questions than it does answers. It's another bedroom, but clearly it's not meant for sleeping. I'm not sure what exactly goes on in here, or whether I really want to know at all. It's like costume and prop central—but with a highly sexual twist.

One wall of the bedroom is lined with what appears to be costumes. I have a vague memory of how much my father loved dressing up for Halloween. However, I didn't need it to be connected to his apparently active and kinky sex life.

I might've been able to get over the costumes and kink, but then I get a load of the elaborate restraint system I apparently missed the first time I glanced at the bed. On the nightstand is a giant economy-size tub of lube. And the cherry on the sundae is the sex swing in the corner.

"Linc, I found something—" Armstrong comes into the room holding what at first looks like one of those adult onesies that have been all the rage. "What the hell is this?"

I rub the back of my neck, aware the tightness isn't going away and that the sudden throb in my temples is likely only going to get worse. "I might be going out on a limb here, but I think it's our dad's sex fetish room."

"Huh." He drops the onesie on the edge of the bed. Upon closer inspection it looks more like a wolf costume. "Well, this might explain why our parents didn't sleep in the same room."

I clear my throat, a million new questions cropping up. Like, did my mother know? How long had this been going on? *Who in the actual fuck would entertain this level of weird?* "It might."

He crosses over to the wall of costumes and pulls a red number off the rack. "I think this is supposed to be a Little Red Riding Hood getup." He checks under the cape and holds up a very lacy, lingerie-style dress. "You think he dressed up like fairytale characters? It kinda reminds me of like those people who dress up as mascots or whatever and screw each other. I went to a party like that once. Some chick dressed like Princess Leia was getting banged by Chewbacca. It was kinda hot."

"Can you shut up before I punch you in the face?"

"You can't punch me in the face. We have that event coming up and that would piss Wren off, and she'll blame me when it's your fault."

"Fine. Shut up before I punch you in your tiny needle dick."

"It's not tiny; it's average," Armstrong fires back, as if it even matters.

"No. It's not. There's even an online support group for the women you've been with called the Armstrong Moorehead Needle Dick Support Group." I'm making this up, clearly. I have no idea if there's a group for my brother's unfortunate castoffs, but if there is, I imagine that would be the name of it.

"That's a lie." He motions to his crotch. "I'm definitely average."

"Compared to what? A Chihuahua?" I wave him off. "Your less-than-averageness doesn't matter, Armstrong. What matters is that this place has clearly been used, probably regularly, and our father obviously had some weird sexual quirks, so there has to be at least one woman out there who knew about this who likely isn't our mother."

He stares blankly at me for a few seconds before he finally replies. "So?"

"So?" I throw my hands in the air. "Who is she? Why was our father living this alternate life where he played dress up and did whatever the fuck they did in here?"

Armstrong shrugs. "Lots of people like weird sex

stuff. Take Amalie, for instance. She was obsessed with sex toys."

"That's because the only person you worry about getting off when you are having sex is yourself. You have to take care of your partner's needs." I don't even know why I'm bothering to say any of this. It's not as if Armstrong has the capacity to think beyond himself.

"She had too many needs. And she didn't know how to behave like a wife. Only mistresses should give noisy blow jobs. Like Imogen. She was very good at being quiet. She would've made a good wife if she hadn't gotten pregnant. Now Wren would probably make a good fuck. She's so uptight. I bet she's hardly been worked in at all."

The more he speaks, the more my skin crawls, and my disbelief mounts. His view on women is barbaric, vile, and demented. So I do the only thing I can that will make him stop and make me feel better. I cock a fist and punch him in the stomach. He drops to the floor, clutching his gut, gasping for breath.

We used to get into it when we were kids. Not a lot, because I wasn't around all that much past the age of ten, but whenever I came home from boarding school, there was sure to be at least one decent scrap.

Armstrong is four years younger, so he couldn't really fight back at the time. He'd pull cheap shots, and I'd have to take it because he was too young to know better, at least that's what my mother thought. Armstrong knew he could get away with it, since I'd be the one to catch heat if I retaliated.

But now, he's just a jackass with a big mouth and zero morals.

I straddle him and bend down, fisting his tie near his throat. "You narcissistic bastard."

He grips my fist with both of his, manicured nails digging into my skin, and his mouth opens and closes as he gasps for air. I realize I'm at the edge right now, that what I've found out about my father explains nothing and everything. And that my brother seems to think his misogynistic, archaic beliefs are acceptable is really more than I can handle.

"Don't ever bring up Amalie or Imogen again with me. Ever." His face is turning red, so I loosen my grip enough that he sucks in another gasping breath. "As for Wren, if you say anything like that about her again, or you so much as look at her the wrong way, I will not hesitate to use your balls for golf practice and your dick as the flag. Am I understood?"

I release his tie. He rolls to his side and curls into a ball.

"Don't make me repeat myself, Armstrong."

"Yeah," he coughs. "Yes. Understood. Christ, calm down." He pulls himself into a sitting position. "You can't tell me you haven't thought about what it would be like to stop her incessant nagging by plugging her mouth with your—"

I grab him by the throat and haul him to his feet, cutting off the end of the sentence. Then, I punch him in the junk and let him go.

He crumples again, cupping himself this time.

"The fact that you've created another human being is a travesty. Thank God, Imogen was smart enough to file for full custody." I leave him lying on the floor in our father's sex room. I also take the bin Armstrong filled with the wine and champagne because my brother deserves nothing, and I need a damn drink.

CHAPTER 12

THE PULL

LINCOLN

It's early evening by the time I get home. My head is spinning, and all I want to do is call Wren, but my phone is dead and my charger is at the office, where I left it. I would search the penthouse for a spare, or go out and get another one, but the need to drown the things I've seen out with alcohol is a bigger priority.

So I uncork a bottle of the white I took from my father's sex pad and down half of it straight from the bottle. It's good, but it's not strong enough, so I grab the scotch and pour myself a very generous glass. I'm about to fire up my laptop when I realize that it, too, is at the office. "Dammit," I say to the sculpture on the side table.

I shrug out of my suit jacket and drop it on the floor, my tie follows, shoes go next, then I unbutton the cuffs on my shirt. I get lazy and decide that's as far as I'm willing to go in the quest for comfort.

I expel a loud expletive. Today has sucked, and the one person I'd like to talk to, who might have some kind of information I can trust, I can't get a hold of. And then I remember Griffin is old school and he still has a landline. My excitement deflates when I realize I have no idea what Wren's phone number is because it's programmed in my dead, useless cell.

I almost toss it across the room, but breaking something expensive isn't going to make it better, so I toss it on the couch beside me and go back to chugging my scotch.

I'm in the middle of debating how hammered I plan to get when the door swings open. I know it's Wren before I see her, based on the way she slams the door and the clip of her heels on the hardwood.

She rounds the corner and props her fists on her hips. It's her go-to pose when she's angry. Her eyes are on fire. Her lipstick is fucking red. I hate it so much. But her skirt is so pretty, the palest gray, with a lacy overlay. Her blouse is white, and it looks so soft, the fabric has a sheer quality to it, so I can see the pale camisole underneath. Her heels are hot pink, which makes me hate that stupid red lipstick even more because it doesn't even match.

I want to kiss that lipstick off and peel the clothes from her body. Then I want to fuck her against the softest available surface. I would like to claim her as mine. I would like to ensure that my brother has no reason to ever fantasize about her again because the only thing he'll be able to imagine is me all over her.

Instead of verbalizing any of these things, which are highly inappropriate and also unlikely with how pissed off she looks, I say, in a tone that matches her expression, "What're you doing here?"

Her jaw twitches. "Excuse me?"

"You let yourself in without even knocking. Again. What if I had company?" I regret the words as they leave my mouth. There's no way I would have company here tonight, or any other night, because Wren is the star of every single one of my damn fantasies. But she doesn't know that, and I'm not sure how she'll react if I issue such an admission. Also, I might be feeling the scotch already since the last meal I ate was breakfast, so I try to backtrack. "What if I were naked?"

"Nothing I haven't seen before." Wren's expression is almost totally blank apart from the slight tic in her cheek. It's very drone-like and unnerving. "Where were you this afternoon?"

We stare at each other, both waiting for something. Maybe she already knows about the penthouse. Maybe she saw Armstrong at the office, and he said something, so she came here to see how I am. That would be nice. I'd like that. Of course, I can't answer the question like an adult; instead, I have to continue to be a prick because I'm in a mood, and she's pissed, and I know she's going to let me have it soon. And I kind of want her to, so I have someone to battle it out with.

"I had some stuff to take care of."

"Well, isn't that nice for you? Thanks so much for letting someone know." She flails a hand in the direction of my phone, which is sitting beside me on the couch.

"My battery died, and I left my charger at the office."

She opens her purse and withdraws my laptop and my phone charger, setting them on the coffee table in front of me. "How very convenient for you."

"You came all the way here just to drop them off?"

She gives me an unimpressed look. "No. I saw them on your desk and figured I was already on my way here, so I brought them with me. You had a tux fitting this afternoon, which you obviously forgot about, so I had to reschedule it for tonight."

My elation over her presence is eclipsed by frustration. Of course she's not here because she wanted to do something nice. She's not here because she's worried about me. She's here because she's doing her job. "Cancel it. I'm not leaving this couch. I'm not in the mood to be prodded."

"I can't cancel. The event is tomorrow night, and they'll be here in a few minutes. I already had to push them back another hour because you can't answer a phone call, and I had no idea where you disappeared to this afternoon. Must be nice to bail on work and not let anyone know where you've gone," she snaps.

"I didn't bail," I reply, just as irritated.

She throws her hands in the air. "I had to rearrange my entire schedule for this. I had plans tonight, and now I don't anymore."

That gets my back up. "What kind of plans?"

"The kind that are none of your damn business."

I set my glass on the table and rub my temples. I thought Wren showing up would make things better, not worse. "Today has been a huge bag of crap, so it'd be real nice if you'd give my eardrums a break and stop reaming me out."

Her expression shutters, and her lips press into a thin line. Her throat bobs with a thick swallow, and she lifts her chin higher. I catch the slightest tremble before her cheek tics again. "I'm trying to help you, Lincoln. I'm sorry if my constant attention is inconvenient for you, but no one knew where you or Armstrong were this afternoon. Everyone was worried, and frankly, so was I."

I drop my eyes from the ceiling. She's not looking at me. She's focused on the wall behind my head. She keeps blinking rapidly as if she has something in her eye. I'm so confused about so many things right now. I want her here, but not for the reason she showed up. "Do we really have to do this tonight?"

"People have bad days, Lincoln. It happens. Imagine what every single day looked like for me when my primary role was keeping Armstrong out of trouble." She's interrupted by a knock at the door. "You need to suck it up for an hour, and then you can go back to moping."

She spins around, and her skirt furls impressively as she stalks out of the room. She shoots an apathetic glare over her shoulder when she reaches the hall. "The sooner you strip down, the sooner it'll all be over." And then she disappears around the corner.

God, she pisses me off and makes me hot at the same time. I've never encountered a woman who I simultaneously want to screw and tell to screw off. I'm angry at my father, at the woman he cheated on my mother with, at Wren for being here for the wrong reasons, at myself for not having asked her to be my date for the goddamn charity event when she dropped that stupid file full of women on my desk.

Five seconds too late, I consider getting my ass off the couch to stop her from opening the door. But I've already made things more difficult, and if I push, she'll push back, and I'll probably say or do something I'll regret. There's a good chance I'll do that anyway.

I'm not going to be any more in the mood for this tomorrow morning than I am now. Actually, I'll probably be in a worse mood, because I plan to get wasted after everyone leaves, so I don't have to think about what I saw in that penthouse. About how screwed up my dad was and how he cheated on my mother, likely on a regular basis. How this might explain why she's a cold, heartless woman.

I mutter my annoyance, but I unbutton my shirt and

shrug out of it, dropping it on the floor with my shoes, tie, and jacket. I slip my belt through the loops and add it to the pile.

Just as I'm pulling my undershirt over my head, Wren returns with two men, both of whom I met before at the suit fitting. "Almost ready for you," I say, my eyes fixed on Wren as I lift my shirt over my head and drop it on the floor.

She, on the other hand, makes a point of staring at a spot above my head, but her gaze flicks down more than once. "So glad you've decided to be compliant."

So much damn snark.

She motions to the two men to her left. "You remember Bradley and Ulrich. Bradley already has the tux ready, you just have to try it on to see if it requires any additional alterations. Then Ulrich can neaten you up."

"I just had a haircut. I don't need another one."

"We're going to smooth out the edges. It shouldn't take long." She looks around the room, then taps her lip. "We should probably do this in the bedroom."

I decide if I'm going to have endure this torture, I might as well get something out of it, like a reaction from Wren. I flick the button open on my pants and drag the zipper down. "You don't think we can do it right here?"

"Bradley will need the mirror, and you'll want to see how the tux looks."

"Why? It's not like I have an actual say in what I'm going to wear and whether I like it. Too bad I can't go like this." I shove my pants over my hips.

"Well, it would certainly get some attention." Wren's gaze slides down my chest.

Ulrich coughs into his bent elbow as I kick the pants off. I should probably switch to black boxer briefs since they do a better job of hiding what's going on than white cotton does. Which is exactly where Wren's attention is focused at this very moment.

I smile, though it's probably more sneer than friendly. "Shall we, then?"

Wren glances at her phone. "I'm going to step out and grab a coffee. I'll be back in a bit."

"Do you really think that's a good idea? I mean, aren't you supposed to be supervising me? You wouldn't want me to have a go at this with an electric trimmer, would you?" I motion to my hair.

Wren clamps her mouth shut. "You wouldn't."

I shrug. "You can't be sure if you leave, can you? Come on, Team Lincoln, let's put me in a penguin suit." I pad down the hall and smile when the angry clip of Wren's heels follows a few seconds later.

Maybe this is exactly what I need. A sexy, angry distraction named Wren.

CHAPTER 13

TIGHTY-WHITIE SHOWDOWN

WREN

I am so annoyed. And turned on. But mostly annoyed.

I hate that I had to give up a movie night with Dani because Lincoln couldn't be bothered to tell anyone where he went this afternoon, and that he's threatened to take sheers to his damn head if I so much as run out to grab a coffee. He's winning the Dick of the Day award, that's for sure.

I should've expected him to take me seriously when I made the comment about stripping down. Lincoln is aware he looks as good out of a suit as he does in one, and he seems to derive particular enjoyment in embarrassing me by wandering around in as little as possible. Or maybe it's because he's spent time in countries where people are worried about important things, like food and shelter, rather than their appearance.

Regardless, his ass is fantastic in those damn underwear. The rest of his body is absolutely magnificent, so as irritated as I may be, at least I have something nice to look at while I deal with his extra-surly mood.

I surreptitiously unfasten the top two buttons on my blouse, partly because it's warm in here, and I get tired of always having to be ridiculously modest at work, thanks to Armstrong. Also, if Lincoln wants to flaunt his entire body, I think it's only fair I flash a little retribution cleavage. I can't decide if he's fully aware of the impact his mostly naked body has on me, or the men in the room, who appreciate it as much as I do.

"Where do you want me?" Lincoln asks once everyone is congregated in his bedroom.

Unsure if he means for it to sound suggestive or not, I give him a dismissive wave. "Right where you are is fine for now."

"Ulrich, the master bath is through there, why don't you set up for the trim? What do you think, tux first, hair second, or the other way around?" I give Lincoln a cursory glance. "Let's do hair first, then I don't have to worry about anyone getting trimmer happy." I also like the idea of him having to hang out in his underwear longer than I'm sure he expected, for my own enjoyment.

Lincoln stands in the middle of the room with his arms crossed while I help Ulrich set up his traveling barbershop. Ulrich obstructs my view of Lincoln's chest when he covers him with the cape, but there's still satisfaction in him wearing only a pair of briefs while he has his hair trimmed.

As frustrated as I am with Lincoln, I can't seem to resist the opportunity to get my hands on him. And not just to throttle him. I stand behind him and run my fingernail along the hairline at his neck and follow it to where it curves around the back of his ear.

He sucks in a breath, and I bite back a smile as goose bumps rise along his skin. "Let's clean all this up." I move around to stand in front of Lincoln and tap my lip with my finger. "What do you think about a fade, Ulrich?" I bend at the waist, aware I'm giving Lincoln a peek down the front of my blouse. He can't see much, a hint of cleavage, maybe a glimpse of the lace edge of my cami.

I don't know what's gotten into me. Maybe it's the way Lincoln reacted to the plus-one conversation and his double standard over me having a potential date. Or maybe I'm just tired of fighting my attraction to him. Not to mention his blatant disregard for the value of my personal time.

Ulrich's face lights up. "Oh! A fade would be fabulous. If anyone can pull that off, it's Lincoln."

I run my hand through his hair at the crown; it's thick and dark, the strands silky between my fingers. "What do you think, Lincoln?"

He has to drag his eyes away from my chest. "What?"

"How do you feel?" I run my fingers through his hair again. "About the fade?"

He clears his throat. "Uh, I don't even know what that is, so whatever you want is fine, I guess."

"Great. A fade it is." I tug the hair at his crown. "But let's keep the length on top."

I step back and clap my hands as if this excites me, which it definitely does, and take a seat on the vanity while Ulrich works his magic. Lincoln's attention keeps drifting to my legs, and then up to the open buttons on my blouse before he focuses on his reflection in the mirror again, his brow furrowed in what I can only assume is aggravation.

The haircut doesn't take long. I snap a couple of pictures for his social media, appreciating the artistry of the style before I post them. Lincoln with a fade is damn well glorious. He asks for a minute before we move onto the tux fitting and ushers us out of the bathroom.

Before I slip out the door, he grabs my elbow and bends until his lips brush my ear. "Stop taunting me or it's going to get embarrassing."

I meet his hot gaze. "Taunting you? I'm not the one always parading around in my underwear. Don't be long. Everyone would like at least part of their evening to revolve around something other than you." I pull the door closed behind me.

A minute later, he exits the bathroom still looking tense. I don't know what happened this afternoon, but I plan to get some kind of explanation once everyone else leaves.

Bradley helps Lincoln into his tux and begins making adjustments. I take a seat on the edge of Lincoln's huge bed, the one he sleeps in naked.

"Why don't we go over your speech while you're being fitted? I sent it to your email yesterday, so you could make any edits you saw fit. Did you have a chance to look at it?" I'm sure the answer to that is no, otherwise I would have received a response to that email. It's already eight o'clock, but if we can finish up here in the next half hour or so, I might still be able to stop by Dani's on the way home for a drink or something. Lord knows I deserve one.

Lincoln eyes me through the reflection in the mirror. This vantage point is ideal since I get to see both the front and the back view. "We can do that after I'm done being prodded. No offense, Bradley."

"None taken, sir." He carefully slips another pin in under Lincoln's arm.

"I can read it to you."

"I can't concentrate on anything right now." Lincoln nods at his reflection, but his eyes skim over my crossed legs.

"Fine. I'll wait." Supervising Lincoln get fitted for a tux might be better than whatever movie Dani and I were going to watch anyway.

Once Bradley is finished, I'm asked for my opinion. I wouldn't be doing my job if I wasn't extra thorough about my inspection. I take the opportunity to straighten and fiddle, particularly around the waistband of his dress pants. I only back off when Lincoln practically growls my name on a whisper and shoots laser beams at me out of his eyes.

The tension between us appears to have ramped up since that almost-kiss in his office. It seems like it's been forever since that happened, but it's really only been a few days. The innuendo-laden comments are getting thicker, and if I'm honest, I'm less pissed off about having to change my plans tonight to include Lincoln than I am that he left work today and didn't tell anyone why.

My feelings are hurt, so I figure I'm within my rights to push him a little as he likes to do to me. However, this is starting to feel more like foreplay than it should, so I give Bradley the thumbs-up, and Lincoln, God bless all that hard labor, strips back down to his tighty-whities.

Sadly, he throws on a pair of baggy gray jogging pants with holes in them and covers all that magic below the waist. One of his ridiculous T-shirts covers his defined chest, but like everything he seems to own, it's two sizes too small, stretching tight across the expanse of cut muscle.

Once Ulrich and Bradley leave, I suggest we look at the speech.

"Are you ever off duty?" he grumbles.

"We only have a day to make changes, and we were supposed to review everything this afternoon; however, you disappeared. I'm still on duty until I can check it off my list, so the sooner you stop bitching about it, the sooner I can get out of your hair and you can get back to moping."

Lincoln fires an aggravated glare my way, which I counter with a raised eyebrow.

"I wasn't moping."

"Is brooding manlier?"

"Much, thanks. I didn't bail on the tux fitting this afternoon on purpose, and if my phone hadn't died, I would've called you. I wanted to call you."

"Is that your version of an apology?"

He runs his tongue across his bottom lip. "I'm sorry I ruined your evening and whatever plans you had with whoever you had them with. I get that you probably can't wait to get out of here, but I could really use a drink, and I think you should have one too, so I don't end up consuming an entire bottle of scotch by myself again."

"You're really selling that drink with your uplifting apology." I cross my arms under my chest, which makes my blouse gape. Now that I'm no longer in the heat of the moment, I feel stupid for unbuttoning it in the first place. "What happened this afternoon?"

He squeezes the back of his neck, like there's a kink in it he can't get rid of. "Can we deal with the speech for now?"

"Sure, okay." Now that I'm not focused on how infuriated I was to find him sitting on his couch like he didn't have a care in the world, I notice he looks exhausted and even sad.

He pours himself a very generous scotch and holds the bottle up. "You interested in this? I have a few bottles of white if that's more your speed."

"White might be better if I want to be able to walk out of here."

"Okay." He leaves the scotch on the bar and grabs a bottle of white wine from the bar fridge. His ridiculously tight shirt pulls in all the right places as he uncorks the bottle. Everything would be so much easier if he weren't so nice to look at.

I wonder what it would be like to have access to all that smooth skin. I wonder what it would feel like to have his hands on me, what his mouth tastes like, how soft his lips are, whether his kisses would be sensual or aggressive. I want to know if he's the kind of man who devours or savors. Or maybe both. I could see both. I bet angry fucking him would be mind-blowing. Maybe I should make him angry again.

"Wren?"

I blink and find Lincoln standing in front of me with the glass of wine. "Thank you," I croak.

"Are you okay? You're flushed all of a sudden." He strokes along my cheek with a single knuckle, and I shiver. "Where'd you go in that head of yours?"

I'm thrown by his sudden shift from combative to concerned, so I brush it off. "Nowhere important. I'm distracted, and it's been a long day. We should go over the speech."

His expression shifts from concern to something like disappointment. "Sure."

I follow Lincoln back to the living room, and he pulls up the email with the speech. I also brought a hard copy, which I retrieve from my bag. Lincoln quietly sips his scotch while he reads it over.

It's about the importance of family and his role in carrying out his father's legacy by stepping in as CEO of Moorehead. It also highlights his family's contribution to the hospital's charity foundation, which is the focus of the night's event. He rubs his forehead and sighs heavily, tipping back his glass and nearly draining the contents in one gulp.

"It's very straightforward. Only about five minutes, which I know will seem like a long time, but it'll be over before you know it. We need you to get used to speaking more formally at events, and this is the perfect opportunity. Do you want to practice it for me? Sometimes it helps if you say it in front of someone else, or maybe you'd be better practicing in front of a mirror." I don't know why I'm rambling, other than I'd like to erase the distress from Lincoln's face, if at all possible.

Lincoln runs his hand down his face. "Can I ask you something?"

"Of course."

"Do you believe any of this?"

I set my wineglass on the table and run my hands over my thighs. "I can't pretend I understand what your relationship with your father was like—"

"I didn't have a relationship with my family, not with any of them except G-mom, really. My father worked long hours when I was a kid, and my parents' relationship was . . . difficult. Transactional? I don't know how to explain it. There was no love in that house. Mostly I remember Armstrong getting into trouble, and my parents fighting about what to do with him because he was a nightmare even then." He closes his eyes for a second, exhaling slowly before he focuses on me again.

"You probably knew Fredrick better than I did for all the time I spent with him growing up. He was never there, and he never tried to be. I spent my summers at camps, or I stayed with G-mom at her summer place so

I didn't have to be in the middle of my parents' love-less marriage or deal with my brother. I went to col-lege out of state, and when I was finished, my father figured I would come work at Moorehead. For whatever reason, he thought I would want to work with him when I didn't even know a damn thing about him. Anyway, I got out of the country. I don't even know these people, Wren, let alone like them, so this family legacy angle is a load of BS. The only reason I'm here doing this, is because I don't want to give G-mom a heart attack, and my brother is mess."

"I'm sorry this situation is so difficult—"

"My dad had a penthouse in Lower Manhattan. Did you know that?"

I'm taken off guard by the sudden shift in conversa-tion, so I stumble for a moment before I respond. "Uh, no. I was unaware."

"I found the deed today, and I figured I should check it out, so that's where I was this afternoon. I thought I'd be gone for an hour or two tops, but uh . . . it wasn't just some apartment. It's where he took his mistress or mistresses."

I don't know how to take all of this. The only ver-sion of Fredrick that I know is the one who protected his son from the media backlash when he got into trouble. "What if it was an alternate work location? Or maybe it was a place he used for out-of-town clients?" I suggest, trying to find a reasonable explanation. Everything Lin-coln's told me shines a very different, unpleasant light on Fredrick. If what Lincoln suspects is true, it makes me wonder if he was condoning Armstrong's behavior with all his cover-ups because he'd been doing the same thing all this time. No wonder Lincoln hates his family so much.

"The location wouldn't be convenient; it's too far from the office. Besides, based on the contents of the place, it's pretty clear it was his sex pad. It's just so in-your-face blatant. I can't get my head around the whole thing." His expression reflects his anger and disappointment.

Despite my own difficult family situation, I can't imagine what it would be like to stumble on something like that, mere weeks after losing his father, regardless of how tumultuous their relationship was.

"You're sure it was his? Could it have been Armstrong's?"

"I might believe that, but I took him with me, and he was just as shocked."

"Could it have been somewhere he took your mother?" I want to give him some kind of explanation that makes sense. It's my job, after all, to fix things. Smooth things over and make them better if I can.

"Uh, definitely not. There were women's clothes in the bedroom that wouldn't fit Gwendolyn." He gives me an imploring look. "I don't even know if it was one woman or more than one. You'd tell me if you knew anything about this, wouldn't you?"

I want to comfort him, but I'm not sure how. "If I knew and you wanted to know, I would tell you, Lincoln. Your parents' relationship always seemed more like a business relationship than one built on love, but I don't know anything else." I cover his hand with mine. "I promise I'd tell you if I knew anything important. And if you want me to look into it, I can."

Lincoln runs his free hands through his freshly styled hair, sending it into disarray. "It was different when I just suspected, but actually seeing it . . . I don't even know who my father was. He had a whole different life, Wren, and he was into some pretty weird stuff that might explain why my parents haven't slept in the same room since I was a kid."

"What do you mean?"

"There was a room with a lot of props and costumes."

"I'm sorry. I don't think I understand."

He shakes his head. "He had a fetish room."

"Oh." I have no idea what I'm supposed to say to that. Sorry doesn't seem right. How exactly does someone deal with finding that out about their deceased parent?

I feel awful for putting him through a tux fitting and a haircut after the afternoon he's had. I know exactly what it's like to be disappointed by a parent in a way that crushes the soul and shakes the foundation of trust. Lincoln is almost better off for not having had any trust to break in the first place.

"I don't even know who I am. I don't want these people to be my family. How is this the legacy I'm supposed to uphold?"

My hand is still covering his. Lincoln flips his so we're palm to palm and threads our fingers together. "You're the only person I feel like I can trust. I don't think even my grandmother will be straight with me. Please, be someone I can count on, Wren. I need you to be that for me." His thumb brushes along my knuckles, and his voice drops to a whisper. "Just please."

I fight the flutter in my chest, because he doesn't mean that the way my stupid body is interpreting his declaration. "You can trust me." I squeeze his hand. "I'll always be straight with you, and I'm sorry you have questions about your father that I can't answer, and if you want help finding answers to them, I can do that."

He nods, gaze shifting back to his laptop. "How am I going to get up in front of all of those people and give that speech with conviction? They'll see right through me, and I'll be a total fraud. That's not who I am."

I move closer and cup his cheek in my palm, trying to get him to look at me. His skin is warm and rough with a day's worth of stubble. For the most part, I avoid making prolonged eye contact with Lincoln because my panties feel like they're going to explode when I do.

It's no different now, which borders on inappropriate because Lincoln is vulnerable and distressed, and no parts of my body should feel excited about our current closeness. But that's the thing about physical responses; they don't always take into consideration what's going on in the brain when they happen.

"Listen to me. You're a good man, who genuinely wants to do good things. I know this is hard for you, and I wish I could tell you something that will make it better, but your family's choices aren't yours to own. You don't have to uphold a legacy you don't feel good about, Lincoln. You can create your own."

"This whole thing is such a mess."

"I know. But I'm here to help you figure out how to manage it, whatever that looks like." I'm still touching his face. I should move my hand. But I'm having a hard time getting the command in my head to make its way down my arm.

Lincoln shifts, his knee knocking against mine, creating another point of physical contact. "I don't think I can do this without you."

"You don't have to."

"Because it's one of your duties as assigned." Something like hurt colors the statement.

I shake my head. "This is me, offering to be here for you, however you need me. Not because it's my job, but because I care and I understand better than you know what it's like to be in your shoes."

I drop my hand, but he catches my wrist. "However I need you?"

The attraction we've been flirting with flares with his gritty tone. Somewhere in my head I acknowledge that this could be a very complicated situation, considering my role. Unfortunately or not, my body doesn't really seem to care that giving in to this chemistry would be a bad idea.

Lincoln is rough around the edges, moody and gruff and cynical. But he's also incredibly sweet and genuine and honest to a fault. And he's gorgeous, which really doesn't hurt. Also, that damn chin dimple is winking at me, again.

So I nod and whisper, "I'm here for you, Lincoln, not because of a contract, but because I want to be."

He exhales a long breath that sounds a lot like a groan. I settle my palm against the side of his neck, and Lincoln's fingers drift along the length of my arm. I notice—stupidly—that his nails are jagged again, and I probably should've scheduled him a manicure.

The minor distraction doesn't last long. I lean in closer, breathing in his cologne.

"Wren?" It's a question and a plea, as his hot eyes roam my face and land on my mouth.

"You almost kissed me in your office." I caress the edge of his jaw, seeking confirmation that I'm not mis-interpreting signals.

"Almost," he agrees.

"If we hadn't been interrupted, I'd know what your mouth tastes like." I run a finger along the contour of his bottom lip.

"Is that what you want?" His voice is low and rough like his stubbled cheek.

"Yes. What about you?"

"I've been thinking about your mouth obsessively since then, before then, even."

I almost want to laugh because of course we can't just kiss; we have to talk it through first. "Obsessively, huh?"

"Very obsessively."

I brush my lips over his, a whisper of connection, and then wait, albeit impatiently, for him to continue.

"I kept second-guessing myself, wondering if I'd read the situation wrong." He speaks against the corner of my mouth. "But here we are again."

"Here we are." I wet my bottom lip, the tip of my tongue touches the corner of his mouth, and I taste the bitter tang of aftershave. "No second-guessing this time."

We turn into each other, and his fingers curve along my neck as he sucks my bottom lip aggressively, teeth skimming the sensitive skin. He releases it only to flick his tongue along the underside of my top lip before sucking that one too.

Well . . . this is a weird first kiss.

Before I can decide whether or not I like it, he pulls back, wearing an oddly smirky grin, which very quickly turns into a frown. "What the . . ." He doesn't bother to finish. Instead, his expression shifts to determination, and he dives back in, this time stroking along the seam of my mouth.

I open, somewhat hesitantly, because I'm worried now that the idea of this kiss is going to be a lot different than the reality, and potentially a disappointment.

Thankfully, he doesn't start tongue-thrusting into my

mouth. Instead, he sweeps inside, slowly, softly, tongue sliding against mine. Okay, this is nice. I can get into this. Especially when Lincoln groans into my mouth, and his fingers slip into my hair and wrap around the strands, tightening just enough to send a shock of heat through my body.

Untwining our still clasped hands, Lincoln wraps his arm around my waist, pulling me closer, which isn't easy since we're sitting beside each other on the couch. I kick off my heels and pull my knees up under me so I don't have to twist awkwardly to maintain the kiss, which goes from sweet exploration to a full-on mouth battle in the span of seconds.

I run my fingers through his hair, gripping the strands tightly as weeks of pent-up sexual tension unravel civility. Lincoln's fingers tighten on my waist, and he lifts me so I'm straddling his thick, muscular thighs.

Any thoughts of why this might not be the best idea disappear as I yank his hair, tipping his head to the right while I angle my own in the opposite direction. I bite his tongue when it slides into my mouth, and his fingers dig into my ass.

We keep going after each other's tongues, sucking, biting, stroking. It's aggressive and fun and hot, and sweet Jesus, I bet this man's tongue skills are beyond incredible in *every* capacity.

He uses my hair to pull me back—not in a forceful, potentially painful way, just firmly. His top lip is curled in the sexiest sneer for all of half a second before his brow pulls into his customary furrow, again. "What the—"

He's still gripping my hair in his fist, so when he comes back in and sucks my bottom lip roughly between his, all I can do is yelp. He backs off again, still wearing that furrowed brow as he rubs over my lips with his thumb. It's tender from all the kissing, so I whimper.

"How is that lipstick still on?" He swipes the back of his hand across his mouth and checks for marks. "It should be smeared all over your damn face."

I bark out an incredulous laugh. "It's a stain. It doesn't come off."

"What?"

"It's a lip stain; it's not supposed to come off. I can eat a burger, and it doesn't go anywhere."

"Well . . . damn." Lincoln is still frowning. "How do you get it off?"

"I have a special remover."

"Oh. Huh." He's still staring at my mouth, still holding my hair while I straddle his lap. "So, kissing you isn't going to make it come off?"

"No."

"Not even if we kissed for, like, the next six hours?"

"I'm sure it would wear off by then, but then, so would my lips. Any other questions?" I'm snarky because this is a bit awkward.

He shakes his head. "No. Uh, actually, yeah." He moves his hand around to cup my ass through my skirt and pulls me in tight against him. "What do you think about taking this to the bedroom?"

CHAPTER 14

FIRECRACKER

LINCOLN

Any concerns I may have had about Wren's lipstick evaporate the second she settles over my erection. It doesn't matter that there are several layers of fabric between us. I'm still painfully hard, and every single muscle in my body responds by trying to contract at the same time.

Then she has to go and roll her hips. I drop my head against the back of the couch, watching her through half-closed eyes. I try to remember the last time I had sex. It's been a while. An embarrassingly long while. But then, when your accommodations lack privacy and hot showers are a rarity, sex really isn't on the brain. Well, that's not true; it's definitely on the brain, but it's not so much a viable option.

Wren makes another slow circle with her hips. I bet she's a good dancer. I bet she's going to be incredible in bed. At least I'm hoping that's where this is headed.

She slides her warm, soft palm—her hand is going to feel so good wrapped around me—up the side of my neck. Her fingernails drag along the edge of my jaw, and she presses her thumb against the center of my chin, right over the divot.

Wren rises, taking away the friction I've been enjoying. "Do you think this is a good idea?"

I know what she's asking. It's the reason I haven't given in to the urge to lock her in my office again and see if we could get that almost-kiss moment back. "I think it's probably the best idea I've ever had." I bite the end of her finger when she skims my lip. "Don't overthink it, Wren. We're already here. If we give in to it, I bet we'll both feel better."

As I say it, I realize it's actually quite true. We've been fighting against the draw pretty much from day one, even when I was being an unbearable, antagonistic ass.

She bites that sexy bottom lip with that stupid lipstick that never comes off and nods once. "Let the record show that I tried to be the logical one for five seconds here, and you had zero interest in listening to reason."

"It wasn't much of an argument, but if that makes you feel better, I'll let you believe you thought about saying no."

Wren shrieks as I grab her ass, slide to the edge of the couch and stand with her wrapped around me. She nibbles along my jaw as I walk us down the hall to the bedroom.

We kiss as clothes come off and drop to the floor. I'd like to say I take my time undressing her, but we're both fairly frantic, stripping the other down as fast as we can to get to bare skin. In all fairness, I'm not wearing much. I take a moment when I get her down to her panties to appreciate what I'm about to unveil, though.

I cup her delicate face between my hands and kiss her again, slow this time, with the intention to savor her and not make her lipstick disappear. She tastes like white wine.

I pull back and run my palms down the sides of her neck, allowing them to roam over the contours of her body, memorizing her softness and this first unveiling. I dip a finger into the waistband of her gray satin panties with red lace accents, and she sucks in a breath as I drag them down over her hips. She steps out of them when they pool at her feet on the floor.

She's tall and curvy and acutely feminine. "You're stunning."

"So are you." She runs her hand down my chest, fingers gliding along the waistband of my briefs. "You should lose these, though."

"In a minute. I want to enjoy you first." Mostly I'm worried that the second she puts her hand on me, I'm going to lose what's left of my control.

She pulls herself up onto the edge of the mattress. Keeping her legs closed, she moves up until she's at the headboard and I prowl after her. I smooth my hands along her shins, over her knees and all the way up her thighs. Instead of parting them, I straddle her and cup her face in my palms again.

"I love touching you." I drop my mouth to hers. "And kissing you."

I don't give her a chance to put her hands on me, though. Instead, I pull back with a grin. "I hope you're ready, Wren. I'm about to make it feel like an apocalypse is taking over your body."

She throws her head back and laughs, a deep throaty sound that turns into a sigh when I kiss my way down her neck. "Pretty sure of yourself, aren't you?"

"I've had weeks to create an elaborate fantasy, and I can't wait to make every dirty thought I've had a reality."

I edge a knee between her thighs and kiss my way over her breasts, stopping to tongue her nipple.

"Oh God." She arches and slides her fingers into my hair, so I do it again. When I get another moan from her, I decide I'm not in the big rush I was originally and settle myself between her thighs so I can spend a little time driving her as crazy as she's made me since she came steamrolling into my life and started bossing me around.

I trail a path over her body until I can press a kiss above her slit, then look up at her. I don't dive right in, and Wren doesn't try to shove my face into her crotch, although based on her expression I'm pretty sure she'd like to. Her nipples are still wet from my mouth, and her chest heaves with each expectant breath.

I nuzzle into the juncture of her thigh, breathing her in.

Wren spreads her legs wider, some silent encouragement to keep going. And I plan to, but it's been a long time since I've been this up close and personal with a woman, especially one as feisty as Wren, so I'm happy to hang out right here for a while.

I kiss the inside of her thigh and suck on the skin there, watching it blush pink. Then I go ahead a give it a little bite.

"Linc?"

"Mmm." I move up an inch and nibble again.

She caresses my temple drawing my attention to her face. She's propped up on one elbow, cheeks flushed and eyes hazy, but lit up with mirth. "I think the spot you're looking for is right here." She taps her clit with a manicured nail and bites her lip, possibly to keep her grin contained.

I arch a brow. "I was making my way there. Am I not moving fast enough for you?"

"Just making sure. You said it had been a long time. I thought maybe you needed a refresher."

I grin and slide my palms up her thighs, framing her sex with my hands. "Why don't you show me what you like, Wren? What makes you feel good?"

"You know what would make me feel really good?" she murmurs.

"What's that?"

She touches herself where she wants me. "Your tongue, right here."

"Here?" I stroke over her fingers, tasting her for the first time.

"Right there," she breathes.

"Again?"

"Yes, please." Her eyes are locked on my mouth, as I caress her a second time and wait.

"And again."

Wet stroke.

"And again."

Long lick.

"And again and again and again," she murmurs, hips rolling, eyes half-closed, lips parted, tongue sweeping across that infuriatingly red lipstick.

She threads her fingers through my hair. "Suck." A half smile pulls at her lips, and she tightens her grip when my eyes flip up to hers. "Please."

I push her fingers out of the way and cover her with my mouth, circling with my tongue before I give her the sweetest little nibble.

She gasps, and then I latch on, sucking hard, causing Wren's hips to lift.

"Again?" I ask against her.

"Please, yes. And if you could keep it up until I come, that would be great."

I chuckle, but do exactly as she asks. Wren is no passive recipient, and I imagine how amazing it would be to have her ride my face—something I plan on trying out another time because this definitely isn't going to be a one-time deal. She grinds against my mouth, body bowing off the bed when the first orgasm hits.

She's glorious when she comes, my name a hoarse cry tumbling from her lips. I have to say I'm pretty pleased with myself that I've already gotten her off, and just with my mouth. I won't feel as bad if I don't have the longevity I'd like.

A lazy grin breaks across her face as I crawl up her body. "That was exceptional." She takes my face between her hands and bites my chin. "I've wanted to do that since I first saw you without a beard."

"Bite me after I've gone down on you?"

"I was referring to the biting part, but the orgasm-by-mouth part has definitely been high on the fantasy list."

"I would really like to hear about that, in detail, later."

"I can do that. It'll be your reward after you practice your speech."

"I love rewards."

"Fantastic, now do me a favor and get on your back." Wren pushes on my chest.

"You're very demanding, you know that?"

"You should be used to it by now. Now roll over, Mr. Moorehead, I want access to what's in those old-man underwear you're so fond of."

I scoff, but flip onto my back. "They're not old-man underwear."

"They are, and they hide almost nothing." She straddles my legs, exhaling a long sigh. "God, you're magnificent, you know that? I was sad that we had to take off all that hair and your beard, because it was kind of sexy in an 'I fight bears with my fists' kind of way, but your face, and this body . . . I spent half of every day worried I was going to soak through my panties when you walked in the room."

"And did you?" I run my hands up the outside of her thighs.

She shrugs and drags her nails over my abs, past the waistband of my briefs. She traces the ridge through the fabric, then wraps her hand around me, giving me a slow stroke before she finally tugs my briefs down, exposing my erection.

"Hmm."

"Hmm? That's all you have to say?" Talk about deflating an ego.

She runs her fingertip along the underside of the head, and I shudder. That smirk of hers appears again. "You're actually quite spectacular everywhere, aren't you?"

"Thanks." I tuck an arm behind my head. "What're you going to do now that you have me naked?"

She taps her lip. "Well, there are just so many options." She takes my erection in her hand. "I should probably offer to blow you, since it's only fair and equitable, but what I really want to do is ride you."

"We can worry about fairness and equity later, if that's what you'd prefer."

"You think? I don't know. It's selfish not to give if you receive."

"You can have a free pass this time." I grab my wallet from the nightstand. I'm pretty sure I have at least one condom in there somewhere. I hope. I riffle around, distracted by Wren's constant slow stroking, and finally find what I'm looking for. I check the expiration date before I hand it over; it's been that long.

Wren plucks it from my fingers, tears it open, and rolls it on. I have to take several deep, slow breaths to manage my level of excitement, which is pretty damn high right now.

Wren grips the shaft and rises, positioning the head at her entrance when she pauses. "Lincoln."

I drag my gaze away from where I'm about to disappear inside her. "Yeah?"

She gives me one of her saucy grins. "Are you ready for the ride of your life?"

I run my hands up her thighs and settle them on her hips. "So damn ready."

"Why can't you be this appeasing all the time?"

"Offer to sit on my cock, and maybe I will be."

"Only if I can sit on your face first."

"That's a deal."

The head slips in, and I'm pretty sure my eyes want to roll up into the back of my head and stay there for the rest of my life. I fight to open them, though, because I don't want to miss this.

"I bet I could get you to promise me almost anything right now."

"Probably." I agree as she sinks down, slowly taking me inside.

When her ass rests on my thighs, she rolls her hips, which is just . . . more than I can handle.

I tighten my grip and give her a warning headshake. "Stay like this, please."

She tips her head to the side and circles her hips again, of course, because she likes to give direction, not take it.

"Don't, Wren."

"Why not?"

She starts to run her fingernails along my abs, which feels incredible, but it's a seriously bad idea if she wants me to last more than thirty seconds. I'm on complete sensory overload. I probably should've let her put her mouth on me, and then I could've gone down on her again or made out for a while or used my damn fingers—at least I wouldn't be worried about going off prematurely.

I sit up in a rush, catching her off guard and flip us over so she's under me.

"Hey! I'm supposed to be riding you, not the other way around."

"Well, you don't listen, so now you get to be ridden instead of doing the riding."

Her lips turn down in a pout. "I was enjoying my view."

"You'll have to settle for this view instead."

She tries to shift under me. I bury my face against her neck, biting the sensitive skin there. "Stop, Wren. Just, please, give me a minute," I murmur in her ear.

She fingers the hair at the nape of my neck. "Lincoln?"

I grab her wrists and pin her arms over her head, pushing up on my forearms so I can look at her face.

"I'm not into being restrained," she says.

"And I'm not into restraints, but I need some time without additional sensory input."

"But I don't—"

"Fucking hell, Wren. I'm at the edge. I'd really like to make a good impression here, and you're making that exceedingly difficult."

"Oh," she breathes, finally getting it.

"Yeah, oh." I take a deep breath. "I'd like to let go

of your wrists, but I really need you to do me a solid here and keep your hands to yourself until I give you the green light, okay?"

"Okay." She bites her lip. It's sweet and sexy, and I don't think it matters how hard I try, this is probably going to be over a lot faster than I'd like.

I release her hands slowly, because while I trust Wren not to bullshit me and tell me the truth when it comes to Moorehead Media, I don't necessarily trust her not to put her hands all over me as soon as I set them free.

Surprisingly, she doesn't move at all, which for some reason jacks me up even more. There's something about seeing her so willingly submissive that's an intense turn-on. Probably because it's rare.

"Lincoln?"

"Yeah, baby?" I stroke her cheek with a knuckle.

"Baby?"

"You like sweetheart or doll better?"

She wrinkles her nose.

"What about little bird?"

"Oh my God, don't."

"I could call you *mon petit oiseau*, if you prefer."

"Translating it into French doesn't make it any better."

"Why don't you come up with an approved list of pet names you think you can handle and we'll go from there."

"Lincoln."

"Wren."

"Have you calmed down enough to start fucking me yet?"

"Should we test things out?"

She reaches behind her, looking for something to grab onto. It's a solid wood headboard—Griffin's taste, based on the dark stain and simple design—so all she's met with is smooth, polished walnut.

I drop my head and kiss her throat, moving up to her chin until I'm hovering over her mouth. I give her a test grind, to see how much I can handle.

"Please do that again," she moans.

I can't very well say no, so I comply. "How's that feel?" I ask against her lips.

"So good, Linc. I would really love it if you could keep doing that for like, an hour, maybe two. Totally doable, right?"

"Oh totally, if by an hour or two you actually mean a maximum of three minutes."

"I'll settle for three minutes as long as you make me come again."

I take her mouth and keep up the slow grind. Kissing her is enough of a distraction that I can keep going, which is a relief. I figure if I make it past the three-minute mark, I'm doing okay, so occasionally I break from her mouth and kiss her neck so I can check the time. I'm at five minutes now, but making it past ten would be a solid benchmark goal.

"Stop looking at the clock," Wren says against my temple.

"I'm not looking at the clock."

"You are. That's the third time. Stop worrying about how long you're lasting, and start worrying about making me come."

I laugh into her shoulder, following it with a bite.

Wren moans, and her fingers slide into my hair. "Do that again."

"Bite you?" I ask against her skin.

"Yes, please."

I give her shoulder a gentle nibble.

"Not like that, like this." She twists her head, and her lips part against my neck. The wet press of her tongue comes first, followed by the firm scrape of teeth and a sweet sting that ends on a soothing suck.

I mimic the same action.

"Again, again," she whimpers. "Oh God, I'm close."

I bite and kiss and suck her neck, worried that I'm going to leave marks, but she keeps murmuring not to stop, so I don't until she comes.

I push up on my forearms, so I can watch her unravel. Her lips are parted, eyes screwed shut, brow pulled down.

"Wren," I say, demanding her attention.

Her eyes flutter open, and she groans as another wave hits her, but she fights to hold my gaze while I keep grinding against her. Her nails bite into my scalp, and she chants "oh God" until the orgasm finally wanes. Which means I don't have to worry about lasting anymore.

I hook an arm under her knee and draw her leg up. And because she's already come—twice—I feel justified in pumping into her in horny desperation.

That drowsy sated look on her face changes to wide-eyed shocked. Her mouth drops open. "Holy mother of—" She grabs onto my shoulders. "God, Linc, that's, oh sh—" The sentence turns into a loud moan.

Because she's coming again.

Because I'm awesome, or just really damn lucky. Which is great since I'm right there with her. There is zero in the way of coordination as I jerk and groan her name, but man, it feels amazing to come in and with another person, especially someone like Wren.

I collapse on top of her and quickly roll to the side, keeping her leg thrown over mine so I can stay inside. I'm half tempted to try to keep going to see if I can get it up again, but I'm wearing a condom, and that's not safe, so I rub her back and kiss along her throat, enjoying the come down as much as the act.

Eventually I pull back. "Hey."

"Hey." That sated peaceful look she was rocking a couple of minutes ago has already disappeared. In its place is wary uncertainty.

I brush the damp hairs away from her forehead. "Overthinking things already?"

Wren buries her face against my chest. "This really wasn't part of my plan for tonight."

"No? You didn't plan to come all over my face?"

"Oh my God!" She pokes me in the ribs.

I catch her wrist and kiss her knuckles. "What about my cock? No plans to come on that either? Not even between the tux fitting and reviewing the speech?"

Her face flushes pink, or pinker than it originally was. "You can stop now."

"I'll be honest, this is pretty much the opposite of how I thought my night was going to go. I figured I'd get wasted on my cousin's expensive scotch and try to forget that my dad had a sex pad. Gotta say, this was way better and a lot less stressful. Actually, come to think of it, this is the most relaxed I've been since I landed in New York." I drag a finger down her spine. "So, I think you should probably stay the night, and we can perform additional stress-relieving activities once I've had enough time to recover and then again in the morning. Maybe we should add them to your special duties as assigned."

A furrow appears between Wren's brows, and her mouth turns down at the corners. "That makes it sound like I'm getting paid to have sex with you."

"It's more like you're getting paid to have orgasms."

Her eyes flare, and she pushes on my chest. "Oh my God. This was probably a really bad idea."

I wrap an arm around her to prevent her from escaping. "This—" I motion between us. "You and me? We were an inevitability. Sooner or later, one of us was going to cave. At least we managed to keep it together and not end up screwing in the copy room, or my office, because Lord knows there's a really damn good chance that Marjorie would've picked that exact moment to ask if I wanted my five millionth coffee of the day."

She opens her mouth, possibly to argue, but then clamps it shut again.

I grin. "See? You know I'm right."

"I was actually going to comment on how much you'd fleshed out that scenario in your head."

"I've been having fantasies about finding out whether or not the panty-less-ness was really an accident."

"As if I would willingly walk around pantiless with Armstrong around."

"I don't think you have to worry too much about my brother. He knows better than to touch my things." I bite back a smile and wait.

Her eyebrows shoot up, and she's back to pushing on my chest. "Your *things*?"

"I'm playing with you, Wren. You're not a thing, or anyone's personal possession, but there's also no way Armstrong would even consider laying a hand on you if he knows we're involved. He might screw with a lot of people, but he won't ever screw with me."

"I don't think people can know about this, Lincoln. How will it look?"

"I don't cut your paychecks. You don't work for me, so I don't see how any of that will actually matter."

"What about the optics?"

"Can you stop doing your job for thirty seconds and enjoy the afterglow with me for a while?"

She sighs, but some of the tension in her body eases. "We need to figure out how to handle this. We need to be professional at work. We can't actually have a scenario where Marjorie walks into your office and finds me bent over your desk, Linc."

"We could do that on a Saturday, you know, to avoid Marjorie, or better yet, there's a home office here and the windows overlook the city. We could pretend we're in the office." I'm actually getting excited about the prospect.

"You're ridiculous."

"I'm horny, and I've been deprived for a long time, Wren. I also haven't had mind-blowing sex in an even longer time, like, probably the better part of half a decade, so I'm not inclined to give it up very easily, and I'd also like to indulge as much as possible. But I get what you're saying, so if we need to keep it professional in the office, I'm willing to give it a try."

"I think you're going to have to do better than try, Linc. Do you honestly think your mother will be okay with us sleeping together?"

"Is there anything in your contract that says you can't?"

"Uh, well . . . no."

"Then technically she can't have a problem with it. Besides, she allowed my d-bag of a brother to bone pretty much every woman on staff, and she had to have known my father had a mistress, or more than one. She really doesn't get to have any kind of opinion on who I sleep with."

"But she pays me—"

"To keep my ass in line and make sure I look good on social media. Come on, Wren. Let's be real here. We spend hours upon hours together. You've seen me in nothing but briefs multiple times at this point. Half the time you're here first thing in the morning, putting my outfits together to make sure I'm not dressed in jeans. People who are attracted to each other can't spend as much time together as we do and not give in to the draw. If anything, it makes sense that we'd end up in bed."

She seems shocked. "Have you been plotting this?"

"Plotting is my brother's area of expertise, not mine. Have I pushed a little? Sure. Have I orchestrated situations in which I'd be mostly naked and you'd be forced to pretend you're not checking out the goods? Definitely. Can't blame me for creating opportunities where I see them."

I skim her cheek with my fingers and smile when she shivers. "You and I both know there's been an attraction from day one. There's no reason to fight it now that we've acknowledged and acted on it, is there? I don't see any reason not to enjoy each other if that's what we want to do. We're adults, making adult decisions, doing adult things that no one needs to know about. As far as I'm concerned, there's nothing to hide, unless of course we decide office sex is a go, but that's why doors have locks."

"While I agree there's technically nothing to hide, I think we need to be smart about how we approach this, especially since your mother cuts my paychecks, and it's my job to make you look good, not create gossip. We have this huge event tomorrow night; we don't need to add more complications."

It's my turn to frown. "Dammit, you're right, which is incredibly annoying."

She smiles. "So we keep this between us."

"Fine. But you're staying the night, and we're having pre-work sex in the morning, so I can make it through the day without embarrassing myself with uncontrollable, spontaneous hard-ons."

CHAPTER 15

TOUCHY, TOUCHY

WREN

Great sex has an incredible, stress-relieving effect. It also throws all good decision-making skills and logic right out the window. I wake up the next morning disoriented.

Until I feel the hard-on pressing against my butt cheek and the rough scrape of stubble across my shoulder.

"I wouldn't be opposed to waking up like this more often," Linc rasps, lips at my neck.

I shiver at his soft hum.

"You know what's fantastic?"

"What's that?" My voice is just as hoarse as his, probably on account of all the loud moaning I did last night, and very, very early this morning.

"We don't have to be in the office until lunch."

"You have a meeting this morning," I remind him. "And we have the event tonight. You still have to practice your speech."

"I rescheduled the meeting, so now we have all morning to practice my speech."

I roll over so I'm facing him, and his smile slowly dissolves as his eyes move over my face. His hand comes up, and I have to wonder if my mascara is smeared all over the underside of my eyes like I plan to audition for the role of a raccoon.

He rubs at my bottom lip. "How is this stuff still on?"

"I told you it doesn't come off."

"What's in it that it stays on this long? Is it even safe to put on your skin?"

"Why are you so obsessed with my lipstick?"

"Because it's the bane of my goddamn existence." At my raised eyebrow, he continues. "You have this incredible face, and these gorgeous full lips, and you wear this lipstick that's just . . . a huge distraction. And it never comes off."

His irritation makes me smile. "Would you like me to take it off?"

"Yes."

I push on his chest. "You'll have to let me up if you want me to do that. I have remover in my purse."

"You stay right here. I'll get your purse." He drops a quick peck on my lips and rolls off me. Popping to his feet, he disappears from the bedroom and returns less than a minute later with my purse in his hands. He's gloriously naked, all those muscles flexing deliciously as he climbs back up onto the mattress and straddles my hips. He's also fully hard.

I pat the head and smirk. "Hasn't anyone ever told you it's rude to point?"

"He's saying hi." He sets my purse between my breasts and gives them a squeeze. "Here you go."

I flip it open and root around for the remover and a tissue.

Linc grabs both from me. "What do I have to do?"

"Put that on my lips like gloss and use the tissue to wipe it off."

"That's it?"

"That's it."

He unscrews the cap and carefully applies the gloss. It's actually quite entertaining since he's so focused on the task. His tongue peeks out from between his lips as he drags the tissue gently across mine. He inspects the pinky-red smear, then goes back and does it a few more times before he's satisfied. He tosses the tissue on the floor and plants his fists on his hips. It's actually pretty comical.

"You need to stop wearing that lipstick."

"Okay," I say, not because I plan to actually stop, but because I don't see the point of arguing with him when he's hard and naked, and being agreeable is likely going to get me what I want a lot faster. Which is him inside me.

His brow furrows. "Okay?

"Sure. No more lipstick." I run my palms up the outside of his muscular thighs until I'm framing his erection.

"You're not even going to ask why?"

"Would you like me to ask why?"

"You're infuriating, you know that?"

I wrap both hands around his shaft and squeeze. "Clearly that's a turn-on for you. Would you like to fuck my mouth, now that it's naked like the rest of me?"

Lincoln drops the lipstick conversation after that, and we spend the next two hours practicing naked stress-relieving activities. Best pre-event pampering ever.

Our awesome morning of sex takes a nosedive into Shitsville when I check my voicemails and realize I never got back to Gwendolyn regarding Lincoln's plus-one. "Dammit."

"What's the problem?" he asks as he sips his third coffee so far today.

"You're supposed to have a date tonight. Your mother wants to know who you're taking and whether they've been vetted."

Lincoln makes a face. "You're my date."

I give him a look. "I can't be your date."

"Why not? Are you going with someone?" His expression darkens. "You need to cancel that now. You're not going with anyone other than me."

I prop a fist on my hip. "Want to try that again without sounding like a possessive douche?"

He runs a hand through his hair and blows out a breath. "Wren, could you please cancel your date for the event tonight so I don't end up all over social media for punching out a stranger?"

"That was so much better." I'm being sarcastic, obviously. "I don't have a date for tonight since I'm on duty and your mother would prefer that I avoid distractions that aren't you and Armstrong.

"Oh. Why didn't you say that in the first place?"

"It didn't seem relevant. Also it annoys me to have to say that out loud." I roll my eyes. "I need to get back to Gwendolyn. She was rather insistent you have a date." My stomach twists at the thought of another woman on Lincoln's arm tonight, even if it's just for appearances.

"Screw that. I'm not bringing a date to appease my mother. I'm going with you. End of story. I'll call her and tell her myself if you think she's going to give you a hard time about it. It's not like either of you can force me to bring someone."

"First of all, we've already established that what's

going on between us has to stay between us. You bringing me as your date is the exact opposite of keeping it
a secret, so I can't be your plus-one. Bringing someone
else will actually be helpful." I choke out the last part.

Lincoln plants his fists on the counter. "Helpful
how?"

"Have you seen the pictures people have taken of us
lately? They're intimate. It would help if people thought
you were dating."

"How would that be helpful? And who cares if I'm
dating?"

"It's good for your public image." I lean against the
edge of the counter.

Lincoln's expression is pinched. "So you're encour-
aging me to take the former cheerleader with the natural
breasts to this event? Is that it?"

I avoid a direct answer. "You need to have a date."

"And you're okay with me bringing some woman my
mother approved because her family has a decent bankroll so we can boost my fucking likes or whatever?"

"It makes you relatable."

He rounds the counter until he's right in my personal space. "You're not answering my question. Tell
me you're okay with me bringing someone else to this
event."

My voice wavers with my reply. "I understand why
Gwendolyn is so insistent about it. It's a logical strategy."

"I don't care about strategy, Wren. I want you to tell
me you'll be fine with my arm wrapped around someone else. Because that's the whole point, isn't it? Photo
ops with someone who looks good on my arm."

"I—" I grit my teeth as the image of that brunette
pops into my head.

Lincoln's dark expression lights up with a menacing smile. "Tell me you'll hate every minute of it."

"Of course I'll hate every minute of it, but Gwendolyn wants you to have a date, and if you don't pick one, I'm sure she'll line someone up for you, whether you like it or not."

"No, she won't because I won't let her. If you can't be my date, I'm not bringing one. I'll tell her I don't need the distraction since I already have enough of those as it is."

"But—"

"Stop arguing with me." Lincoln's mouth covers mine, ending the conversation.

I'd be lying if I said I wasn't relieved that he's refusing a date, even if it would look better for us if he had one.

Surprisingly, Gwendolyn is not nearly as upset about Lincoln's lack of date as I anticipated. She says something about it probably being for the best, all things considered. Whatever that means.

Despite my protest that we should arrive separately at the event, Lincoln insists we take one car. That way he can review his speech again on the way. When he stumbles on a word, he lifts a hand to his hair, and I have to smack it away before he can mess it up since it's been styled with product.

"I really hope I don't mess this up tonight." he says, then starts the whole thing from the beginning again.

"You'll be fantastic," I assure him. "It's only five minutes. It'll be over before you know it."

"I know." He taps his fingers on the armrest. "This whole event is just . . . not really my thing. I don't do tuxedos and five hundred dollar a plate dinners."

"It's not for nothing, Linc. It's a fundraiser for a brand

new wing in the NICU, and support for families who need it. I know you're used to projects with more tangible, visible results, but you're still supporting something that's going to help a lot of people. Even though you believe your family is hosting it for the wrong reasons, your intentions are pure." I put a hand on his knee and squeeze. "You need to approach it from your own moral standpoint, Lincoln. You would do this for the right reasons, so stand behind those."

He slips his fingers between mine. "Is your lipstick the kind that rubs off?"

"What?" I thought I'd done a great job at giving him a pep talk, and he's asking about my lipstick again. "Are you seriously still on this? It's not red."

"Is it or isn't it the kind that rubs off?"

"It doesn't rub off, but I have to eat dinner and pose for pictures. I can't—"

His mouth covers mine, tongue sweeping inside, softly, tenderly. After a few long seconds he pulls back and trails gentle fingers along my cheek. "I don't know how every man who crosses your path doesn't fall in love with you. Everything about you is incredible."

I laugh, embarrassed. "I don't know about that."

He shakes his head. "Don't dismiss the compliment, Wren. I have a lot of words I want to say, but I'm pretty sure none of them are appropriate at this very moment, so I'm going to leave it at you being incredible and me being lucky enough to have captured your attention. Also, you look stunning tonight. And if you don't have plans, I'd like it if you spent the weekend with me."

"You're kind of all over the place right now, aren't you?" I smooth out his lapels, even though they don't need it.

"Yes, I am, but I meant what I said, and I'd really

like it if you said yes to spending the weekend. It would make the rest of this night a lot easier to manage."

"This seems an awful lot like coercion."

"You can call it that if you want. I'm sure it will give us something to argue about later."

I chuckle. "I'd love to spend the weekend with you. We'll have to stop by my place at some point, though, since this isn't exactly casual wear." I motion to my simple black dress.

"Or you could spend the weekend naked."

"What if I get chilly?"

"You can wear one of my T-shirts."

"What if someone happened to catch me getting out of your car on Sunday wearing this dress?"

"Hmm. You make a good point." He taps his lip. "I guess it would be nice to see your place. We could spend a night there if you want. We can make that fantasy you have about me screwing you senseless on your kitchen counter a reality."

"I don't have a kitchen-counter fantasy." Although, it's not a half-bad idea.

"You do now." He winks.

Our conversation is put on hold when the car pulls up in front of the hotel. Media already line the entryway, which of course, makes sense. Lincoln's easy mood quickly fades. "That's a lot of cameras."

"You'll be fine. Just smile and be your charming self."

"I think I'm only charming when I'm making you come."

"You're far more charismatic than you give your-self credit for, although you are particularly enchanting when you're giving me an orgasm." I pat his cheek.

The driver opens the door, and Lincoln exits the

vehicle first. Cameras flash, and Lincoln looks like he's debating whether or not he wants to get right back in the car and go home. I slide over, and he offers his hand. He attempts to pull me in when there are photo ops, but I give him a warning smile and tell him I need to take a few pictures. I'm mindful not to fuss over him, considering how the tabloids have been spinning those kinds of images lately.

He keeps reaching for me as we make our way into the hotel, and I have to elbow him more than once and remind him to keep it friendly and professional. He shoots me a purse-lipped, displeased smile but backs off.

Despite his nerves, he's charming and articulate. People express their sympathy over the loss of his father, and while I can sense his tension, no one else seems to pick up on it. I introduce him to my parents, who are chatting with a group of local politicians. As expected, Lincoln is eloquent, and my father is his charismatic self, asking Lincoln all about his pursuits in Guatemala.

Photographers request pictures, as is typical at these events. My father insists that Lincoln join us for a few of them. They'll be great for social media, both Lincoln's and my father's, so I make sure to take a few of my own so I can post them during speeches.

My parents are pulled into another discussion, and Lincoln bends to speak against my ear. I'm hyperaware every time he gets too close, worried about all the cameras and the attention he's getting tonight. I feel transparent, as if it's written all over my face that I've slept with him. I'm about to remind him, again, of how we need to be careful how we appear in photos, when Lincoln turns to address a huge man with dark hair and the same icy blue eyes as Lincoln. "Hey, cousin! It's good to see you under better circumstances."

Now, Lincoln is a gorgeous man. He has the kind of features that take your breath away. The man he's currently talking to looks like he was carved out of marble and brought to life. I remember seeing him at the funeral, but I'd been too busy keeping tabs on Armstrong at the time to be able to pay much attention.

Beside him is a woman who looks like a human Barbie doll, but not in the sense that she's plastic. She's incredibly elegant and poised with long, wavy blond hair and a flawless face I recognize.

The human Adonis grins and pulls Lincoln in for one of those manly hugs with a hearty back pat. I can definitely see the family resemblance between Lincoln and his cousin.

"Wren, this is my cousin Lexington and Amalie." Now I know the name. She's Armstrong's ex-wife, or ex-whatever since their marriage lasted only a handful of hours. "Lex, Amalie, this is Wren, she's my—"

I cut in, before Lincoln says something that could cause more problems than good. "I manage Lincoln's PR and make sure he doesn't wear ripped jeans to fundraising galas," I say, with a smile.

"And here I thought Linc actually had a date." Lexington takes my hand in his. They're huge, like the rest of him.

"Going solo, tonight," Lincoln says tightly, but I can feel his eyes on me, and Lexington gives him a questioning look.

A small dark-haired woman pushes her way between Amalie and Lexington. "You two need at least six inches between you at all times, otherwise you're at risk of spontaneous humping." She hands Amalie a glass of champagne and then finally notices Lincoln and I.

We go through another round of introductions, and I meet Ruby, the petite brunette, and her husband, Bancroft, who is the youngest of the Mills brothers, but amazingly is bigger than Lexington.

While Lincoln catches up with his cousins, I chat with the women. Amalie works for Williams Media and Ruby performs on Broadway. They're fun women, the kind I wouldn't mind sharing a table with. Unfortunately, we have assigned seating, and they're two tables over from us.

Based on the place cards, Lincoln and I are seated with his mother, a couple who are huge contributors to the foundation we're raising money for tonight, Armstrong, and someone named Jordan Cromwell. I don't know why that name is familiar. Maybe it's an associate of some kind. Armstrong is already seated and based on the place cards, I'm supposed to sit between them, Lincoln switches mine with Jordan's, who maybe isn't here yet, pulls out my chair, and takes the seat beside me, leaving the one between him and his brother empty.

Armstrong gives him the eye, but doesn't comment. Although he does start muttering about Lex and Amalie and how he can't believe they're attending the event. Lincoln gives him an incredulous look. "They own the hotel, and Amalie does charity work for the hospital. Of course they're going to be here. If you don't like it, you know where the door is, and if I find out you so much as breathed in Amalie's direction, I'll be the one holding your arms behind your back while Lex gives you another black eye and a broken nose."

"Boys, no fighting," Gwendolyn says sternly as she

slips into the seat across the table. "You're the center of everyone's attention. People are watching and they'll notice dissension."

I squeeze Lincoln's thigh under the table. He leans in and whispers, "If I survive tonight without committing a crime, it'll be a miracle."

I turn my head until my lips are at his ear. "As long as it's not an indecent exposure charge, we can get you off."

He chuckles and says quietly, "Give me a few hours and I'll be getting off all right."

Gwendolyn smiles tightly, although that's pretty much the only way she can smile. "What are you two whispering about?"

"Nothing I care to share," Lincoln says with a smile.

I kick him in the shin. "I was telling Lincoln about the time my dad took me to my first gala event like this. My mother couldn't go, so I attended instead. I was only fourteen, and I felt like a total princess."

"Isn't that sweet?" Gwendolyn continues to smile. "Unfortunately, Lincoln didn't have much of an opportunity to attend these kinds of events in his youth. He was very focused on his studies from a young age. Penelope thought a private boarding school would be best for him, so he would be challenged. At least now you're doing something of value with all of that education, isn't that right, Lincoln?"

"I was doing something of value before I came back to New York," Lincoln says coldly.

"I've been doing something of value for years, but apparently it's not enough," Armstrong gripes.

"Sticking your dick in everything that moves is not something of value," Lincoln snaps.

"Lincoln!" Gwendolyn looks like her eyeballs are about to pop out of her head and roll onto her bread plate.

"Do I need to sit between the two of you?" I cut in.

"No!" Lincoln and Armstrong say at the same time.

I grace them with my don't-push-me smile. "Then let's practice what we learned in kindergarten. If you don't have anything nice to say, don't say anything at all."

The bickering stops, thankfully, since a woman approaches the table. And suddenly I know why the name is familiar. She's the vetted interior designer from the profiles Gwendolyn provided for Lincoln.

She's wearing a very pretty, formfitting green dress that matches her eyes and complements her hair. "Hi." She waves at the table. "It looks like I'm supposed to be sitting at this table tonight. I hope that's okay." She eyes the empty seat between Lincoln and Armstrong.

"You've got to be kidding me," Lincoln mumbles so only I can hear.

She rounds the table. "Oh yes! Here I am. Jordan." She has a bubbly personality, and I'm sure she's quite nice, but considering it's obvious Gwendolyn took matters into her own hands where Lincoln's date is concerned, I've decided I hate her.

Lincoln and Armstrong both push back their chairs and stand. Armstrong, being the lecherous vulture he is, is quicker, which for once doesn't bother me in the least. If Gwendolyn is going to pull this kind of thing, she can deal with her youngest son and his smarminess. I have more important issues to manage tonight. Like this beast called jealousy.

"Jordan, your dress is exquisite, as are you. Armstrong Moorehead, Junior CEO at Moorehead Media. It's a pleasure." Armstrong kisses the back of her hand,

and I suppress a shudder and a snarky comment about his new, self-imposed title.

Jordan looks taken aback, her gaze flitting to Gwendolyn, who appears unimpressed, possibly because her plan isn't working the way she expected.

Once she's seated, Armstrong does the honors of introducing Jordan to the table. She seems to perk up when Armstrong grudgingly introduces Lincoln. He's polite, but not overly friendly, and Armstrong quickly dominates her attention.

When he finds out she used to be a college cheerleader, he turns into his smarmy, disgusting self. "That must mean you're flexible. Did you travel with the team often?"

Jordan falls right into it. "Oh yes! To both. I still practice yoga at least five times a week, and I can do the splits. We used to travel to state championships all the time. Did you play football in college?"

While Armstrong butters up his next victim, Lincoln spends a good part of dinner whispering things in my ear. I elbow him in the side, intent on getting him to stop because he's drawing his mother's attention with how focused he is on me.

Once dinner has been served and cleared—it was delicious and horrifyingly expensive, I'm sure—speeches begin. Lincoln is the first to take the stage, which is both a blessing and a curse because there's no buffer before him.

The MC takes the podium, and Lincoln turns to me with a ridiculous grin. "Do I have anything in my teeth?"

I bite back a giggle so I don't interrupt the speaker. "Nothing in your teeth." I smooth out his lapels and adjust his tie, but avoid the compulsion to touch his hair, aware Gwendolyn is watching. "You'll be fabulous. You know this inside and out. Five minutes, then you can relax."

For a moment I think he's going to lean in and kiss me. Thankfully, the MC calls his name, and he pushes back his chair, making his way through the crowd to the podium.

I get my phone ready and adjust my chair, which is situated in such a way that I don't even have to get up to be able to record him.

Lincoln takes the podium and holds up his cue cards. "I feel like it's seventh grade again and I'm giving a speech in front of the whole school. Don't worry, though. I'm not going to picture you all naked." He scans the crowd, eyes landing on me for a split second. "I'll picture you all in tighty-whities instead."

A ripple of laughter moves through the room.

He clears his throat, and the crowd falls silent. Then he shows everyone who he really is, including me. He's eloquent, charismatic, and commanding. He's expressive and giving and emotive. He pauses a couple of times to collect himself when he speaks about the legacy his father left behind, about how difficult it is to fill his shoes. No one but me understands the real reason he struggles through this part. It doesn't matter that they misread his emotional response; it gives them what they need, a leader they can relate to and empathize with.

I record his speech, and as soon as he steps away from the podium, the entire room erupts in applause. I stand and clap along with everyone else, wearing a proud, silly grin. He stops to shake a few hands on the way back to his seat, to me, which is where his gaze is fixed. When he reaches me, I remember where we are and that Gwendolyn is watching. So I turn my head away when he pulls me in for an impulsive hug. I pat him on that back, hoping it looks friendlier than it does intimate.

"I told you you'd be amazing." I drop back into my chair as soon as he lets me go.

"I did all right?" Lincoln takes his seat beside me, angling his chair in such a way that his foot brushes my calf.

"Better than all right. You were a natural up there."

I can feel his eyes on me, and Gwendolyn's vulture-like stare drifts our way every so often—either that or I'm being paranoid.

I consider how incredibly eloquent Lincoln is, how despite not having been part of the family business, he's stepped in with grace. If he wanted to, he could easily take over permanently and make Moorehead into something amazing. But he's said on more than one occasion that he can't wait to get out of the city. My contract is up when he goes, so I'm not sure this warm feeling in my chest is a good thing. I worry I'm setting myself up for heartbreak.

Once speeches are over, I excuse myself to the bathroom while Lincoln is pulled into a discussion with some influential people. Now that the hardest part is over, I can breathe easier. I stop at the bar to grab a scotch for Lincoln and a glass of wine for myself. I'm on my way back into the hall when Gwendolyn's cold hand wraps around my elbow.

"A word, please, Wren," she says icily.

"Of course, what can I do for you?"

She pulls me away from the guests to a private corner. "What exactly do you think you're doing?"

I look down at the drinks in my hand. "Now that the speeches are over, I felt it reasonable for Lincoln to have a drink. I thought he was exceptional."

Her grip on my arm tightens. "Don't play coy with me, Wren. You're far too intelligent for that. I'm paying you to make sure Lincoln looks good in the eyes of the media and that he presents a good face for the company."

I roll my shoulders back, a hot feeling creeping up my spine. "And that's exactly what I'm doing."

"Lincoln was supposed to bring a date, and you couldn't even ensure that happened. And now Armstrong has commanded the attention of the woman I invited for him."

"I had no idea Jordan was supposed to be Lincoln's date. I tried to convince him it was in his best interests, but—"

"Are you sure about that, Wren? I see the way you look at my son and how he's been looking at you."

"I don't know—"

"Don't think for a moment I don't see what you're doing here," she whispers angrily.

The accusation in her tone gets my back up. "I'm sorry. What exactly am I doing?"

"You know what this company could be worth with the right management. You're trying to get your claws into my son so you can cash in on what's his. I can understand the allure. He's quite a catch, but you're rising above your station, Wren. Lincoln is too many rungs above you on the ladder for it to be a good match. You need to be careful about allowing yourself to get too distracted. I wouldn't want you to lose sight of your goals."

I've never felt any particularly warmth for Gwendolyn, but this is a side of her I've never seen before. I don't have a chance to respond—which is a good thing, seeing as I doubt it would've been anything less than scathing—because Lincoln's voice breaks the silence stretching between us.

"You disappeared." Lincoln's warm breath caresses the back of my neck, indicating how close he is. "I've been looking everywhere for—oh, Mother." He looks between us. "Everything okay?"

"Everything's fine. I thought you might like a drink." I pass him the scotch. "Gwendolyn and I were discussing how well the speech went."

"And how important it is that people see how capable you are. Make sure you post on social media tonight, Wren."

Lincoln takes the glass from me and shoots his mother a look. "Lighten up. Wren's been on all day. I think it's safe to say she's done her job for the night and deserves to enjoy herself for a few minutes without being hounded." He settles a hand on my lower back, but I step out of reach.

His smile is stiff. "Come on, Ruby and Amalie were asking where you went. If you'll excuse us, Mother."

"Of course, enjoy the rest of your evening. You would've made your father proud tonight."

Lincoln gives his mother a curt nod, and I follow him back to the hall. "Everything okay? That looked intense."

"Everything's fine. She really just wanted to make sure I wasn't shirking my responsibilities." He's in such a good mood, totally in his element, and I won't take that away from him. He needs to see he can do this, that he's good at it, and that his presence here will only make this a better company.

But what his mother said sticks with me for the rest

of the night. As much as I care about Lincoln, I worry about Gwendolyn's ability to come between us, and exactly what kind of recourse will follow if she finds out what's really going on.

CHAPTER 16
SETTLING IN

LINCOLN

"I'm not kicking you out of your penthouse. I'll get out of your hair for a few days so you can have the place to yourself," I tell Griffin. I can see about staying at Wren's, but that could be complicated. In the weeks since we started sleeping together, it's been pretty standard for her to come to the penthouse, and it makes sense since she's contracted to work with me, but the other way around is tricky.

I don't necessarily care if my family finds out we're sleeping together, but I get why Wren is so adamant that we keep it between us. I don't want to compromise her contract or her reputation, and I get what the optics are like, even if they're a pain in my ass.

"The penthouse is huge, and you know you're welcome to stay as long as you want. Besides, Cosy and I are only in town for three days, and then we're back out again."

"I should really get my own place."

"What's the point if you're leaving in a few more months, anyway?"

"I don't know. I just don't want to be in the way."

"Or maybe you're getting comfortable in the concrete jungle."

"Just thinking it might be a decent investment."

"Can't argue with real estate. Anyway, we're traveling for two more months. We didn't expect to stop in New York at all, so you don't need to worry about being in the way. Oh, and the penthouse across the hall might be available soon, so if that looks like something you'd be interested in, let me know and we can get you into that."

"You sure you want me for a neighbor?"

"Better having you all up in my business than my brothers nosing around, as they do. How's the city treating you? You managing okay?"

I consider how things have changed in the past few weeks, particularly since Wren and I stopped fighting our attraction. I'd call it dating, but mostly it's the two of us holed up in my cousin's penthouse in the evenings since we can't do the whole dinner and a movie date in public without all the speculation that comes with it. Naked movie watching is my new favorite pastime. "It could be worse."

"Hey, we still have that place upstate, right? I've got a meeting as soon as I land, but I'm free after that. We could head out there, get away from the grind, drink too much beer, eat hotdogs for dinner and breakfast like we used to when we were in college."

I tap on the arm of my chair. Wren and I are supposed to spend the weekend together. Out of necessity, I've been quiet about what's going on between us with everyone except Griffin. He's a vault, and I trust him not to say anything about my relationship with Wren. "Would Cosy come?"

"She doesn't have to if you need it to just be you and me."

"Nah, I'm supposed to spend the weekend with Wren, so I want to run it by her."

"This sounds like it's getting serious there, cuz."

"I like her, but I still have projects out of the country lined up for the next year." I rub my chest at the sudden twinge that thought brings with it. It's too soon and we're too new for me to start merging what I want and what she wants into something we could take on together. At least I think it is.

Griffin chuckles. "A lot of things can change in a few months."

I avoid commenting on that, because he's sure as hell not wrong. "Let me talk to Wren and see if she'd be interested in roughing it for a night."

"Okay. We're getting on the plane now, so just message and let me know."

"Sounds good, safe travels, cuz." I end the call and head back inside, peeking in the bedroom. Wren's still sleeping, although, it's early and a Saturday, so it's understandable. Also, I kept her up pretty late last night.

I'm hoping I can convince her that a camping trip with my cousin and his girlfriend is a great idea.

I drag the sheet down—she's naked underneath it— and watch goose bumps rise on her skin as I brush her hair away from her face. I look forward to waking up with her in my bed several days a week. I hate New York and my job less, and work isn't painful when she's in the office. She makes things better, brighter, more alive. She makes me believe that Moorehead Media could be something good with the right leadership.

I sit on the edge of the bed and bend to kiss her neck and then her shoulder. She hums in her sleep and rolls over onto her back, exposing her lush, full breasts. Her nipples peak in the cool air, so I circle one with a fingertip.

She slaps my hand away and covers her eyes with her arm. "What time is it?"

"Almost eight."

She peeks out from under her arm. "We went to bed at two in the morning. You know I'm grumpy when I get less than seven hours."

"Your nipples don't look grumpy." I lean down and suck the right one, flicking it with my tongue.

Her fingers slide into my hair and she arches. "If I'm bitchy later, it's your fault."

"You can take a nap later if your attitude is a problem for me." I release her nipple long enough to pull my shirt over my head and drop my briefs on the floor. Then I latch back on as I fit myself between her legs.

Half an hour later, Wren is stretched out beside me, head resting on my chest. "How do you feel about camping?"

"In tents?" she asks.

"Or a trailer."

"I was a Girl Scout, so I have some tent experience, and I've done the trailer thing a few times." She props her chin on my chest and gets a faraway look in her eyes. "When I was little, my parents rented a huge RV and we went on a three-week camping trip. It was so much fun. We stopped wherever we wanted. It's probably one of my favorite childhood memories."

"That sounds like a great family trip."

"It was. Did you ever go on family vacations?"

"Not with my parents, but me and my cousin Griffin have done a lot of traveling together. He and his girlfriend are flying in for the weekend, and he suggested we head upstate, get away from the city, and relax for a night. What do you say?"

Wren's expression grows wary. "I don't know if that's such a great idea, Linc. How are you going to explain your handler tagging along?"

"Griffin knows what's going on, Wren."

She pushes off my chest, pulling the sheet around her. "I thought we agreed to keep this between us."

This isn't quite the response I was going for. "You haven't even told your best friend about us? Dani?"

They spend a night every week binge-watching some show and drinking wine or whatever. All I know is Wren doesn't sleep over that night.

She makes a face. "Well, yes, Dani knows we're . . . involved."

"And you trust her to keep it to herself, yes?"

"We've been friends since grade school."

"Well, I got you beat. Griffin and I have been tight since our mothers were pregnant. He's a fortress, and he knows to keep that information to himself. Come on, Wren. Let's do something normal and coupley and fun. I want to share how awesome you are with the people I actually care about."

"It'll just be Griffin and his girlfriend? What's her name again? Casey?"

"Cosy."

"Like cozy up next to me? Or a tea cozy?"

"Either works, but the British spelling of the word."

Wren's nose wrinkles. "I think I like her already."

A few hours later, after I firm up the details with Griffin, we stop at Wren's place to pack a bag of camping-appropriate gear. While she tosses things in a bag, I check emails and sift through social media posts. It's hot in her apartment, so I shed my hoodie and drape it over a chair, leaning on the counter as I scroll through my alerts.

"Okay. Ready to go." She drops her bag on the counter. It looks like she's packed for a week, not a night.

Most of the time I get to see Wren either in dresses or naked, so I'm digging the faded jeans and T-shirt ensemble.

"Oh no, this is no good. Obviously I need to change." She spins around and takes a step toward her bedroom.

I grab her wrist before she can get too far. "What? Why? You look hot."

She motions from her chest to mine and then to the full-length mirror on the other side of the room. "Look at us. We're all matchy-matchy."

I take in our reflections. We're both wearing white shirts and jeans. "This is like the perfect couple selfie opportunity, isn't it?"

Wren rolls her eyes. "We look ridiculous."

I wrap my arms around her from behind and kiss my way up her neck to her ear with a chuckle. "I'll put my hoodie on, and no one will know but us."

"It's too warm for hoodies," Wren argues.

"We can wear them just until we're in the car. Then we can lose them." I kind of like the matchy-matchy, so I take a bunch of crappy selfies while Wren tries to free herself from my hold.

We both cover the T-shirts with hoodies—not matching ones—and shed them once we're in the protective cover of the vehicle's tinted windows and head out of the city toward the campground. It's about an hour upstate. We're going early, so we can make sure it's all set up when Cosy and Griffin arrive.

I'm not sure camping after a six-hour flight and a meeting would be something I'd jump at, but apparently Cosy is superexcited, and Griffin does pretty much anything to make that woman happy.

"Can I ask you something? It's kind of personal, though." Wren's sitting in the passenger seat, hair pulled up in a loose ponytail, lips glossy. She went for highlights a week ago, so there are more blond streaks. It softens her face and makes her look sun-kissed. She's mind-numbingly gorgeous.

"Sure."

"How did you and Griffin manage to stay so close when you were in boarding school?"

"We wrote letters to each other until computers became a thing, then we'd email and stuff. He'd keep me informed as to what was going on with Armstrong, since there was usually some trouble."

"Even back then?"

"Armstrong was always . . . different, I guess. I don't really know what's wrong with him, but he's always been an instigator. He used to push my buttons constantly, and then when I snapped on him, he'd go crying to the nanny or Gwendolyn. It drove me up the wall, honestly. He had a hard time with rules, as if they didn't apply to him."

Wren covers my hand with hers, fingers laced between mine. "That must've been difficult."

"It was frustrating. At first when I got sent to boarding school, I'd been so angry. I'd considered it a punishment because they were taking me away from everything familiar. Griffin and I spent a ton of time together. I spent weekends at their place and so would Armstrong. He and Lex were super tight back then, actually."

"You mean the Lex that's with Amalie? His ex-wife?"

I grin at how shocked she is. "It's like a soap opera."

"It really is."

"Anyway, it was hard at first, because Griffin and I were close, but he'd come up for a weekend once a month. After a while, I realized it was better for me to be out of that house and away from all the dissention. The more distance I had, the more I realized I was always the one Gwendolyn favored, and Armstrong could never seem to meet her expectations. It was a difficult position to be in.

"Whenever I came back for holidays or whatever, it seemed to make the animosity between us grow. So I stayed where I was, or found camps or charity stuff to do during the summer. When we were a little older, Griffin would do the same thing, so we'd have those months together."

"And that's how you stayed close."

I nod. "Exactly. We went to the same college and shared an apartment for four years. In a lot of ways, he's like another sibling. We were both the oldest; we both liked to travel. We have the same core values. Griffin was always a relationship-oriented guy. He was with the same girl all through high school, and then he dated the same girl all through college, but then, his parents were solid, so I guess it makes sense."

"Wow, that's uncommon in this generation."

"Mmm, it can be, depending. Anyway, early last year I spent some time in China between projects, and Griffin was there. It was before everything imploded with Imogen, and we had time to just be guys and hang out and do good stuff. Griff excels at the hotel business, and he likes it, but he's always taking extra side trips, doing volunteer work where he can. He never says anything about it, just works it into every trip he goes on, makes it part of the job."

"I wonder if you could do that."

"Do what?"

"Connect your outreach projects to Moorehead. I know you don't want to give that up, but it seems like maybe you're starting to settle into your role, and you're so good at leading people. It's something to consider." Her smile is soft and almost hopeful.

As much as I dislike the city, I might be able to get used to it if Wren was a constant and I could find some kind of happy medium.

CHAPTER 17

PERSPECTIVE

LINCOLN

Griffin and I sit on camping chairs in the sand while the girls do flips on the floating trampoline. Wren is quite agile, and it's entertaining watching the two of them out there, spotting each other for roundoffs. A group of guys in their late teens, possibly early twenties, loiter close by. They're like a bunch of peacocks, squawking and preening as they check out Wren and Cosy.

"Please tell me we didn't act like assholes around girls when we were their age." I nod at the guys as one of them crushes an empty beer can on his forehead.

"I don't remember doing anything that stupid, but you never know." He sips his beer. "I'm on the fence as to whether or not I want one of those guys to hit on Cosy, so I can see her shoot the SOB down."

"Same." I clink my bottle against his.

"So, you saying this isn't serious is bullshit, eh?" Griffin asks, pulling my attention away from Wren in her sexy red bikini. I may not like it when she wears lipstick that color, but those little scraps of fabric are a whole different story.

"As serious as it can be for something that can't be public."

"Well, her contract doesn't last forever, does it? Once it's done, you're free to make out with her on every street corner in New York."

"Yeah, but I have that project in Costa Rica, and I've already had to push back the start date because I'm here. Besides, she has her own plans, and I don't know that Costa Rica is going to fit into them."

"I've said it before and I'll say it again. Plans can change." He side-eyes me. "And who says you have to go to Costa Rica and stay there? Your project in Guatemala is going pretty damn smooth despite you being here."

"Yeah, but that's the thing I miss. Being part of the project. I don't want to manage them remotely all the time."

"I get that, and I'm not saying you have to step back completely, but what if you had everything in place so that you could set the project up, get it rolling, and then come back to New York and manage Moorehead?"

"I don't know if I want to manage Moorehead permanently. Dealing with Armstrong for six months is one thing, but to commit to every damn day?" The thought alone makes me both nauseous and irritable.

Griffin makes a sound in the back of his throat. "Do you really think you can walk away, though? Armstrong is never going to be able to handle running that place. It'll sink if you don't stay."

"Me and G-mom are going to find a replacement."

He gives me a look. "Come on, Linc, do you really think that's her plan? It'll take a good year or more to train anyone new. I know you want to believe you're here for a few months, but I think you might need to reframe your future plans. I'm pretty sure your grandmother's idea was to groom you for the role and keep you around long enough that you'd get settled." He motions to Wren, who's in the middle of doing some kind of walkover thing.

She's damn bendy. And Griffin is 100 percent accurate. G-mom probably had no intention of finding someone to take over for me, because without me keeping Armstrong in line, the company will likely go under or we'd have to sell it. "Dammit. G-mom played me."

Griffin grins. "As a good business woman does."

I'm going to give her shit the next time we video chat. "I don't want to give up the work I'm doing. I can't run Moorehead and organize projects in South America."

"Why can't you, though? You have this huge media company and all these resources at your fingertips. Why not shift the Moorehead focus and diversify? You could have an entire magazine dedicated to your outreach projects."

Wren mentioned something like that on the way here. I've been so wrapped up in learning the ropes, I haven't had a chance to look at what Moorehead Media is missing, and this could be it. "That actually might work."

"Look at what Amalie does for William's Media with all those makeup tutorials for the pediatric cancer unit. That video she did for the Christmas gala thing they threw kicked up their ratings something like fifteen percent, which is big revenue dollars. You could do something similar with your outreach projects, couldn't you?"

"Yeah, maybe." And Wren's big into charity work

with wanting to start her own foundation. I know she volunteers at the neonatal unit at one of the hospitals with her mom every week. It's not quite the same as outreach and creating sustainable communities, but at least our goals sort of seem to align.

"I haven't seen you this into anyone since . . . well, ever. I'm just saying, if you want this to work, Linc, there are ways to make it happen."

Several hours and many beers later, we're all sitting around the fire roasting marshmallows. Well, Wren is roasting marshmallows like it's her profession, and Cosy is charring hers. So far, she's lit every single one on fire. Wren, on the other hand, inspects her perfectly toasted ones before offering to share with me. Her cheeks are pink from the drinks she and Cosy have been consuming.

"So, how exactly did you two meet?" She motions between Griffin and Cosy.

I chuckle. "Oh, please do share this story."

Griffin gives me the cut-eye and opens his mouth to speak, but Cosy interrupts. "He was buying a double-headed dildo."

"What?" Wren's eyes bug, and the word comes out garbled since her mouth is full of marshmallow.

Griffin rolls his eyes, but his cheeks heat. "You love leading with that, don't you?"

"I love watching you blush." Cosy leans in and kisses the end of his nose, but her chair tips toward his and she has to scramble to right herself.

"Cosy used to work in an adult toy store."

"Called the Sex Toy Warehouse," Cosy adds.

"I drew the short straw and had to buy a bunch of stuff for a bachelor party," he explains.

"Why didn't you buy it all online?" Wren asks.

"It wouldn't have arrived on time."

"Not even with express shipping?" she presses.

I burst out laughing, because this was exactly my question.

"I couldn't risk it," Griffin grumbles.

We spend the rest of the night talking, sharing college stories, and I love that Wren fits in so seamlessly with the people who matter most to me.

By the time we finally get into bed—we get the trailer and Griffin and Cosy take the tent, although it's big enough to sleep ten people and it's set up on a platform, complete with a king mattress—Wren is drunk and languid. "I had fun tonight." She sidles up next to me and throws her leg over mine.

She's not wearing panties based on the sudden heat against my thigh.

"So did I."

"Thanks for inviting me." She trails her fingers down my chest. "I know time with Griffin is pretty rare, so the fact that you'd included me was nice."

"You're my girlfriend, why wouldn't I include you?"

She lifts her head. "I'm your girlfriend?"

"Uh, is that actually a question?"

"No. Yes. Maybe. I don't know." She bites her bottom lip. It's still a soft shade of pink. At least it's not the red I find so distracting. "I hadn't defined us in my head."

I grin because she looks unsure now. "So up until now, how would you have defined me in your head? Am I the project whose bed you've been sleeping in and whose cock you've been riding?"

Her mouth drops open, and her eyes go wide with something like horror. "What? No! Of course not. It's not, you're not . . . I just—" She scrambles for an explanation.

I roll her onto her back and edge my thigh between

hers. She parts them automatically. "Am I your fuck buddy? Is that it?"

"I've never had a fuck buddy."

"Really?"

"Why do you sound so surprised? It's more a guy thing, isn't it? I bet you've had loads of fuck buddies." She sounds annoyed at the possibility.

"Actually, it's never really been my thing either." Have I had casual, no-strings sex? Sure, but it's never been something I was all that comfortable with, nor was it something I sought on the regular. I prefer to connect with the person I'm sleeping with, whether it's on a superficial level or deeper—like what I have with Wren.

She runs her fingers through my hair, allowing them to trickle along my neck until she cups my face. "You must've had a few in college." I think it's supposed to come across as playful, but her expression is serious and somehow sad. I don't understand why this conversation has taken a sudden serious turn.

I draw a line across her temple and down to her chin with my fingertip. "Not a lot. I lived with Griffin; he was the king of monogamy. It felt wrong to bring home an endless stream of women who didn't matter. I didn't ever want to be like my father, uncommitted and absent."

"I'm sorry," she whispers.

"It's okay. I was mostly absent too, so I wasn't exposed to most of it. I never wanted to be that way when I was in a relationship, whether physically or emotionally. I didn't find the thrill in things that were meaningless, so I didn't pursue meaningless things."

Wren nods. "I was the same." She presses her thumb against my chin and slowly drags it down my throat. "You're everything and nothing like I expected you to be."

"What do you mean?"

"Well, in my head, you were this elusive introverted mountain man, which I mean, you kind of were at first. But I was positive I would find out all of these horrible things about you, that the image you presented couldn't possibly be authentic and you'd be just like Armstrong, or maybe even worse because you made it look like you cared. But you're nothing like Armstrong. You honestly couldn't be more opposite. If you didn't have at least a couple of physical similarities, I'd be hard-pressed to find any real way to connect the two of you." She bites the tip of her tongue. "I'm rambling. I do this when I'm drunk. I get all introspective, and then all this stuff comes out of my mouth and I don't really have control over it."

"I think I might want to get you drunk more often."

She giggles, then nibbles my chin. "Your dimple does things to me."

"I noticed that."

"As a good boyfriend does," she murmurs. Her eyes lift to mine. "Saying it out loud makes it real, doesn't it?"

"It's always been real, Wren. This is you and me choosing to acknowledge it and own it. Now we see where it goes from here."

I end the conversation with a kiss that becomes more. We have soft, slow sex that feels like it's weighted down with words that mean more than either of us are willing to say for fear of breaking the spell we're under.

And I fall more in love with the woman who fits so perfectly into my life, like she's always been part of it, like she's somehow been sewn into the fabric of who I am, without either of us realizing until now.

I don't know how I'm going to keep my feelings for

her masked much longer. As I wrap her up in my arms and wait for sleep to come, I consider how deep I am with this woman. All the things I thought I wanted are changing, and it's all because of her.

CHAPTER 18

TRUTH DOESN'T SET YOU FREE

WREN

Lincoln slides into my office and closes the door behind him. Most of the time we're extraordinarily careful about the way we interact at work, and I make a concerted effort not to fix his tie or smooth his suit jacket when we're anywhere a photo could be taken. As a rule, we also keep our office doors open when we're together. I'm about to remind Lincoln of this, however, his expression is tense, not playful.

I stop typing and give him my full attention. "What's up? Everything okay?"

"Can we make a stop on the way home?"

My stomach flutters when he says things like that. I'm sure it's subconscious, and that he's just referring to his place as home—which isn't even technically his— because it's easier. But in my head, it sounds like he's referring to it as *our* home.

"Yeah, of course."

"You almost ready to go?" He drums his fingers on the doorknob.

He's obviously antsy about something. "Give me five?"

"Yeah. Okay. I can do that." He doesn't make a move to leave, though.

"Would you like to sit while you wait?" I motion to the chair across from my desk.

"Sure." He crosses the room and drops into the chair, crossing one long leg over the other. The finger tapping resumes, this time on the arm of the chair.

I don't bother finishing the email I was about to send. He's clearly on edge. Instead, I shut down and start packing up my things. "Where are we going that has you so agitated?"

He glances at the door and shakes his head. "I'll tell you once we're out of the office."

Well, that's cryptic. I throw my laptop in my purse and double-check that I have everything I need so I can finish up the last few emails once we're at home. Penelope should be back from her cruise soon, but she's been in regular contact as long as she has reception. Mostly, she checks in to make sure Lincoln is managing okay and that Armstrong isn't causing problems.

I sleep at Lincoln's at least four times a week. He would probably like it if I stayed every night, but I have to justify paying my rent, and I need time with Dani and my family. My mom and I have made volunteering at the hospital a weekly event followed by dinner. Sometimes I go back to Lincoln's afterward, but other times I need space since it can be emotional.

Lincoln doesn't say much on the elevator ride down to street level other than to exchange pleasantries with a couple of people heading home for the day.

"Okay, what's going on?" I ask as soon as we're in the car and Lincoln has given the driver the address. "Why are we going to Lower Manhattan?"

"You know that penthouse my father had?"

"The one you think he used to see his mistress?" Even the word makes my skin crawl.

"That's the one." Lincoln runs his hands up and down his thighs. "Someone's been in there recently, and I want to check it out."

"How do you know someone's been there?"

"Every time a person enters the penthouse, I get an alert. I cancelled the housekeeping service after I discovered the place, so there's no reason for anyone else to be there. And I checked with Armstrong, and he said it wasn't him."

"And you believe him?"

"He said, and these were his words, playing dress up in Dad's old fetish gear isn't how he wants his sex to go down."

"He's unbelievable."

"He certainly is that. Anyway, I wanted to check things out, because obviously someone else has an access code for the penthouse besides me and Armstrong, and I'm assuming it has to be a mistress."

"Have you managed to dig up any other information about the property?" I ask.

"Honestly, I've been too preoccupied with everything else that's going on, and there are so many files to go through. I have some I want to look over this weekend, see if any of it links to this place." He runs a hand through his hair and sighs.

"Anything I can do to help, you let me know." I reach over and squeeze his thigh. "You know, Dani's a PI, so say the word, and I can ask her to look into it for you."

He frowns. "Really? I thought she worked in IT."

"That's part of her job." Often she finds backdoor ways to get information. I don't ask a lot of questions about how she comes by it. I just know she has access to things I know nothing about it.

He laces our fingers together. "Let's see what we find when we get to the penthouse."

He doesn't let go of my hand until we have to get out of the car. The ride up to the penthouse floor is tense with Lincoln nervously tapping against the handrail.

I follow him through the penthouse, wondering who Fredrick met here, and how that person felt about being the other woman. Did she consider how it damaged the relationship he was already in? Was she the reason he never connected with his wife? Who else was hurt because of their affair besides Lincoln and Armstrong? There are too many unknowns and what-ifs in a situation like this.

Lincoln stops in every room. The drawers in the master bedroom have been emptied, as have the closets. The sex room appears to be untouched, so I get to see, in three dimensions, exactly what Fredrick got up to in the bedroom, at least with his mistress. I honestly can't see, and don't want to imagine, Gwendolyn taking part in any of this.

Lincoln spends only a few seconds in there before he closes the door and returns to the kitchen. He opens the fridge to find it bare. "I wonder if his mistress has been here." He strides across the room and yanks open a door, which leads to an empty pantry. "This was full before, and there was stuff in the fridge."

"Do you think she came to clean it out?" It's obvious someone did, but I don't know what else to say.

He turns to me, looking lost. "Is it wrong that I want to know who she is? I just want to understand all of this."

"I don't think it's wrong. It's human, Lincoln, and understandable. This is a part of your father you don't know and that doesn't make sense to you. But even if you find out who she is, you'll never really get the answers as to why, as least not from your father's side." For a moment I consider telling him that I'm a product of an affair, that the man I call my father doesn't share any of my DNA and the man who does gave up his legal rights without a fight. That I've spent the last ten years wondering if my mother looks at me and sees her biggest mistake. That I'm ashamed of how I came to be, or that I'm here, and my sister, their *real* child, didn't even survive three days. But I don't want to shift the focus away from him and his pain, so I keep it where it's safest—a weight in my chest I can't ever seem to unload.

"Knowing something seems like it would be better than knowing nothing." Lincoln crosses through the living room and opens another closed door. This one leads to an office. It's a gorgeous space with built-in bookshelves, floor-to-ceiling windows and a view of Manhattan's skyline. Based on the setup and the top-of-the-line computer, this office was used regularly.

"I didn't come in here last time." Lincoln walks the perimeter of the room until he reaches the desk. He drops down in the leather executive chair and runs his hands across the smooth wood surface.

I have no idea what he's thinking about, but I know where my mind has gone. This office says more about the relationship than any other room in this penthouse. It says that he spent time here, that this wasn't just a place to sneak away for sex. There was an emotional connection, at least on some level, and it took him away from his family, dividing him between them.

Lincoln opens drawer after drawer, riffling through the contents. He finds a set of keys taped in the back of one of the drawers, which unlocks the filing cabinet. He pulls out several folders, so I round the desk to stand beside him, uncertain what he needs from me. He flips through phone bills, heating bills, laundry and dry cleaning bills, and receipts for takeout, fetish websites, expensive lingerie, and dress stores.

"He had an entire life I didn't know about," Lincoln says, voice low and rough.

"Do you think your mother knew?"

"I don't know how she couldn't."

"What about Penelope?"

"If she knew, she would've told me. At least I think she would." He spins in the chair and spreads his legs wide. Pulling me closer, he rests his forehead against my stomach and wraps his arms around me. There's nothing sexual in his actions or mine. It's comfort sought and given.

"The only way to find out is to ask."

"I just want to understand why."

"I know."

He lifts his head, and my heart aches at the sadness in his eyes. At the what-ifs probably going through his head. How maybe things would've been different, how his life might've been different if this didn't exist. It was exactly how I felt when I found the paperwork that told me the father I'd grown up believing was mine, wasn't.

I'd gone through all the what-ifs. It all came down to one single truth: I would never know anything different because this was the path my parents took, and there was no way to produce a different outcome than the one that already was.

It didn't stop me from wanting answers, though. So when Lincoln packs up the contents of the filing cabinet and spends most of the night poring through them, I'm right by his side.

And when we fall into bed in the wee hours of the morning, exhausted and bleary-eyed, no closer to an answer than we were before, I don't deny him the escape he seeks in me. Because it brings us closer together in ways he can't understand yet. And because I'm what he needs.

The next afternoon, I'm dragging. I have enough caffeine in my system to fuel a plane, and I'm so jittery, I don't think I could take a steady picture if my life depended on it. So when Gwendolyn calls me into her office for a chat, I immediately break into nervous sweats.

"Have a seat." She motions to the chair opposite her desk, face expressionless—which isn't unusual, but today it's putting me on edge.

I feel like I've been pulled into the principal's office and I'm about to get handed a month of detention.

She steeples her fingers and tips her head while she inspects me for a few very long seconds. "I need your help with something important."

"Of course." I clasp my hands in my lap and cross my fingers it doesn't have to do with Armstrong. It's been nice not dealing with him as often.

"You and Lincoln are sleeping together, am I correct?" It's less question and more statement, which is unnerving on so many levels. I thought we'd done an excellent job of remaining professional in the office and when people are watching us.

"I . . . uh . . . I don't think that's—"

She waves an impatient hand in the air. "I know my son, and how he's behaving is atypical, which means one of two things, he's either developed a problem with hard drugs or he's getting laid regularly. Based on the way you're blushing and sputtering, I'm going with option two." She taps on the desk. "Now I may not like it, or approve, or think you're a good choice for Lincoln, but I can't control where he decides to unload his stress, and he could certainly do worse."

I'm about to say something I'll definitely regret, but she raises a hand to stop me.

"I'm being candid, Wren, something you should appreciate. Since you're holding my son's balls in your hand, I need your help with this situation." She pushes a folder toward me. "Do you recognize this?"

I flip it open and try to keep my eyes from flaring. My tone is intentionally placid. "Should I?"

I think she may be narrowing her eyes at me, but I can't be 100 percent on that. "I know Lincoln was at the penthouse in Lower Manhattan, and I know you were with him, so there's no point in pretending." She pauses for effect. It works. "He needs to stop looking into it."

I sit back in my chair, confused. "You know about the penthouse?"

She makes an exasperated sound. "Of course I know. I'm not stupid, and my knowledge is irrelevant. What's important is you persuading Lincoln it's not worth looking into any more than he already has."

"But—"

"This is not a *but* situation, Wren. This is the kind where you follow my direction and do as you're told. Now, I understand your loyalty to Lincoln, especially considering what's going on between you; however, you'd do well to remember that your contract is up in a few months. Actually, Lincoln adapted quite well, better than I anticipated, so you may very well be able to finish out your contract early." She stares coldly at me, a sneer distorting her upper lip. "Not that it matters either way. Lincoln will likely go back to whatever impoverished country he feels would benefit from his altruism, and you'll want to move on, which will be exceedingly difficult with a bad reference, won't it?"

This seems a lot like blackmail. "With all due respect, Gwendolyn, I can't tell Lincoln what he can and can't do."

A slow, creepy smile wavers on her lips. "Now, Wren, as a woman, I'm sure you know that's untrue. There's a lot you can do to distract Lincoln. So that's what you're going to do. Distract him however you can. Keep him from digging any deeper than he already has. The legacy of the Moorehead family is counting on you."

She leans back in her chair, wearing a calculated, malevolent expression. I see so much of Armstrong in her in that moment. "In a few months, you'll walk away with quite a hefty amount of money, and as I promised, a glowing recommendation. I'll honor my promise to you, but in exchange, I expect you to do this for me. Everyone has a dirty secret or two, don't they, Wren?"

A shiver fights its way down my spine at what sounds very much like a threat. I can't imagine my mother confiding such personal, shameful information to her.

Gwendolyn doesn't give me a chance to respond, not that I know what to say to that since I'm beginning to think trusting her is a very bad idea. "It would serve you well to protect Fredrick's secrets if you'd like me to protect yours."

"You can't blackmail me with money and a recommendation, Gwendolyn. I don't need either of those things from you—"

She pushes up out of her chair and rounds the desk.

"You're not understanding me, Wren, if you think all that's at stake here is your paycheck and a recommendation." She leans in close, gripping my elbow to keep me from stepping away. "One little mistake can ruin an entire family, can't it, Wren? How would that look on your father's campaign if it came out that the 'Family First' politician has a daughter who's a product of an affair and he's kept it a secret for years? Such a pitiful scandal, isn't it? Especially since he lost his *real* daughter before he even had a chance to love her."

My stomach drops as the threat settles around us. "But you can't—"

"Imagine how quickly the public will lose faith in your father if they find out his whore of a wife cheated on him while he was starting his career. You of all the media must know how quick people are to pounce on scandal. Your father's career will end very quickly, and then what will you have other than your family's shameful past smeared all over your father's 'Family First' campaign? He is running for governor next election, isn't he?"

Panic sets in, and I try to find a way to get myself out of this without someone I care about getting hurt in the end. "You can't do this to my family—"

"Oh, but I can. And I will expose your family for the frauds they are if you don't do what I ask. Don't even think about telling Lincoln about this conversation, or I'll drop an exposé on your father so fast your head will spin." She steers me toward the door. "You know, I didn't understand your fascination with neonatal charities at first, but it all makes sense now, doesn't it? You're the bastard survivor, and your poor little defective sister was the punishment for your mother's infidelity.

It's amazing how the balance is set no matter what our choices are, isn't it?" Her smile is far from sympathetic. "The truth doesn't always set you free, Wren. Sometimes it becomes the noose around your neck. You'd be wise to remember that."

CHAPTER 19
NOT MY BED, BUT I'M LYING IN IT

WREN

My stomach rolls and knots as I leave work that afternoon alone. I cut out while Lincoln is in the middle of a conference call, like a coward, and head straight for Dani's. We'd already planned to hang out tonight, but normally I'd wait until Lincoln was finished with his call. We'd debrief, look at tomorrow's schedule, and he'd persuade me to come to his place instead of going to mine when Dani and I are done talking about how great he is in bed.

I need space and some time to think before I can talk to him. I don't know how to get myself out of this situation without someone I care about getting hurt. I may have a great poker face, but Linc and I have been spending a lot of time together. Enough that he's learned how to read my facial expressions and body language. I won't be able to keep this from him, and while I certainly trust him with my family's sordid secret, I don't know that I'll be able to lie about his mother threatening me by exposing my father and my family.

I need perspective. The kind I can only get from Dani.

She opens the door and her smile drops. "Uh-oh, what's wrong?"

"Pretty much everything." I drop my purse on the floor and cross over to the fridge. I'm relieved to find she has something other than beer, even if it is one of those horrible sugary drinks I normally avoid because they give me the worst hangovers.

I pop the top and chug half the bottle. It's like drinking liquid sugar, but I don't care, I need to take the edge off.

Dani grabs the bottle from me. "That's not alcohol, you loon, it's black current syrup." She holds it up so I can see the label.

"Awesome, so I consumed enough sugar to send myself into a coma." I can't even get drunk properly.

She turns me toward the living room and gives me a push. "Go sit. Let me get you a water and maybe a glass of wine."

"The whole bottle would be better." I throw myself on her couch and run my hands down my face. I've probably smeared my eyebrows down to my chin, but whatever.

Dani returns a minute later with a glass of water and a carafe of wine with a straw. I'm sure it's meant as a joke, but I take the carafe and leave the water. Dani takes the cushion beside me. "Did something happen with Lincoln?"

"No. Yes. Sort of. Not directly with him, but it involves him."

She motions for me to go on, but I hesitate, the damn NDA I signed taunting me. While I have some leeway with Dani since she's a PI and I've used her on past occasions to help sort out some of Armstrong's less-than-savory situations, this would be a direct breach. I figure I could do worse things than break an NDA, considering I'm now being blackmailed by the person who wrote it.

So I explain the trip to the penthouse last night and how Gwendolyn pulled me into her office this afternoon. I pinch the bridge of my nose. "My mother must have told her about the affair. I mean, that's the only logical way Gwendolyn could've found out, isn't it?" My parents have been very careful to cover all the necessary tracks, not because my father is unwilling to admit I'm not his, at least not in the biological sense, but to protect me and my mother. "Why would she do that? Why tell someone something so private and shameful?"

Dani blows out a breath. "Well, based on what you've told me about Gwendolyn, she seems to be pretty good at manipulating, so I can only assume that's what she did to your mom. Maybe she was looking for leverage?"

"Leverage for what, though?"

"Think about it, Wren. You have all this sensitive information about her family, particularly Armstrong. Gwendolyn and Fredrick covered everything he did up by paying people off, which tells you a lot about who they are and how they conduct business. They need dirt on you, so you don't expose the dirt you have on them. Gwendolyn was looking for a way to get something on you, so she could hold it over you if she needed to. And now she's found something big enough to do a lot of damage to the people you love."

I tap my lips, anxiety making my stomach twist. Or maybe it's the half bottle of syrup I drank. Until recently, I didn't see Gwendolyn as a potential threat, but obviously she was prepared to treat me as one. "How am

I going to convince Lincoln not to look any deeper? I'd want answers if I were him. I wanted to know when I *was* him." I sip the wine, considering how bad my hangover will likely be if I drink this whole thing after that syrup. I'm not sure I actually care. "Maybe I need to break it off with him."

"How is that going to help anything?"

I rub my temples, working it out in my head. "There's no winning here, Dani. Not for me. If I don't get Lincoln to stop looking into this, Gwendolyn is going to ruin my father's career and potentially have me blacklisted from charity organizations in this city. If I tell Lincoln his mother is blackmailing me, she's going to expose my father anyway. No matter what I do, someone I love is going to get hurt. How awful will it look for the senator who prides himself on 'Family First' to have raised his wife's illegitimate child from an affair and have kept it a secret for years? I can see exactly how Gwendolyn would spin this so it would have the most devastating impact, Dani. It'll be a nightmare. He'll know something is wrong the second he sees me. There's no good way out."

"And you think breaking it off with him is going to make it somehow better?"

I stare up at the ceiling, spinning my wheels, trying to figure out how I can get through this with the least amount of damage possible. "I don't know. There's no answer I like, Dani. I don't want to drag him into this. Gwendolyn will destroy my family either way, and she'll turn Lincoln into a martyr. The public will eat it up, and Lincoln will be right in the middle of the mayhem. And all for what? Because he wants to look into a damn penthouse with a fetish room? It doesn't make any sense. None of this does."

"Okay, let's put feelings and emotions aside for a second, which I get is hard since you're clearly in love with the guy—"

I immediately go on the defensive. "I'm not—" I can't finish the sentence because she's right. Somewhere along the way, I fell for Lincoln, for his cynical attitude, for his unapologetic lack of fucks given when it comes to status, for his altruism and his generosity. I drop my head in my hands. "I'm so screwed right now."

"Let's not panic, yet. We need to look at the facts and assess them with logic."

"Easy for you to say, your life isn't a billion shades of messed up right now."

"I think the Mooreheads' penchant for drama is rubbing off you."

"This isn't a joke, Dani."

"I'm not trying to be funny. Just hear me out. Gwendolyn knew about the penthouse, and probably has for some time. So there are two possibilities we're working with. Either she's the one with the fetish, or she knew about the mistress. Regardless, she has something to hide. If she didn't, she wouldn't be trying to stop Lincoln from looking for answers."

"So what do I do?"

"You find out what she's hiding and blackmail her right back."

"I can't blackmail my boyfriend's mother."

"I'm not sure you have another option, Wren. Not if you don't want Gwendolyn to blow the lid off your family's secret."

"I can't let that happen." I take an extra-big gulp from the carafe. "God, what if my mother didn't say anything?"

"What do you mean?"

"What if Gwendolyn tapped my phone? What if she's been listening in on all my calls? Maybe that's how she knew about me and Lincoln. Oh my God! What if there are cameras in Griffin's penthouse? What if they're in mine? What if she's seen what we do behind closed doors?" The thought alone is terrifying, and actually a whole lot gross.

"Honestly, Wren, stop freaking out. All anyone has to do is look at the pictures of you and Lincoln together, and they can guess what's going on. He looks at you like you're the beginning and the end of his world. You would have to be legitimately blind not to notice how enamored he is with you."

She has a point. I've seen the candid pictures. "Okay, fine, but that doesn't explain how she knew I went with Lincoln to the penthouse in Lower Manhattan unless—oh my God. Lincoln gets alerts when someone enters that building, and if Gwendolyn knows about it, then she must get alerts too. Is that possible?" Which makes me wonder if she knew about his first visit to the penthouse.

Dani takes the carafe of wine from me and sets it on the table. "That makes logical sense."

I rub my temples, trying to understand how quickly my life has been upended. "I don't get it. How could she know about the penthouse and be okay with it? How is someone ever okay knowing their spouse is cheating on them?"

"I don't know, Wren. Maybe they had some kind of arrangement. She has to be hiding something if she's throwing out blackmail, though."

"Now I just need to find out what."

CHAPTER 20
BAD VIBES

LINCOLN

My conference call took three times as long as I would've liked thanks to how much Wentworth Williams likes to jerk off his ego. But the end result was positive, so the time wasted is something I'll gladly forfeit. The deal I struck with Williams Media means I no longer have to fire twenty people, and I'm pushing a brand-new initiative that will focus on things I actually care about, like helping people. It's a win all the way around. The best part? Amalie—Armstrong's former fiancée—will be heading up the initiative.

Financially, we're putting out more than we're getting back, but I think it's a smart decision in the long-term. Also, my conscience feels lighter, especially after I call G-mom and tell her the news. I may be in my thirties, but it still makes me feel good when she tells me she's proud of me.

Unfortunately, there's still a weight in my gut that hasn't eased up since the visit to my dad's secret penthouse, and it's grown exponentially this afternoon.

I leave my office in search of Wren, because if any-one will share my excitement over the deal with Wil-liams, it's her. Also, seeing her might help with this uncomfortable, pervasive feeling I can't shake.

Except she's not in her office and her laptop isn't on her desk. Maybe she had to run an errand or she got pulled into a meeting. I fire off a message and wander down the hall.

I could ask Marjorie where she is, but then I might get pulled into a conversation with her about whatever healthy *blah blah blah* she's into, and I don't feel like pretending to be interested.

Instead, I take the long way around to bypass my as-sistant's office and check in with Lulu. Everyone has to go by her to leave the building unless they take the stairs. Since we're on the twenty-seventh floor, that doesn't happen very often, apart from fire drills.

"Hey, Lulu." I smile and glance around the mostly empty reception area.

She looks up from her computer and gives me her customary wide smile with her too-dark lipstick. "Hello, Mr. Moorehead, how can I help you?" Lulu is always extra polite with me, and nervous, but she's warming up slowly.

"Have you see Wren around?"

She glances at the clock. "She left the office about forty-five minutes ago."

"Did she say when she'd be back?"

"I believe she left for the day. Is there something you need? Anything I can help you with?"

There sure is something I need, but Lulu definitely can't help me. "Uh, no. I'm good. Thanks." I rap on her desk and head back to my office, the unsettled feeling growing. Usually Wren checks in with me before she leaves. I would've at least expected a text.

When I return to my office, I find my mother standing behind my desk, riffling through my files. "I hear you saved twenty jobs today."

I can't tell whether or not she's pleased by this. I appeal to the business-driven side of her, the part that's focused on money and company optics. "I thought a deal with Williams would look better for the company than cutting all those people loose and sending them directly to the competition."

"It was very smart thinking, Lincoln. I always knew you'd do well if you chose to come back and take over the company."

"Well, it's not really a choice, is it?" Although, even that's not entirely true anymore. I'm starting to see how I can make changes that will drive this company in a direction I like a lot better. But she doesn't need to know that right now.

She smiles and runs her hand across the back of the executive chair. "You could've walked away, Lincoln, gone back to Guatemala right after the funeral, but you didn't. You've embraced your role at Moorhead, and you're showing exactly how capable you are. Your father would've been proud."

Not once in any decision I've made since coming back to New York have I considered whether or not my actions would make my father proud, mostly because I didn't have much respect for him. "Excuse me if I don't take that as a compliment."

My mother sighs. "Your father wasn't a bad man, Lincoln."

"Everyone keeps saying that, but I fail to see any of

the good in him. He was a shitty father, and he certainly lacked a moral compass from what I've witnessed."

"He had too much of one," my mother says.

"I don't understand how you can say that."

She sneers. "Your father was ruled too much by his heart."

"I think you mean his dick."

She gives me a hard look. "Enough, Lincoln. The crassness is unnecessary."

"I honestly don't get it. How could you stay with him? How could you condone what he let Armstrong get away with? How could you be with someone who was obviously unfaithful to you? Did you know he had a penthouse in Lower Manhattan?" I shudder at the thought and try to suppress the memory of the sex room before it becomes vivid and contains my mother.

"Of course I knew. I'm not stupid, Lincoln. I'm pragmatic." Her expression shifts to disgust. "What that penthouse represents is a disgrace to the Moorehead legacy, but I forgave your father for his transgressions. I let it go, and you need to as well. It doesn't do anyone any good to hold onto the kind of anger you harbor for someone who's not here to receive it."

"But he chea—"

She slices an angry hand through the air. "I said enough, Lincoln. Everyone makes mistakes. Take a look at what you're doing. I may not approve of this tryst you're having with Wren, but clearly your physical needs require attention."

"My physical needs? That's not what this is about."

Gwendolyn turns to the mini fridge. She frowns at the contents, which consist of still and sparkling water in recyclable and reusable bottles. "I hired Wren to manage you and your social media, not your personal needs. But I imagine she must look fairly appealing after the last couple of years. Just remember who you are and who she is."

That hot feeling in the back of my neck crawls down my spine. "What's that supposed to mean?"

She gives me a look as she paces the office. "Oh, come on, Lincoln, don't tell me you're so blinded by lust that you can't see what she's doing."

I cross my arms. "Please, enlighten me."

She rolls her eyes and sighs. "Men, so driven by your libidos that you fail to see when someone is using you for their own personal gain. Wren is the daughter of a senator, and she's taken a job working for the top media company in the state. She could've found a position in a charity organization if she wanted to. She didn't have to sign the contract to work with you, but she saw an opportunity and she took it. I can't blame her. Look at you." She motions to me, and her mouth approximates a smile. "You look so much like your father when he was your age. So handsome and charming. It's no wonder Wren stayed on, but don't be fooled by her interest in you, which I'm sure seems quite genuine. She's like everyone else out there, looking to climb the ladder the quickest way she knows how."

My mother settles a palm on my shoulder. For a moment she meets my gaze, looking almost sad. "Everyone uses everyone else to get where they want to go, Lincoln. No one's motives are pure. Don't mistake lust for something it's not."

"Of course you'd believe that, since that's how this whole family operates, isn't it?" I don't believe what's happening between me and Wren is simply based on lust. And now I can't shake the horrible feeling that Wren's sudden absence this afternoon and this conversation with my mother are somehow connected.

On my way out of the office, I finally get a message from Wren.

Left work early. Didn't want to interrupt your call. With Dani. Chat later.

It should assuage me, but all it does is ramp up the worry. I respond with: *Everything okay?* It takes far longer than it should for her to reply with a thumbs-up. Wren never responds with emojis, which means that the unsettled feeling grows even more.

I leave the office early and pick up pizza on my way home, hoping when she's done with dinner and a movie with Dani that she'll come over, spend the night, and alleviate my anxiety.

Except I still haven't heard from her by ten o'clock, which is atypical. At ten thirty I'm debating whether it makes me look slightly desperate if I text for an ETA, when my phone finally buzzes on the coffee table.

It doesn't even make it to the end of the first ring. "Hey, baby, when are you getting your fine ass over here?"

"I didn't realize we were in the pet names stage in our relationship." The voice on the other end of the line is not even remotely feminine.

My excitement deflates like a sad puffer fish. "Oh, hey, Griffin. I thought you were Wren."

"Yeah, I figured with the fine-ass comment. I mean, my ass is pretty amazing, but you acknowledging that would be crossing some lines I'm not comfortable with."

I laugh, but it comes out flat.

"You okay, man? You sound morose."

"Screw you and the morose bullshit." Although he's probably right.

"Seriously, what's up? Things okay there?"

"Yeah. No. I don't know. Things are screwed up as usual in my family."

"The same as usual, or something different this time?"

I fill him in on the new developments with my dad's secret penthouse, the conversation I had with my mother about letting it go, and what she said about Wren being a ladder climber.

"Wait. What? Why would she contract Wren to work with you if she thought she was a ladder climber? That doesn't add up."

"My thoughts exactly. I don't know why she's pushing this angle all of a sudden. It doesn't make any sense. None of this does. I don't get why my mother would accept that my father was cheating on her, let alone forgive him for it. I get that maybe theirs was a marriage of convenience or whatever, but it's like he didn't even try to hide it from her. And she's adamant I let it go. Everyone says my father wasn't a bad man, but he never made an attempt to be part of my life until I had an MBA from Harvard, and everything I've seen points in a very different direction. Nothing adds up."

"I get where you're coming from, Linc, but knowing doesn't always make it better," Griffin replies carefully.

"You're not the first person to say that." I look up at the ceiling, wishing revelations were written there. "I don't know what I'm supposed to do here."

"If it's eating at you this badly, then you dig, even if Gwendolyn doesn't want you to. Just be prepared to get answers you might not like."

* * *

At eleven, Wren finally calls. "I'm sorry it's so late."

I don't know if it's my state of mind or what my mother said or the conversation I had with Griffin, but I'm hyperalert and she sounds off.

"You don't usually leave work without saying good-bye." It comes out sounding more like an accusation than a question. I need to be careful how I tread with Wren on this. I can't project my own insecurities onto her.

"I know, I'm sorry. I didn't want to interrupt your call, and then Dani and I got talking and I lost track of time."

"Are you on your way over now?"

That off feeling I've had all afternoon grows when Wren's silence stretches out before she finally answers. "I'm already at home."

"I thought you were going to Dani's."

"I was, but we had a change of plans and ended up here."

"Oh, okay. Want me to come to you tonight, instead?"

"Coming here isn't really a good idea, is it?"

Normally I'd say she has a point, but my mother clearly knows what's going on, so I'm not sure we need to hide it any longer. However, Wren might not know this, and it's definitely not a phone discussion. "I could send a car to pick you up, then."

"That's really sweet of you to offer, Linc, but I'm pretty beat and I'm not really feeling one hundred percent."

"Is everything okay?" It seems like that's the only question I'm asking lately.

"I'm just feeling under the weather. I'm sure it's noth-ing, but I don't want to pass it along. We have that big meeting early next week, and I don't want to risk getting you sick. I'm going to take some vitamin C and go to bed. Try to get a solid seven, which definitely hasn't been happening lately. I'll see you in the morning, okay?" She yawns.

"Okay. Sure. You'll spend the night tomorrow, then?" Other than nights like these, when she's with Dani or her mom, she's been sleeping in my bed.

"We'll see how I'm feeling tomorrow. Night, Linc."

"Night, Wren."

I'm even more off after she ends the call. She's noncommittal about tomorrow night, and she didn't even ask how my conference call went, which is very unlike Wren. She's usually all about the business and making sure things are going smoothly, so maybe she really isn't feeling well.

Even still, I can't settle, so I end up going through more of my father's files from the penthouse. I stumble on a cellphone bill, but when I call the number associated with the account, it's been disconnected.

I fall asleep on my desk and wake up to the sound of birds chirping, with a stiff neck, a sore back, and the same bad feeling from the night before.

My morning doesn't improve when I find Wren's office empty at work. Her laptop still isn't on her desk, which I assume means she's either not here or already in a meeting.

I fire off a message and pop my head into the conference room, but it's empty as well. Wren still hasn't messaged back—although, to be fair it's only been a minute—so I stalk down the hall to my assistant's desk.

"Good morning." It comes out more bark-like than actual greeting.

Marjorie startles and knocks her jar of pens over,

spilling them across her desk. "Oh! Good morning, Mr. Moorehead. Can I get you a coffee?"

Of course that's the first question out of her mouth. "I'm fine, thank you," I grind out with a smile. "I'm actually looking for Wren. Have you seen her this morning?"

"Oh, uh, no, I haven't. Would you like me to check her office for you?"

I tap on the edge of her desk, unhappy with this information. "I've already done that. I'll check with Lulu."

"I can call her for you. Right now. Let me call her." She picks up her phone before I can argue and punches in Lulu's extension. "Hello, Lulu, it's Marjorie. Mr. Moorehead is looking for Wren, have you seen her yet this morning?" There's a brief pause while Lulu asks her something too muffled for me to catch. "Lincoln not Armstrong . . . ah, okay. I'll let him know." She hangs up, that odd smile of hers still stretched across her face. "I'm sorry, Mr. Moorehead, but it seems Wren has called in sick this morning."

"She never calls in sick."

"Until this morning, that statement would be correct." Her eyes light up with some sort of odd excitement, and her smile widens. "Is there something you need help with? I'd be happy to be of assistance."

I wave her off. "No, no. It's fine. It can wait until Wren is back." I turn on my heel, phone already in my hand, thumbs flying across the tiny, stupid screen. I have to delete half the message thanks to autocorrect mistakes. I abandon the message entirely when I reach my office and call her instead.

Of course it goes to voicemail.

My stomach twists with anxiety. First, that conversation with my mother yesterday, then Wren bailing on me last night, and now she's calling in sick.

Something's going on, and I'm almost positive it has to do with Gwendolyn.

I send a text to go with the voicemail and wait for a response.

And wait.

And wait some more.

It's fucking infuriating.

I suppose now I know how Wren felt every time I ignored her calls and messages in the beginning. I can't say I like it very much.

CHAPTER 21

PICKLE

WREN

After a restless night and a headache that's likely a result of the lack of sleep and the four million grams of sugar I consumed last night, on top of a half a bottle of wine, I called in sick this morning.

I need to tell Lincoln what's going on, but first I need to give my father fair warning. While I'm not responsible for my parents' choices, I can at least let them know what they're about to be up against. There are enough secrets being kept; we don't need them between us as well.

My stomach twists uncomfortably as I walk up the front steps to my parents' house. It's ridiculously early, as is the plan. I wanted to catch my father before he left for work.

"Hey, sweetie, this is a surprise." He opens the door and ushers me in, pulling me into a hug. When he backs up and takes me by the shoulders, I force a smile, but I'm sure it looks as flat as it feels. His own falls. "What's wrong? You look exhausted."

My shoulders curl forward, and I drop my head, unable to hold eye contact as the tears I've been fighting a losing battle against fall. "I have a problem."

"It's okay, whatever it is, it'll be okay." He pulls me in for another hug. My dad doesn't balk at tears and tell me to buck up, probably because I'm not much of a crier, so he knows it can't be good if I'm in his foyer, ruining his suit with tears.

When I'm composed enough, he leads me to the living room, where I tell him all about Gwendolyn's threats to expose our family if I'm unable to keep Lincoln from looking into the penthouse further.

My father is a warm man, genuine and approachable. It's why he's such a perfect fit as a senator. People like and respect him because he shows strength of character, and he's fair and just. But right now, he looks like he could go a round in a boxing ring and win.

"I'm sorry, Dad," I say, gathering my courage. "I know I'm putting our entire family in a difficult position and that I probably shouldn't have gotten involved with Lincoln while working for Gwendolyn." I summon the courage to tell him the rest.

"Wren, honey—" my father interrupts, but I cut him off.

"Let me finish, please, Dad. I can't lie to Lincoln. I know it's going to make things complicated for everyone, but I love him, and I won't let someone blackmail me into keeping my mouth shut, least of all his own damn mother." I rush on, trying to get the words out before I break down in another fit of tears. "I know this has the potential to hurt your campaign, but I can't let Gwendolyn push me around like this. I just need you to understand." I hiccup loudly, my panic gaining momentum as I consider, truly, the ramifications of my actions.

He puts a gentle hand on my shoulder. "Sweetheart, take a breath."

I inhale loudly and release it slowly, trying to stay calm. My dad regards me with a sad smile. "I'm so damn proud of you right now."

I blink several times. "But I'm putting you in a horrible, awful position."

"You're being blackmailed, Wren. It's out of your hands. If anything, you're the one being put in a horrible position."

"You're not angry with me?" I exhale some of the anxiety that's been keeping my stomach in knots.

"Of course I'm not angry with you. I'm immensely proud of you for holding onto your morals, especially when you've been surrounded by one of the most morally gray families I've ever had the misfortune of knowing." He reaches for his Rubik's Cube, something he's had on his desk for as long as I can remember, and starts twisting it, breaking up the perfect color patterns on each side until they're a rainbow mosaic.

"There's no way out of this without someone getting hurt. I've tried to come up with an alternative, but Gwendolyn has backed me into a corner."

"Well, that's what she's good at, isn't it? Gwendolyn sure knows how to play the game. I didn't realize how twisted she really is. I questioned when Gwendolyn and your mother started spending time together, knowing what I do about that family. But then, I think your mother felt bad for her, considering all the rumors about Armstrong. And of course, they were both so committed to working on charitable projects, I thought it was good for your mom. I should've been more careful, and I should've discouraged you from working with that family."

"I just wanted to make things better with Mom. And it's not as if she was wrong about the job. Gwendolyn has amazing connections, and it was an opportunity I couldn't pass up," I admit.

My mother appears in the doorway, her surprise turning to concern as soon as she sees my face. "Wren, honey, is everything okay?"

My dad's smile is sad as he sets the Rubik's Cube on the table, one side already uniform again. "We have a situation on our hands, Abigail." My dad fills her in, and with each admission, her face grows paler, and I begin to second-guess myself. My mother may have made a mistake all those years ago, but she's genuinely a good person. I see it every time we volunteer at the hospital together. I suddenly realize she's spent her entire adult life trying to make up for a lapse in judgment.

"Maybe we can find another way." Even as I say it, I know there isn't one. "I don't want anyone to get hurt by this. It's not going to look good for your campaign."

My dad dismisses the idea. "Forget about the campaign, Wren. That's not what this is about."

"But if everyone finds out I'm adopted—"

"This is my fault," my mother says softly.

"This isn't yours to own, Abigail—"

My mother puts up a hand to stop my dad. "It is, though. I ultimately made the decision that's led to this. It's me you were protecting all those years by keeping the adoption a secret. We should've addressed it when Wren found out." My mother turns to me. "I'm so sorry, honey." She takes my hands in hers, expression imploring. "You're in a bad situation because of my choices."

"This situation is as much my fault," my dad interjects.

My mother gives him a soft, sad smile. "We can both own it."

In all the years since I found out I was the product of an affair, neither of them has ever really talked about it with me.

My mom squeezes my hands. "We wanted to protect you. *I* wanted to protect you. When your dad and I found out you weren't biologically his, I was devastated, not because I was pregnant, but because I'd made your life so difficult even before you were born. I didn't want you to grow up being ashamed of me and how you'd come to be. But if it hadn't been for you, Wren, I don't think your dad and I would still be together."

All the knots in my stomach tighten. "I don't understand."

"You were our wake-up call, Wren. You were the reason behind the 'Family First' platform. I pushed your mother to make a decision she regrets because I was absent. We were both at fault, she *and* I. It's not just one of us who's culpable. I was too focused on my career and not focused enough on our relationship. I ignored all the signs. I pushed aside your mother's needs and placated her with things instead of love. You were the reason I finally opened my eyes and saw what I was doing to the person I loved the most."

My parents look at each other, and I don't see any regret, only love.

I voice the one thing that has eaten at me all these years. "I always wondered if you looked at me and saw your biggest mistake. Especially since you lost Robyn, and she was really *yours*."

Tears spill over and cascade down my mom's cheeks. "Oh, sweetheart, no. Losing Robyn was painful for all of us, but it was also inevitable."

"I don't understand."

My mom and dad exchange a remorseful look before she continues. "We should've explained this years ago, but talking about it was just so difficult. Your father and I are both carriers of a rare genetic disorder. We can't have children together, but with you, I didn't pass on the gene. So if it weren't for you, we would have no children of our own. You were our miracle, Wren. You always have been. You're the reason for everything good in our lives. We always wanted you, both of us. Your father signed the adoption papers because as far as we were concerned, you were ours in every way that counted."

They envelop me in a hug, one that's full of the promise of healing.

"I don't think either of us fully considered the ramifications when you were born, Wren. And then, when you found those documents when you were a teenager, we should've handled things differently so we could've avoided putting you in this kind of position. You should never have carried this burden. We'll make this right for you, Wren. For all of us," my father says.

He pulls me and my mother into another hug so tight, it's almost hard to breathe. We stay like that for a long time, letting go of emotions tied to a past we can't ever get rid of and a pain that suddenly feels fresh.

Eventually, he releases us. "I'm so sorry the decisions your mother and I made are causing you such turmoil."

"I know you are, both of you." I squeeze their hands. "There's nothing I can do to stop Gwendolyn from exposing you."

"We've always been prepared to tell the truth, Wren. We should have done it a long time ago," my dad says.

"Gwendolyn will turn it into a scandal."

My mom's expression goes icy. "Not if I have anything

to say about it. She's sorely mistaken if she thinks she can take advantage of you, or anyone in this family."

"She can only turn it into a scandal if she's the one doing the exposing. I don't have anything to hide, Wren. I can talk to my publicity team and find a gentle way to address this publicly. Gwendolyn can't blackmail you if she doesn't have anything to hold over your head."

In all the time I've known about the affair and where I came from, I never really looked at it through my mother's eyes, maybe because I'd found out as a teen when my whole world revolved only around me and how things impacted me. I'd blamed her for it, was ashamed of her and for her, and myself. But learning this, knowing that I'm wanted and always have been, regardless of how I came to be, helps soothe away some of the hurt I've carried in my heart all these years.

Now, I understand better my father's reason's for protecting her, us. It's never been about him or his career; it's always been about keeping us safe from the media showdown. They could rip us apart, and my parents never wanted to put me under such scrutiny. "Does this mean you're going to make a statement?"

"Your mother and I will do whatever it takes to make sure you're not the one caught in the middle of other people's bad decisions, or forced to make choices you'll regret."

CHAPTER 22

TAKE A MOTHER DOWN

LINCOLN

By ten, I'm about ready to pack it in and go on a mission in search of Wren. My mother is absent from the office, G-Mom just returned from her cruise so I've yet to see her or speak with her, and last I heard, Armstrong missed another putt in his office game of golf and broke his computer monitor. Again.

And still nothing from Wren.

I've gotten all of absolutely nothing done this morning, apart from looking through more financial files, in search of something, *anything* that will give me some answers as to what my father was hiding and why my mother is so intent on keeping it that way. Every time I find a large withdrawal from my father's business account, I underline it and set it aside, prepared to cross-reference until I find something that might get me off this hamster wheel.

My cell rings as I find yet another transfer of funds in excess of twenty-five thousand dollars. I glance at the screen, spit the highlighter out from between my teeth, and slam my thumb down on the answer button so hard that my phone shoots off my desk and clatters to the floor.

"Hold on." I push out of my chair and it hits the wall behind me with a loud thud as I scramble around my desk. "I dropped my phone. I'm here." I snatch it up, relieved the screen hasn't spiderwebbed, and bring it to my ear. "Wren? Are you okay? Are you sick? Do you need anything?" Wow. My calm and collected needs some work.

"It's me. I'm . . . okay. Are you at the office?" Her voice sounds hoarse, like maybe she has a sore throat.

"Yeah. Yes. I'm at the office. Are you at home? Can I bring you anything? Soup? Tea? Ginger ale?"

"I'm . . . no. I don't need anything, and I'm not at home."

"Did you go to the doctor's? Your voice doesn't sound great. You should've called. I would've taken you."

She clears her throat. "I'm not at the doctor's. You don't have any meetings this afternoon, do you? I didn't schedule anything for you."

"No. Nothing. Are you coming in?" Her tone ramps up my nerves.

"No. Um, but I think we need to talk."

"Okay. Sure. Shoot."

"Not over the phone. What time do you think you're going to leave work? Maybe I could come over, then?"

"I can leave right now. I can be at my place in twenty, or more like half an hour, depending on traffic."

"Okay. I'll meet you there."

"Are you okay?" I start packing up my things, shoving them into my messenger bag. "You really don't sound okay."

"I'm—" She hiccups. "No. Not really. I'll explain when I see you."

"You're worrying me a lot, Wren."

"I know, and I'm sorry, but it's really not a phone conversation."

"I'll be there as soon as I can." I end the call, shove the file folders I was going through into my messenger bag, and bust my ass to the elevator.

"Oh! Mr. Moorehead! I was about to stop by your office!"

I take a deep breath and grit my teeth. Marjorie has no idea how stressed I am, and I don't want to take it out on her simply because she's had the misfortune of running into me right now.

I plaster on what I'm sure is a horribly disingenuous smile and turn to face her. "I'm on my way out, Marjorie. Can it wait until tomorrow?"

"There's a call from Wentworth Williams."

Dammit. Wentworth likes to talk. A lot. Whenever I have a call from him, I budget an hour and make sure I have another meeting lined up afterwards—real or fake. Unfortunately, since he's the reason I didn't have to fire twenty employees, I should probably field the call. "Fine. I'll take it."

"He's on line two."

Despite telling him I have a meeting in ten minutes, he keeps me on the phone for fifteen. On the upside, the merger seems to be going well so far. By the time I finally leave, I should almost be at my place, so I text Wren and let her know I got held up by a call and to make herself comfortable.

Of course, the trip back to my place can't be smooth. There are two fender benders clogging up traffic on the way to the penthouse, and it's everything I can do to keep from rolling down the windows and screaming bloody murder at the idiots who are blocking two lanes.

During the exceptionally long trip back to my place, I roll around a million different possible scenarios. I can hear Wren in my head, telling me I'm being a drama queen and asking if I need my crown, but any conversation that can't be had over the phone is a serious one. And serious conversations are rarely good.

Even the elevator seems to take forever, and when I open the door to my penthouse—my *cousin's* penthouse—and finally lay eyes on Wren, I should feel some form of relief, but I don't.

I find her sitting on the couch in the living room, a glass of water in front of her. She's wearing one of her pretty dresses with a full skirt. But her eyes are red-rimmed, and she looks exhausted. She pushes to a stand and gives me a weak, tremulous smile. A lone tear glides down her cheek, and she smooths a hand over her stomach.

I track the movement, and all of a sudden, that heavy feeling in my gut, the one that's been weighing me down since last night, finally lifts.

"Oh fuck." I drop my messenger bag on the floor with a loud clunk, which probably isn't good for the laptop inside, but I don't give a shit. I rush over and pull Wren into me, wrapping her up in a hug that I try to keep as gentle as possible. "It's okay, babe. There's no reason to be upset. We'll figure it out." I release her and tuck stray hairs behind her ear. "I'll take the penthouse down the hall as soon as it comes available. You can move in here with me, or I can stay with you if that's better. Whatever you want, we'll do this together." I place a hand over her stomach. "The three of us." Jesus. I never thought I'd be excited about the prospect of having a kid, especially a surprise kid, but after the last twenty-four hours of speculation, this is definitely better than any of the alternatives.

Wren's brows pull together, and she makes this pouty face. It's so fucking cute. "The three of us?"

"Yeah." I press a gentle kiss to her lips. They taste salty. She must've been worried about how I'd react to the news. "You, me, and our baby."

"What?" She looks down at my hand covering her stomach, and her eyebrows shoot up along with her hands. She gives her head a vehement shake. "Oh, no. No, no, no. I'm not pregnant, Linc."

I drop my hand and step back. "You're not?" Despite only having been together a couple of months, I'm irrationally disappointed.

"Why would you think I'm pregnant?" She runs her hands self-consciously over her stomach. "Am I bloated or something?"

"What? No. Not at all. I just . . . It made the most sense? You not feeling good, taking the morning off, not being able to tell me over the phone, all the tears. I just thought . . . you being pregnant was logical."

"We use a condom every time."

I shrug. "Maybe my sperm are bionic, and they can blast through a condom."

Wren drops to the couch and barks out a humorless laugh. "The last thing I need right now is to be pregnant."

"Would it be so bad?" I'm not sure why I'm offended. Maybe because she sounds so incredulous.

And now she looks incredulous too. "Is that a serious question? Lincoln, we've been together for all of two months, and it's not even public. Do you realize the kind of field day the media would have with that? You knock your personal handler up?"

I motion between us. "Well, we wouldn't have to keep it a secret anymore, then, would we?"

"Imagine how the media would spin that. I'd be the wannabe socialite senator's daughter who seduces the CEO of Moorehead Media. They would shred me."

"Whoa. Where is this coming from?" This conversation has taken a swift right turn into Shitsville.

Wren rubs her eyes. "Because your mother told me I was reaching above my station by being with you, and that I should learn where my place is."

I stop pacing the length of the living room and turn to face her. "She said *what*?"

Wren tips her chin up, defiance making her eyes burn. "She accused me of being a ladder climber. And that was right after she threatened to expose my family if I can't get you to stop looking into your dad's penthouse."

I hold up a hand because I'm not entirely sure how to process all of that information. "My mother is blackmailing you?"

"Apparently."

I give my head a slow shake. I shouldn't be surprised to hear this. I should expect nothing less of my mother. I always assumed Armstrong's sociopathic tendencies were an anomaly, now I'm not so sure. "I'm sorry. I'm really fucking confused right now. I think you need to back this bus up and start over, so I can understand why the hell my mother is blackmailing you."

"Have a seat. We'll start at the beginning." She motions to the cushion beside her, so I take it.

By the time she finishes, I'm both horrified and devastated for her. "I'm so sorry, Wren, about all of this, but especially about what happened to your family. I can't imagine how difficult that would've been."

"I wasn't even three at the time. I don't really remember Robyn. I mean, I have pictures of me standing by her incubator in the NICU, but she only survived a few days."

"That would've been awful." All those months spent waiting for a life to come into the world, only to lose the baby days after she was born. I can't fathom how painful that would be.

"It was. My only real memories of that time are how sad my mother was. Obviously she blamed herself for it. First she unknowingly conceives me with someone who wasn't her husband, and then she loses the child she did conceive with him. Our relationship suffered when I was a teenager because that's when I found out I wasn't my father's biological child."

I take her hand in mine. "Wren, I'm so—"

"Sorry. I know. Me too. I wasn't keeping this from you on purpose. It's just not something I tend to talk about with anyone. I'm sorry I didn't come to you as soon as your mother threatened blackmail. I needed to think. I didn't know how to handle it, and I don't want to drag you into my circus."

I sit dumbly for a moment, absorbing her words. "Are you kidding me right now?"

She looks down at her hands for a moment before she lifts her chin. "I had to make a difficult choice today, Lincoln, and I needed time to sort that out before I could come to you."

"You don't have to make any choices. There's no way I'm going to sit back and let my mother blackmail you."

"There's nothing you can do to stop her, though. If she finds out I told you, she's going to go public with my family scandal. If I can't get you to stop looking into that damn penthouse, she's going to expose us. Either way, it's coming out. There's no way I'm going to stop you from finding out the truth about what was going on with your father. You deserve to know."

"There has to be a way to stop her. We have to be able to do *something*."

"I've already done something. I went to my dad this morning and explained the situation."

"Explained how?"

"I told him I couldn't keep this from you. That you deserved to know, and I was prepared to handle whatever the consequences might be. I care about you too much to let your mother try to scare me with blackmail."

"You're putting me in front of your family?" I'm pretty freaking stunned, to be honest, because the only people in my family I'd do that for are G-mom and Griffin. And maybe Bane and Lex, context depending.

"I love you. It sort of trumps everything and everyone else, doesn't it?" Her confidence wavers for a moment, and her throat bobs with a nervous swallow. She opens her mouth and ducks her head, as if maybe she wants to call those words back.

"Yes, it does." I cup her face in my hands, smooth my thumbs over her damp cheeks, and lean in closer. "I love you right back, Wren." I press my lips to hers briefly. "But I'll be honest, I really wanted to be the one to say that first, so I'm a little annoyed that you beat me to it. But considering the circumstances, I'll let you get away with it."

Her incredulous laugh turns into a surprised gasp when I kiss her again. I wish this moment were framed in something other than conflict, but I'll take it, because whatever happens next, at least we're facing it together.

I reluctantly pull back. "I'd really like this to follow up on that kiss with more of the same, but I think we have to deal with some crap. We need to find a way to stop Gwendolyn."

"My father's taking care of that," Wren says darkly.

"How?"

"You can't blackmail someone if you don't have anything to hold over them, can you?"

"And that means what, exactly?"

"He's planning to make a statement before Gwendolyn can."

I run my hand through my hair. "He's going to go public about your mother's affair?"

She nods. "If your mother exposes my family, it will be a PR nightmare. At least this way, he'll have control over how it comes out. I don't think it'll be fantastic, no matter how it shakes down, because let's face it, having a daughter who's the product of an *affair* when your whole campaign is based on 'Family First' is less than ideal, but it's better than the alternative."

I can see exactly how my mother would spin it to crumble Wren's father's platform, much like the way they tried to make it look like Armstrong had been set up at his wedding, and that Imogen had made false accusations regarding her pregnancy. "How is he going frame it?"

"I don't know. But it's going to get messy. We may want to avoid being seen in public until it blows over, the media will probably have a field day with it." Of course she's already going into PR-triage mode.

"Screw that. I mean, I get it if you want stay out the public eye, but I'm the very last person who cares how this will reflect on me or my asshole family. And frankly, I'm not above airing all of my family's dirty laundry as counter-blackmail, so let's not worry about the optics."

"I think we need a strategy going forward. A plan on how we're going to handle this, should it blow up."

"My plan is to rip my mother a new asshole for threatening to blackmail you." I've never had the warm fuzzies for my mother, but this seems like a new level of low for her. Or maybe I haven't been around her enough to experience how low she really can go.

"While I appreciate your desire to stand up for me, you can't do that. We need to buy time until my dad makes a statement."

"So, just let her get away with this? She has to be hiding something, and it has to be bigger than your mother's affair, otherwise she wouldn't be blackmailing you in the first place."

"And it has to be connected somehow to the penthouse," Wren adds.

"So if we find that link, maybe we can stalemate Gwendolyn, and your dad doesn't have to make a statement," I finish.

"It doesn't matter what we find. He'll make a statement anyway, but you deserve to know what secrets she's keeping from you."

I trace the edge of her jaw. "Can we make a deal?"

"What kind of deal?"

"Until last night, you've always been straight with me. I grew up in a house full of lies and deception. My parents' relationship seems to have been a complete farce, and I never want to be like that. Can we promise each other that we'll keep being honest, even if it's difficult?"

Wren pulls her knees up and shifts so she's facing me. "Of course. I just needed to process everything, and I'm used to doing that on my own."

"Next time, we figure it out together."

CHAPTER 23
ADD IT UP

WREN

We spend the rest of the evening going through the files Lincoln found in the Manhattan penthouse, cross-checking numbers and looking for any oddities or links that might give us a lead. I have no idea how Dani does this all day, every day. My eyes feel like they're going to be crossed forever.

By the time Lincoln and I fall into bed, it's the wee hours of the morning. Even though we should be too tired for anything but sleep, he still manages to make love to me, whispering those words against my lips. And I know that no matter what happens, I made the right choice.

At five thirty in the morning, my mind turns on. I sneak out of bed, not that I need to do much sneaking, Lincoln can sleep like the dead. I make myself a coffee and leaf through my notes from last night while the sun rises.

I keep flipping back through the statements from August more than a decade ago with those large withdrawals in similar amounts. They continue for four years, and double for the two years following it before they disappear. They could be tuition payments for a four-year undergrad and a two-year MBA. I make a note to check it out when I'm done going through the rest of these statements. Based on the timing, it seems like it could be Lincoln's tuition.

Lincoln wakes up around seven—I might've crept back into bed at six fifty-five after freshening up and acted as his personal alarm clock. Relieving stress before we create more seemed like a smart idea. We order in breakfast, make fresh coffee, and sit at the kitchen table where I've spread all the files out.

"Okay, question, how old were you when you graduated from Harvard?"

"Undergrad or MBA?"

"Either? Both?"

"I was twenty-two for my undergrad and twenty-four for my MBA, why?" He bites the end off the sausage speared on his fork.

I refrain from commenting on the semi-phallicness of it. "Hold on, I'm trying to see if something connects." I filter through the dates on the bank statements, looking for the ones I highlighted. "Okay. So that's about a decade ago, and you went there for six years, correct?"

"Yup, sounds about right."

"Do you know what tuition cost back then, and how much was covered by your scholarship?"

"Umm." Lincoln taps on his chin, right where his little dimple is. I don't know why I'm so obsessed with that particular feature. "Wren?"

"Yeah?" I drag my eyes back up to his.

"Distracted by the sexy?" He points to the dimple. "Maybe I should consider growing a beard again to keep it from being such a problem."

"I was thinking. And don't you dare or that laser appointment will happen faster than you can blink."

"You'd think after all the orgasms you've had in the past twenty-four hours, you'd be nicer to me."

"I was fully responsible for making my own orgasm happen this morning. You just laid back and enjoyed the ride." I point to the computer screen. "Now focus, please. Your scholarship, what did it cover?" I pull up a browser on my phone and look up tuition costs at Harvard for an undergrad ten years ago. I get a list of top Ivy League colleges and their rising tuition costs over the past decade.

"My undergrad scholarship covered tuition in full, and I'm pretty sure it covered fifty percent of my MBA."

I glance up. "That's impressive."

He shrugs, cheeks flushing. His embarrassment is cute. "School and me got along. I liked learning."

"Me too." I probably would've had the biggest crush on him if we'd met in high school. Smart, and a chin dimple. All the ovaries exploding everywhere.

"So, it looks like tuition would've been about thirty-five grand a year, but your scholarship would've negated that, so it doesn't line up the way I want it to."

"Doesn't line up how?"

"These withdrawals. I wondered if they were tuition-based. They start the same time you went to Harvard, but the numbers don't add up." I turn the files toward him, so he can see what I'm talking about.

While he looks them over, I check out the tuition costs associated with the top schools in the country. "Hold on a second." I grab the files, nearly knocking over Lincoln's coffee. "Here! Oh my God! Look as this!" I stab the highlighted withdrawal and the tuition for Princeton. "These match exactly."

"I didn't go to Princeton."

"Did Armstrong?"

"No. He went to Harvard too, and this is four years too early for him."

I slump back in my seat. "Dammit. It's probably a coincidence."

"Maybe." Lincoln flips through the bank statements and scrolls through the chart on yearly tuition hikes. "Except it matches the cost of tuition four years in a row. One year I can see being a coincidence, but four?"

"It seems highly unlikely." I shift closer. "So, whose education was he paying for? What about Gwendolyn?"

He shakes his head. "She was involved in charity stuff and event planning when I was a teenager. Her and my aunt used to host all the events for Moorehead and Mills Hotels." He rubs between his eyes. "Who would you put through college, especially Ivy League, apart from your kids?"

"I don't know, Linc, but I know someone who might be able to find out for us."

CHAPTER 24

DIG DEEPER

LINCOLN

My head is spinning as we make the short trip to Dani's—who I haven't met in person yet. I'm shocked when she opens the door. She doesn't appear old enough to be a PI, but then maybe the innocent look is exactly what makes her a good one. I guess I'm about to find out.

She throws open the door. "Girl, I have a drama llama dancing around my apartment!" She looks past Wren to me, and she lets out a low whistle. "Wow. I thought all those pictures were airbrushed or something, but clearly you really are this hot without any help." She makes a circle motion in the air beside her head, maybe referring to my face. "You've got some excellent genetic engineering going on. Good work, bestie." Her hand shoots out. "I'm Dani, Wren's best friend for forever. If you happen to have any single family members apart from your asswipe of a brother, I am totally available. I'm not looking for anything serious either. Straight hookup is fine with me."

"Dani, dial it back a little," Wren says, but there's laughter in her voice.

"Right. Yeah. Sorry. It's nice to meet you outside of social media posts. Come on in." She leads the way into her small studio apartment. There's a desk in the corner, foot-high stacks of paper surrounding a laptop, and three huge monitors. "Excuse the mess. I work from home, obviously."

She offers us something to drink, and I accept a glass of water. My mouth is dry, and my palms are sweaty.

Wren puts a hand on my knee. "It'll be okay."

I nod, but my stomach is doing that churning thing again.

Dani drops down on the chair across from us. "Soooo . . ." She motions to the papers strewn across the coffee table. "After Wren told me about the blackmail threat, I looked into Fredrick's properties, since that's the impetus, right?"

"Right." I squeeze Wren's hand.

"Now, Fredrick had what appears to be quite a few investment properties, which isn't uncommon for people with lots of money. Real estate is usually a good place to store your dollar bills. But, then I started researching the properties, and I noticed something interesting." She taps a picture of the high-rise where my parents' penthouse is. "His condo in the city is a Mills Property, which makes sense since you're related to them, correct?"

"Yeah, by marriage. My aunt is married to Harrison Mills."

"Right. So, of course, you'd buy from family, which I totally get. And over the years, most of your father's condos have been associated with Mills real estate. But there are four properties over the past three decades that aren't related to Mills buildings, which again, wouldn't be a red flag, since some of them are houses and the Mills only do condos and hotels." Dani's knee bounces, and she gets this odd gleam in her eye. "But here's where it gets interesting. Fredrick used a different account to purchase those four properties. And based on the statements I've been looking at, he strategically funneled money into that account through Moorehead Media. He was actually really sneaky about it. It's pretty genius."

I rub my temples, already feeling lost. I get buying the Manhattan condo on the sly, since that's where he met with his mistress, but what would be the purpose of the other properties? Unless he had multiple mistresses or fetishes that required their own place. "Can you explain that further?"

"Yup. For sure. Let me start at the beginning." Dani slaps her thighs and then rubs her hands together. "A little over three decades ago, your father bought a five-bedroom house in Jersey."

"As an investment property?" I ask.

"That's what I thought, until I checked into the deed. At first he was the sole owner, but a couple of years ago Jacqueline Mercier was added to it."

"I don't recognize that name."

Dani nods. "I wouldn't expect you to, but we'll come back to that. Seven years after he bought the house in Jersey, he purchased the condo you discovered in Lower Manhattan. And about a decade ago, he purchased an apartment in Princeton, very close to the university."

"Was this one an investment property?"

"At first I thought maybe he'd bought it for you or brother, but neither of you attended Princeton. Also, he sold it four years later, so roughly how long it would take to earn an undergrad. Then he bought another condo, this time in the city."

"So, there are four properties my dad kept a secret?"

"It looks that way, unless maybe your mother knew and never said anything."

"Well, she knew about the Manhattan penthouse, but I don't know about the other properties," I say.

Dani's knee continues to bounce. It's making me anxious. "I figured it might be a good idea to look into this Jacqueline Mercier woman, because she seems to hold the Jersey connection. And this is what I found." Dani opens a folder and spreads a series of images out over the table.

"Holy shit." It isn't the woman in her late fifties who catches my attention. It's the woman beside her who does. Because as much as she resembles her mother, she also bears a lot of similarities to me.

The woman in the photo has the same mouth, chin dimple, and a more feminine version of my nose, but the features are there. She's a total hybrid between my father and this woman. "He had another family? Jesus. Do you think my mother knew about this? This has to be what she's trying to hide." I look to Wren, as if she'll have the answers. "This is unreal, right? Like this whole thing is just . . . nuts." I pick up the picture of the Jacqueline woman and the younger woman who looks to be close to my age. "This isn't, like, some photoshopped trick?"

"No. I pulled it from her social media."

I let it digest for a few seconds before I turn back to Wren. "I have a sister? And my father kept her a secret from us for her entire life? Why would he do that?"

She puts a hand on my thigh. I wish I could feel the contact, but my whole body seems to be numb. "I don't know, Lincoln, but there must've been a reason."

"I have an address and a phone number for Jacqueline. Her daughter's name is Hope," Dani offers.

"Hope." I press my palms against my eyes, trying to absorb this new reality. "I thought the sex room was bad. This is a whole different level of messed up." I look at the pictures again, trying to unsee the similarities between Hope and me, but I can't. We are very much related.

"I'm going to give you two some privacy." Dani pushes up off the couch and rounds the coffee table. "Wren, let me know if you need anything else."

"Thanks, Dani." Wren leans in and presses a kiss to my shoulder. "What to do want to do, Linc?"

"I want some answers. I want to see with my own eyes that this is real." He motions to the spread of pictures.

"Do you want to take a trip to Jersey to see if we can get some of those answers?"

"Yeah. Okay. That sounds good." I don't actually know if it sounds like a good idea at all, but I need to do something other than sift through this pile of information with no history to tie it to. At least not one that I can understand.

"Why don't we go back to your place and get Griffin's SUV?" Wren says softly.

I push up off the couch, my body feeling like it's disconnected from my brain. I don't track anything during the cab ride back to the penthouse. Wren grabs the keys for the SUV, and then I'm in the passenger seat, staring out the window as we head toward Jersey.

She gives my hand a squeeze when we're stopped at a light. "We're going to deal with this together, Linc. You're not alone."

I turn to face her, those gorgeous gray eyes ringed

in navy, so serious and stoic, meet mine. "Why does no one in my family seem to work on any normal plane of existence where they're culpable for their actions? I don't get it. How could my dad keep this whole other life a secret? Why lead it? Why would someone willingly be the other woman? I get that Gwendolyn isn't a good person, but why not leave, then? Why would she be okay with this?"

"I don't know, Linc, but hopefully we'll get some answers to those questions."

She adjusts my collar before the light turns green. I've come to realize it's more of an excuse to touch me than anything else. "We can just pass by the house. If there's a car in the driveway and you feel up to it, you can see if she's home. No matter what happens, I'm right here with you."

It takes almost an hour and a half to get to Jersey, thanks to all the stupid weekend traffic. The house isn't anything grand, not like my parents' penthouse in the city or the house in the Hamptons. However modest, it's a beautiful home, and something I can appreciate. I wonder if this is the life my father saw for himself, but never had. Or maybe he did have it, and that's why he was never part of mine.

There's a Lexus sedan in the driveway; it looks to be a fairly new model, maybe only a year or two old. The front garden is neatly tended. Everything looks well maintained and pristine.

I grip the door handle, my stomach somersaulting, mind racing. "What do I do? Knock and see if she'll answer? I don't know what protocol is here? Do I call first?"

Wren runs her nails softly down the back of my neck, an action meant to calm me. "I don't think there is a protocol, so whatever you think is going to be best for you is what you should do. But I do think you might want to keep in mind that based on the little we know, there was obviously a relationship here, and that your father's death could be a significant loss. Let's not go in guns blazing, okay?"

"Okay. Yeah. Don't be a jerk, then?"

Wren nods. "Exactly."

I take a deep breath. "You'll come with me?"

"Of course." Wren cuts the engine.

It's warm today, and my palms are damp as I step out of the SUV. I wipe them on my thighs and reach for Wren's hand as we cross the quiet street and walk up the driveway. Jacqueline might not be home. She could have two cars. She could be out shopping, or with her daughter. *My sister.*

I take a few deep breaths before I press the doorbell. A dog barks and the patter of nails across tile grows louder.

"Toby, sit!" The woman's voice gets louder with the click of the lock. The door opens a second later, and the woman from the pictures appears.

She sees Wren first, but as her gaze shifts to me, her smile drops and her face drains of color. "Oh my God." She exhales shakily and reaches out.

I take a quick step back, and she presses her fingers to her lips. "You're so much like him. It's almost like looking at a ghost. I'm so sorry, Lincoln."

I slip my hands into my pockets because I don't know what else to do with them. "You know who I am."

She smiles sadly. "Of course I know who you are. I wasn't sure if Fredrick had a chance to tell you before he passed. We'd talked about it—"

"Tell me what?" I snap.

Her face falls again. "About him and me. About Hope."

"He didn't tell me. I found the penthouse, and it led me here."

"Oh." Her fingers go to her lips again. "This isn't how he wanted you to find out."

"Find out what exactly? That he had two totally separate families? How exactly does one bring that up with their kid? 'Hey, just wanted you to know that I've been cheating on your mother for our entire marriage, and by the way, you have a sister I never told you about, but it's cool, right?'"

Wren squeezes my hand, likely because my voice is rising and we're standing on my father's mistress's front porch, drawing attention.

"I understand you're upset, Lincoln, and you have every right to be. If you'd like to come in, I'll explain my side of the story as best I can." She steps back, inviting us in despite my outburst, which tells me a lot about her relationship with my dad, I suppose.

I came here for answers, and she's apparently willing to provide them, so I accept the invitation to come inside.

Pictures line the fireplace mantle. Most of them are of Jacqueline and Hope, but more than one include my father. I pick one up, noting that they look very much like a real family, and my father's smile seems genuine.

"I'm sure this is quite a shock for you. I think it would be best if I started from the beginning." Jacqueline motions to the couch.

"That would be good." There's nothing normal or comfortable about this situation for either of us.

Jacqueline clasps her hands in her lap and gives me a small smile. It's clear my presence unnerves her, possibly because she's right about me looking like my father. "I met Fredrick in the final year of my undergrad while he was finishing his MBA. We had similar study habits and were often in the library at the same time. When we first started talking, it was innocent enough, and while I found him attractive, he was dating Gwendolyn, so I kept my distance."

"Something obviously changed." I glance at the pictures of Hope lining the fireplace mantle.

"It did." She takes a sip of her water. "I had no intention of breaking them up. I never would've pursued your father if he was in a happy, committed relationship. But one evening I ran into Fredrick, and he confided that his parents had set him up with Gwendolyn. They both came from influential families who were intent on pushing them together, but it wasn't what he wanted. It was difficult, though. There were expectations for both of them."

I think about the way my parents always were with each other: formal, cold, businesslike. It never felt or looked like love. "But there was something between you?"

"Initially, we were just friends. I admit I was enamored, but I tried to keep it platonic. At least until Fredrick broke up with Gwendolyn. He didn't want to hurt her, and I didn't come from the same kind of affluence, which was an issue in itself." She clasps her hands in her lap and smiles sadly. "We kept it quiet and tried to be discreet, but eventually she found out and confronted me. It was . . . unpleasant. By then, I was in love with your father, and I wasn't so willing to walk away."

"And you didn't, obviously, even after he married my mother." I can't keep the disapproval from my voice.

"It wasn't so simple as walking away. A few months

after Fredrick and I started seeing each other, Gwendolyn announced that she was pregnant with Fredrick's baby. She had tests and proof, or at least that's what it looked like. I was devastated, Fredrick was . . . beside himself, but he was nothing if not an honorable man who intended to do the honorable thing. So I did what I thought was right; I stepped back and he married Gwendolyn. It was all very rushed. They eloped, and later had an official wedding. I was heartbroken, but I didn't want to be a home-wrecker."

I bite back the scathing words I want to say, because based on what I'm seeing here, she was one anyway.

She looks up at me, expression full of sadness and remorse. "We found out later that Gwendolyn had faked the pregnancy as a way to force Fredrick to marry her." She clears her throat and dabs at her eyes.

"How do you know she faked it?" I ask.

"Because you were born just shy of ten months after they eloped."

I can't seem to feel anything but shock. As a child, my mother called me her honeymoon baby with so much pride. Now I understood why. She'd tricked my father into marrying her. No wonder their relationship resembled a two-dimensional cutout. I don't know how my father could stand to look at her every day for all those years. And suddenly so much makes sense, and instead of hating this woman, I feel bad for her, and maybe I understand why my father was so absent from my life. It doesn't make it better, but at least it makes sense.

"To make a bad situation worse, two months after they eloped, I discovered I was about three months pregnant. College was over. I didn't want to make Fredrick's life more difficult, so I kept my pregnancy from him. I severed ties and moved out of the city."

"But you obviously couldn't stay away from each other based on this." I motion to the pictures, evidence that he was very much a part of her life.

"I tried, Lincoln, sincerely I did. I raised Hope on my own. I wanted to be able move on, truly, but three years after Hope was born, I ran into your father. I took her to Central Park. Fredrick and I used to go there when we were in college. I missed him. I'd been so in love with him; it was painful to see him in Hope every day and not have him in my life. I just wanted to be close to him. I never expected I'd actually see him." She wipes away tears and takes a moment to compose herself.

"I was pushing Hope on a swing when he came strolling through the park that day. You were with him. You and Hope are only months apart, and you both looked so much like Fredrick, even then. My God, I remember it as if it were yesterday. It felt like the shattered pieces of my heart mended as soon as I saw him." She reaches for a tissue, more tears falling with her memories. "He quickly came to the conclusion Hope was his. He'd wanted to leave Gwendolyn, but then she announced she was pregnant again, and I knew that he couldn't do that to her or you. Their relationship was never built on love. It was a business transaction and a way for Gwendolyn to get what she needed out of life." She pauses. "I'm sorry. I shouldn't speak this way about your mother."

I wave off the comment. "She's blackmailing Wren right now to keep me from finding all of this out. I'm aware my mother is a manipulative bitch, so the apology is unnecessary."

Jacqueline seems taken aback by my crassness, but

she nods once and continues. It's hard to argue with the truth. "Fredrick tried so hard to make it work with Gwendolyn, and I tried to stay away from him, but he wanted a relationship with Hope. He was trapped in a loveless marriage. He knew Gwendolyn would make the custody battle a nightmare and he feared what would happen if he left Gwendolyn to raise you and your brother on her own. He didn't want to tear his family apart, and he didn't want me and Hope dragged into it. So he stayed, and eventually Gwendolyn realized there was no way to keep me out of his life. He couldn't walk away. He supported Hope and me financially, and emotionally, as best he could."

"He really had two separate families." Every time a question is answered, more new ones rise to take their place.

"And he tried his very best to support them both. By that point, his and Gwendolyn's relationship was nothing but a shell. There wasn't any love to hold them together, so she made a bargain—he would stay married to her, and as long as Hope and I remained a secret, we could continue to see each other and she wouldn't bleed him dry in a divorce."

It sounds exactly like something my mother would do. "And you were okay with that? Being a secret?"

"Of course not, but there were no other options. I loved Fredrick, love him still, even though he's gone. I didn't want to tear him away from you and your brother. I didn't want to ruin your family, but we were . . . soul mates. In a different life, maybe we would've ended up together the way we should have, but it wasn't that simple or easy."

"You were the other woman." It sounds harsh, but it's the truth.

"As a result of circumstances beyond my control, yes. I'm so sorry, Lincoln. I'm sure this is painful to hear, but your father was a good man with a good heart. He was trying to do the right thing for everyone, although we all suffered for it, you the most, I think."

I don't know if that's true. I wonder how much Hope suffered, having a father she couldn't name. But the connections finally come together in my head, memories making more sense than they did before. My mother's outbursts, my father's stoicism, the way she'd break down on me and tell me if it weren't for me, she'd have nothing. G-mom always swooping in when she went into one of her emotional tailspins. And then I'd been put in boarding school. From my perspective, I'd had a shitty father who was a cheater. And in a lot of ways I understood his absence and maybe even his infidelity, because there was nothing loving about my self-absorbed mother. And now I know where it all came from, but it sure doesn't make it any less painful. We were the second-string family he was forced into keeping.

While this certainly explains a lot, it doesn't explain everything. "That room in the penthouse . . ." I let it hang there, because what the hell else can I say?

Jacqueline makes a face, and her cheeks flush. She shifts uncomfortably. "I'd hoped to have cleared that out before anyone discovered it. I'm not sure there's an easy explanation. He ran a massive company and was always in charge. Gwendolyn essentially blackmailed him into staying married. It all took its toll on him, I think. He was a complex man who tried to do the right thing, despite the pain it caused him and everyone he loved."

I hold up my hand. "I don't need more of an explanation that that."

"That's good because I wasn't planning to elaborate

further. I couldn't bring myself to go to the penthouse for a long time after Fredrick passed."

"But someone cleaned out the closet."

"Your mother went."

"Why would she do that?"

More tears stream down Jacqueline's cheeks. "He was with me at the penthouse the night he suffered the heart attack. It was a sensitive situation, and Gwendolyn had to be called, which was difficult for everyone. He passed on the way to the hospital. If I had to guess, she came to the penthouse to get rid of the evidence of my existence."

I blow out a breath. "This is a lot to take in."

"I'm sure it is. He never wanted to hurt you, or anyone. And if you have more questions, I'll do my best to answer them. Talking about him helps ease the loss, at least for me."

"What about Hope?"

Jacqueline looks down at her hands. I notice a ring on her right one, opposite where a wedding band would go. A simple gold band and diamond decorate her finger. "It's been difficult for her, obviously, losing her father, being unable to attend the funeral. The lack of closure is challenging."

I can relate to that feeling. After hearing all of this, I'm lacking closure too, because I didn't even know my father. I think about those times over the years after I graduated when he gently requested that I consider coming back to New York to work at Moorehead. More than that, I remember those tense times when it seemed like he had something he wanted to say, but never did. This secret was the divide between my father and me. "Do you think . . . I'd be able to meet her one day? Do you think she'd want to meet me?"

Jacqueline seems surprised. "Is that something you'd want?"

"She's my sister. I'd like to know her if she'd like to know me."

Her smile is both sad and hopeful. "I can speak with her."

CHAPTER 25

BLOW IT ALL UP

LINCOLN

The following morning, Wren decides the best thing for her to do is go to work like everything is normal. As much as I don't want to send her right into the wolf's den, she's right. If she doesn't show up, it's going to raise suspicions.

So Wren heads to Moorehead, and I make a stop at my g-mom's house before I do the same. My plan was to keep her out of this as long as I possibly could, but considering my mother is blackmailing my girlfriend and pretty much blackmailed my father into staying married to her—and making his life and everyone else's miserable as a result—it's time she knows the truth. Or a version of it. Also, I don't want her to find out she has a granddaughter she never knew about from anyone other than me.

She answers the door in a pair of yoga pants and a shirt I bought for her two Christmases ago that says WORLD'S BEST G-MOM. She pulls me into a hug. "Lincoln! This is a surprise! Did I forget a meeting?"

"You didn't forget, G-mom. I should've called to tell you I was coming by."

"Well, it's a lovely surprise. Come in. I was just making my morning tea. You should join me for a cup." Her smile falters as she looks me over, suddenly on alert. "Is everything okay? You look tired. Did something happen with your brother while I was away? I knew I should've postponed the trip."

"Nothing happened with Armstrong. Well, nothing that Wren and I couldn't handle, anyway." I pull out a chair and motion for her to take it. "I have something to tell you, G-mom, and I think you might want to sit down for it."

She slips into the chair and folds her hands on the table, waiting for me to take the seat next to hers. "Is Wren pregnant?"

"What? Why would you . . . we're not—"

She gives me her don't-bullshit-me face. "Oh, come off it, Lincoln. I see the way you two look at each other." She smiles wistfully. "It's exactly the way Norman used to look at me, God rest his soul." She makes the sign of the cross. My grandfather died of a sudden heart attack when I was a baby. G-mom never remarried, and I guess I can understand why, if she loved him the way I love Wren. I don't know that any other love would be enough.

"Wren isn't pregnant."

She looks momentarily disappointed before she purses her lips. "Has Armstrong gotten someone else pregnant?"

"Not that I'm aware." I shift my chair so I'm facing her.

"What's going on, Lincoln? You're all"—she motions to me—"helpful and fidgety."

"I'm always helpful."

She gives me a look. "If you say so. Now, tell me what's going on."

"Did you know Dad had a mistress?"

Her entire demeanor changes, and she looks down at her hands.

"G-mom? Did you know?"

"Lincoln." She reaches for my hand, but I yank it away.

I push my chair back and stand. Based on her guilty expression and her complete lack of surprise, the answer is yes, she did know. "Did you know I have a sister too? Did you know Dad had a whole separate fucking family?"

G-mom's expression shifts from guilt to confusion. "I—what?"

I'm relieved she doesn't know, otherwise it would mean the one person in my family I trusted had let me down too. "I have a sister named Hope. According to Jacqueline, she was pregnant with her before Dad married Gwendolyn, but she didn't find out until after they eloped." I give her the abridged version of the story Jacqueline told me.

"Oh, Fredrick." G-mom's eyes fall closed, and she shakes her head sadly. "This explains so much."

"About what?"

"Why your father refused to leave Gwendolyn. Why he continued his affair with Jacqueline even after Gwendolyn found out. I knew he worried about what would happen to you and Armstrong if he tried to leave your mother, but this . . . now it all makes sense."

She sighs and rubs her temples. "I'd suspected for a long time that your father had someone else, and it wasn't a surprise, since Gwendolyn built their relationship on lies and deceit right from the start. After you were born things seemed . . . better. But when she fell pregnant again with Armstrong, their relationship seemed to just implode. Things between them continued to get worse, and I had to intervene. The house was toxic, and I couldn't stand to see you being dragged through their misery. It was the reason I pushed to have you sent to boarding school when you were ten."

She squeezes my hand. "I'd wanted to take Armstrong out of that environment as well, but your mother wouldn't allow it. I used the fact that you would run Moorehead as an excuse, and your father supported it, but he wouldn't allow Armstrong to go as well. I thought when you were adults, he would finally divorce Gwendolyn, but he continued to stay. When I tried to reason with him, he told me he stood to lose too much if he did, and now I finally understand what he meant." Regret and sadness pull her mouth down. "Your father was trying to make the best out of an impossible situation. I wish he'd have come to me. I would've helped him figure it out if I'd known the whole truth. All these missed years . . ."

"Gwendolyn tried to blackmail Wren to keep this from me." I explain my mother's threats to expose Wren's family, and the events of the past twenty-four hours. By the time I'm done, G-mom looks like she's ready to go to war.

"Your mother needs to be knocked off her self-imposed pedestal," G-mom says through clenched teeth.

"That's why I came here this morning, to warn you that I'm going to take her down."

"I'm coming with you. That woman has ruined

enough lives." She pushes away from the table. "She's not putting Wren and her family in jeopardy because of a secret she has no right to keep."

While G-mom changes, I message Wren, but I don't get a response, which is worrying.

The trip to Moorehead is tense. The anger builds the closer we get. "I'd like to be the one to confront her," I tell G-mom on the way up to the twenty-seventh floor.

"Of course." She appears calm, but I don't think I've ever seen her this furious. Not even when Armstrong set off firecrackers in her garden when we were kids and destroyed her award-winning rosebush.

"And I'd like to check on Wren before we go in there."

"Understandable. Is she doing okay?"

"She's got bigger balls than most of the men on staff. She can hold her own, but I'd prefer she doesn't have to under the circumstances."

"She really is an amazing woman, isn't she?" A brief smile appears.

"She is," I agree.

"You two will make a formidable team."

"I think so too."

The elevator dings, and we pass Lulu, who shoots up out of her chair. "Mr. Moorehead, Ms. Moorehead, good morning. Mrs. Moorehead has been asking after you this morning. She seems . . . agitated, and I don't believe it has anything to do with Armstrong. She asked that you report directly to her as soon as you arrive."

"Thank, Lulu." I keep walking past her desk, but instead of heading toward my mother's office, I make a left and head for Wren's.

"But, Mr. Moorehead—"

"I got it handled, Lulu. Don't worry."

"That woman deserves a raise for dealing with your mother and your brother."

"Agreed. I'll see what I can do about that." I knock on Wren's office door and peek inside, but her chair is empty. Once again, I get that terrible, sinking feeling as I stalk down the hall to my mother's office.

Armstrong pops out as I'm about to pass, blocking my way. "Where have you been this morning? Do you know how many people have asked for you? If you're going to take the morning off, you should at least tell someone."

"He was with me."

Armstrong grimaces when G-mom comes into view. "Oh, Grandmother. I didn't see you there." He turns his attention back to me. "If you'd bothered to call your secretary, we would've known you were going to be late."

"It was an unexpected emergency," G-mom snaps and grabs my elbow. "Come on."

"Where are you going? You know Mom wants to meet with you, don't you? She's not happy with you and whatever's going on with our handler. Also, it's not really fair that you get all the perks and I don't get any. She was mine first, and then you stepped in and took her away from me."

I spin around and grab him by the tie. "Wren was never yours, not even for half a second. She tolerated you because she had to. You're an annoying job to her."

He sneers. "What're you, other than the dick she's riding on her way up the social ladder?"

I raise my fist, ready to punch him, but G-mom grabs my arm. "Keep your head, Lincoln. Armstrong, shut your damn mouth. No one wants to hear you spew your narcissistic garbage."

I release my brother's tie with a shove. He stumbles into the wall. Of course, being the asshole he is, he can't let it go. He trails after us. "Why does Mom want to meet with you? What'd you do now?"

I ignore him, because answering means he'll ask more stupid questions, and I can't deal with whatever his response will be. The door to my mother's office is closed, so I knock once and barge on in.

What I find makes me see red. Gwendolyn's fingers are wrapped around Wren's wrist, and she's trying to force a pen into her closed fist. It would almost be comical, since Gwendolyn is clearly at a disadvantage strength-wise.

The door slams against the wall, startling them both. "What the hell is going on?"

Gwendolyn releases Wren and takes a step back. "We're amending Wren's contract. Where have you been this morning?"

Wren drops the pen and pushes to a stand. "If by amend, you mean blackmail with another one of your NDAs, then I guess that's what we're doing."

My mother jerks as if she's been slapped. "I'm trying to protect my family from money-grubbing bottom-feeders like yourself."

Armstrong's eyes light up with malicious glee, and he claps his hands together. "You knocked Wren up, didn't you?"

Wren throws her hands in the air. "Why is that the first conclusion everyone jumps to?" She turns to Armstrong. "I'm not pregnant."

"Oh." Armstrong stuffs a hand in his pocket and motions between our mother and Wren. "So, what'd you do now, Linc?"

"This doesn't concern you," I retort.

"Well, actually," G-mom cuts in.

I give her a look. "Seriously?"

"Might as well have everyone involved present. Take a seat, Gwendolyn. You too, Armstrong. We all need to have a talk."

Wren takes an uncertain step toward the door, but I catch her hand. "You should stay. I need you to stay."

"She's not part of this family; she needs to leave." My mother points at Wren.

"Wren's involved in this discussion, so she stays," I reply coldly.

Wren squeezes my hand and moves in closer so her shoulder touches my arm, which gives me enough calm not to lose it on my brother or Gwendolyn. Yet.

"Oh for Chrissake! We need to have a private conversation, Lincoln. I'm trying to protect you, and you're making decisions with the head in your pants instead of the one on your shoulders. Isn't there a man in this family who uses his brain when it comes to women? She's only with you because she wants your status and what's in your bank account. She'll drain you dry and make you miserable, like all bottoms-feeders do."

"Sounds like you're talking about yourself, not Wren."

Her face turns a bright shade of red. "Don't you dare to talk to me like that! I'm your mother!"

"You're giving yourself a hell of a lot of credit there, Gwendolyn," I scoff. "The only thing you did was give birth to me. Aunt Mimi and G-mom are the ones who raised me."

"Penelope was the one who suggested you go to boarding school. That was not my decision. She took you away from me, and she wouldn't have stopped there either, if she'd been given more opportunity to take the things that belonged to me." Gwendolyn shoots G-mom a hateful glare.

"Things? That's how you refer to your children, Gwen? I was saving Lincoln from a lifetime of misery," G-mom spits angrily. "Too bad I couldn't save Fredrick from the same fate."

"Fredrick was the one with the wandering eyes! I stood by him the entire time."

I snort my incredulity, uncertain if she believes the lies she spews, or if she's been putting on an act for so long that she's perfected the role of martyr. "I'm so sick of the bullshit, Gwendolyn. The lies end now."

"I-I don't know what you're talking about," she sputters.

I slap the file folder on the desk. "Open that."

"What is it?" My mother takes a reflexive step back, as if she's afraid either me or the file is going to bite her.

"Open it and find out."

"This is some kind of trick. I don't know what you think you're doing, Lincoln, but you'll regret it. This woman . . ." She points to Wren. "She has nothing but bad intentions when it comes to you. I tried to tell you—"

"This has nothing to do with Wren, apart from the fact that you tried to blackmail her. Open the goddamn folder!" I yell.

She seems shocked by my outburst, although she shouldn't be. If anything, my family is good at pushing every single one of my damn buttons.

She reaches out tentatively and opens the folder, revealing a picture of Hope. Her eyes go wide, wider than they were before, and her hand flutters around in the air. "Wh-where did you get this?"

"From Jacqueline. I met her this weekend." I wait for her reaction, and I'm not disappointed.

Her spine straightens and an approximation of a sneer curls her lip. "Whatever she said, it was a lie. She tried to ruin our family!"

Armstrong cranes to see what's on the table and frowns, then points to Hope. "Who's that? Is she one of Dad's girlfriends?"

"Shut up, Armstrong, or I will knock every single one of your overly bleached teeth out of your goddamn head."

"It was just a question." He takes a step back.

I turn back to my mother and pin her with a glare. "If anyone ruined anything, it was you. I find it more interesting that you thought you could keep this from us forever by blackmailing my girlfriend. You threatened to expose Wren's family to the media for no other reason than to protect yourself, as per fucking usual."

"I was protecting my family and the legacy we've built! Do you realize how difficult it's been to keep all of this quiet over the years? All the time and energy I spent building connections and standing by your father's side. We built this empire. As if I would let some middle-class ladder climber take it all away from me! That woman was reaching above her station, just like this one." She flicks a hand in Wren's direction.

I slam my palms on the desk. "Don't you dare insult Wren. You kept our father tethered to you and made our lives miserable, so you could have a cushy life and endless amounts of money at your disposal."

"That stupid bitch was going to take your father away from us, and I stopped that from happening." She points at her own chest.

"He was in love with her."

"He was reckless and infatuated. He wanted what he couldn't have."

I pin her with a look of disgust. "He wanted a life with someone he loved, and he had it, even with you standing in the way."

"He had an affair because that's what men do."

"No." I shake my head, seeing exactly who my mother is, and how much Armstrong is like her. "He took care of them. If it were just an affair, why would he put Hope through college?"

"Because that home-wrecker threatened to go public with Hope." Her hands shake as she slams the folder closed, cutting off the view of Hope.

"Who the hell is Hope?" Armstrong asks.

"Your sister," G-mom grinds out.

"Wait. What? Since when do we have a sister?" Armstrong seems completely confused. "Is this some kind of ploy to divide up the Moorehead shares? If anyone has to give anything up, it should be Lincoln."

I ignore my brother, as does everyone else. The alternative is throwing him through a window, and I would like to avoid a murder charge today. I keep my focus on my nervous, edgy mother. "I think it was you doing the threatening, Gwendolyn. Dad bought Jacqueline a house, and he bought Hope a house too. That penthouse they had together? It looked like it was used often. For as long as you've been married to him, he was in love with her, and you're so caught up in your bank account you kept him tied to you."

"I did it for you and Armstrong." Gwendolyn's voice shakes along with her hands.

"Bullshit! Everything you did was for you! You shackled yourself to misery to spite him and took us all down with you. Congratulations on ruining every single relationship you had because you were too selfish and materialistic to let Dad go. I suggest you leave Wren and her family off your path of destruction. I think you've done enough damage to the people who are related to you by blood. You don't need to add to the pain you've caused everyone."

My mother blinks several times, maybe absorbing what I've said, or maybe she's thinking about all the money she stands to lose now that there's another potential hand in the cookie jar. "What're you going to do? You can't go public with this. Think of the scandal. How will it impact Moorehead Media? You'll drag your father's name through the dirt, and for what? To get back at me for trying to do what was best for my family?"

"I don't get what the big deal is. So Dad had an affair? Like that's anything new. At least she dealt with it instead of pulling an Amalie, running off like a bratty, little girl and screwing the first available asshole who showed interest in her," Armstrong says.

It's honestly a miracle that my brother has survived this long without having his entire face rearranged multiple times. I turn to Wren. "What does it take to invoke your self-defense clause?"

"And Mom's not wrong." He motions to Wren. "Obviously this one sees an opportunity. Wrap your rod, brother, or next thing you know, she'll be telling you she's having your baby and you need to marry her."

"I'm gonna punch him," I mutter to Wren, who nods in agreement.

So I do. But I don't aim for the stomach. I aim lower. He falls to his knees, sucking in high-pitched breaths while he cups his balls.

"Not sure why you didn't expect that, you dumb twit."

"Lincoln!" Gwendolyn shrieks.

"Oh, shut it, Gwendolyn. He deserved it. Can't keep

his mouth shut or his pants zipped for five seconds. Also, what he's accusing Wren of is exactly what you did to my son. You stole his future, forced him to ostracize his own blood, and you're the reason Armstrong has no moral compass." G-mom gestures to Armstrong, still folded in half, cupping his balls. "Enjoy the perks you have right now, Gwennie, because you won't have them much longer."

"You can't take what Fredrick left me!"

G-mom crosses her arms. "The only thing he left you in the will was the house and ten percent of the shares in Moorehead. Everything else is to be equally divided between his children, or didn't you listen when Christophe was going over the will?"

"I devoted my life to Fredrick!" Gwendolyn shrieks.

"You devoted your life to spending his money, and while you might have sat on the board of every charity, I'm well aware that your contributions have been minimal. I wonder what else I might find out if I dig deeper, Gwendolyn."

"I was pregnant first."

"You lied about that and tricked Fredrick into marrying you. If you hadn't gotten pregnant on the honeymoon, he would've left you and you know it."

"He wasn't supposed to end up with her! I saved this company by being the best partner for him. I did everything I needed to maintain order and present a strong front."

"But you didn't love him." The sadness in G-mom's voice is etched into her face.

Gwendolyn throws her hands in the air, exasperated. "Love is a worthless emotion. More than lust, even. I did what I had to do to make a better life for myself and my family. I gave us power and status, and what did that other woman do? Stole his attention once in a while when he needed a fix, and left a stain on Fredrick's name. She might have had his heart, but I had everything that matters."

I stare slack-jawed at the woman who birthed me, and wonder how I managed to make it out of that house without turning into my brother. It's no wonder he's the way he is. "His bank account?" Sarcasm and venom lace the words.

She raises her chin in defiance. "His loyalty."

"You threatened to bleed him dry if he left and told him he'd never see his children again. There was no loyalty there. Maybe he pitied you, or maybe he feared that leaving us with you would destroy us. He took the only option you gave him. You divided his entire life, and if you attempt to blackmail Wren, or me, or anyone else I know, I will expose you for the manipulative con artist you are."

CHAPTER 26

ANOTHER FRESH START

LINCOLN

I'd like to say the weeks following the confrontation with Gwendolyn were easy, but that would be a lie, and I've dealt with enough of those for a lifetime. I bought out her company shares—turns out she wanted the money more than the headache of having to deal with me on a regular basis.

My brother imploded, as he often does, and ended up going on a bender that landed him in prison, thanks to an indecent exposure charge, reckless driving, and a DUI. Since the contract with my father had long expired and the one Wren signed for Gwendolyn was considered void once she was bought out, there was no obligation for Wren to help manage what was or wasn't leaked all over social media. When Armstrong screws up, he doesn't half-ass it. No amount of bandaging could keep him under the media radar.

While my mother was busy trying to manage the mess from the sidelines, I gave a public statement indicating my brother was struggling with the demands of Moorehead and the loss of our father, and he would be taking some time off while he sought help. In doing that, I recognized that I was fully prepared to embrace the role of CEO of Moorehead. And in a lot of ways I already had, I just needed to acknowledge it outside of my head. Leaving New York wasn't an option anymore, not with a company that needed a real leader, and of course, New York had Wren.

Senator Sterling obliterated any chance at being blackmailed when he blew the lid off his own "scandal." It was a well-orchestrated media leak in which paperwork regarding paternal rights and Wren's birth father agreeing to sign his over appeared on one of the biggest gossip sites.

He followed up the media firestorm with a press conference in which he openly spoke about his love for his daughter and his wife, and how they'd dealt with the circumstances at the time. It wasn't easy for any of them, but being the charismatic, devoted family man he is, the senator was able to spin the entire thing so he shouldered the blame and made Wren their saving grace. He followed it up by setting up a charity event to revitalize an adoption center in Haiti that had been destroyed in a recent hurricane. His poll numbers have skyrocketed since it all came out.

Two weeks after the media circus, I decide Wren and I need a break from everything, so I book us a weekend at a cabin three hours upstate. I'm in the middle of going through her bag to make sure she has all the things I like—it's totally fair, considering she pretty much dresses me every day like I'm an oversize toddler—when my phone rings.

"It better not be work-related." I snatch the device up from the bed, and my heart stutters as the name *Hope* appears on my screen. Jacqueline gave me her number and I reached out recently, but until now, I haven't heard from her.

Wren comes up behind me and wraps her arms around my waist, one hand slipping low as her lips move against the back of my neck. "Do you need me to answer and say you're indisposed?" Normally I'd be all over whatever she's offering, but right now, I have to take a rain check.

"I need to get this," I choke out.

"Is everything okay?" Wren ducks under my arm and looks at the screen. "Oh my God." She takes me by the shoulders, turns me around, and forces me to sit down. "I'm right here if you need me. Go ahead and answer."

I swallow, take a deep breath, and bring the phone to my ear. "Hello?"

"Hello, hi, um, is this Lincoln?"

"It is." God, my mouth is dry. "This is Hope?"

"Yes. Yeah. Sorry. I, uh . . . got your message last week. I'm sorry it took me so long to get back to you, I just . . . this isn't . . . I don't know how to do this."

"Me either, so I think we're on even ground with feeling awkward."

She laughs and I laugh too, but we both sound pitchy and weird.

"Um, I know this is odd for both of us, but I was wondering if maybe you wanted to talk about . . . things. You mentioned having some stuff to share with me."

"Yeah, I do. I don't know what your schedule is like. I'm going away for the weekend, but—"

"I know this is short notice, but are you in the city tonight? I met a friend down here, and I thought—"

While we talk, Wren runs to the kitchen and brings me back a glass of water, which I gladly accept since

I've developed an acute case of cottonmouth. I almost choke mid-sip. "Where are you? We could grab a coffee? Or maybe shots would be a better idea."

She chuckles again. "I'm in Midtown. Where are you?"

"I'm downtown." I look at my current attire. I'm wearing holey jogging pants and a stained T-shirt. "I can come to you."

"Or I could come to you," Hope offers.

"Do you want to come to my place? Would that be awkward? There's a restaurant in my building; we could get coffee or shots there since they serve both."

"It's only awkward if we make it awkward, right?"

I think I like her already. "Exactly. Want the address?"

"Fire away."

Once she has the address, we agree that she'll text when she's in the lobby.

I think I'm in shock as I end the call. "I'm going to meet my sister, and she seems pretty cool."

Wren steps between my thighs and settles her palms on my shoulders. "That's great, babe. I'm so glad she called."

"Me too." I jump up, nearly sending her toppling backward. I grab her waist to keep her from falling over. "I need to find something else to wear." I make sure Wren is steady before I release her, but pause to kiss her before I disappear inside the closet. "Should I wear a suit? I don't know what to wear."

Wren appears in the doorway. "It's not a job interview. You're meeting your sister; jeans and one of your fun shirts would be reasonable."

"Okay. Yeah. Good idea."

Wren helps me pick out jeans and a shirt because I'm incapable, quite literally.

I pass her a brush and let her style my hair because my hands are shaking. "This didn't feel real until right now. I have a sister, Wren, and I'm about to meet her. I want to like her, but part of me already resents her too."

She smooths her hands down the sides of my neck. "It's okay to feel conflicted, Lincoln. You can know it's not her fault that your dad was so absent from your life and still be upset with her."

"But she didn't do anything wrong, so how is that fair?"

"Emotions don't always take fairness into account, do they? I spent my teens and most of my early twenties blaming my mother for having an affair. I never took into consideration what pushed her to make that choice. Was it a bad one? Definitely, but if she hadn't made it, I wouldn't exist and my parents' marriage may have failed. I assumed my mother saw me as a mistake instead of her salvation."

"But I kept my dad and Jacqueline apart; I didn't bring them closer together."

"You aren't the reason they were kept apart, Linc. Besides, if Gwendolyn hadn't done the things she did, you wouldn't be here and then I wouldn't have you in my life."

"I wish it could've been different. I wish I could've known my dad. If he'd just told me, I wouldn't have spent my entire life thinking he was a bad father."

"I know. All the what-ifs are the hardest things to deal with, but I think in meeting Hope, you might get to know him, at least indirectly, and maybe you can stop being so angry at him."

"I just want some peace." I wrap my arms around her and pull her closer, breathing her in. "Will you come with me?"

"Why don't I wait with you in the lobby, but when she gets here, I'll come back up to the penthouse and you can message if you need me."

"Yeah. Okay. That would be good."

Wren waits with me, as promised, until Hope shows up.

She's wearing a pair of jeans and a long-sleeve shirt. I can see pieces of my father in her face, which means I can also see pieces of myself. It's pretty surreal.

"Hope?" I approach her, and she looks up from her phone, nervously worrying her lip.

A tentative smile curves the corner of her mouth. "Lincoln?"

"Yeah. Hey, hi." We both step in awkwardly. I'm unsure if I should shake her hand, or hug her, or what.

We laugh at the same time, so I pull her into a hug, because she's my sister and she seems a hell of a lot cooler than the stupid asshole brother I grew up with.

"Thanks for going out of your way to come here." We take a seat in a private corner of the restaurant, and embarrassingly enough the servers address me as Mr. Moorehead.

"This place is pretty swanky," Hope observes. "You live here?"

"I'm staying at my cousin's right now, but it's in this building. They own it. The building, I mean. I'm planning to buy here soon, though. One of the penthouses is supposed to be available in a month or so." I'm nervous and rambling.

"Pretty convenient to have restaurant right inside your building."

We fall into a brief awkward silence, which is broken, thankfully, when the server brings us our drinks. I went with scotch and Hope ordered the same.

"You really look a lot like Dad." She drops her head. "I mean, Fred. You look so much like him."

"You called him Dad?"

She gives me a tentative smile. "Our relationship was unconventional, but he was very much my father, even if he wasn't fully present in my life."

"Can you tell me about him? About your version of him. I get the sense I didn't really know him very well."

She tips her head. "But you grew up with him."

I fill her in on my childhood, on my father's absence from the family, his long working hours, my years spent in boarding school, and then college out of state, and my job abroad until recently.

Hope's expression turns sad. "I'm so sorry. I feel like this is my fault, like I took him away from you, and you never got to know all the really great parts of him. He was fun to be around. We went on a lot of trips together, mostly vacations to secluded cabins and places out of state where we wouldn't be seen by a lot of people, I guess. As a kid, I didn't understand why he never flew with me and my mom, but as I got older, it started to make more sense. I mean, as much sense as it could."

It's difficult to swallow past the lump in my throat. "You went on family vacations?"

She looks almost guilty as she nods. "Did you?"

"I skipped out on things like that. My brother, *our* brother"—I motion between us—"is an asshole and difficult to deal with."

She spins her glass between her palms. "I've seen the stuff in the news. I wasn't sure how much of that was real or fabricated to create drama."

"He's really that much of an asshole."

She nods. "Dad seemed to worry about him a lot."

"He talked about us with you?"

"Not when I was young, but when I was older and I understood better the dynamics of his relationship with my mother, he did. They seemed so in love with each other. It was hard to see my mother so upset every time he went back to you guys, and there was a lot of resentment on my part. But as I got older, we talked about it, how complex it was. He thought the world of you."

"He said that?"

"He was so proud. I was jealous of you a lot." She ducks her head, maybe embarrassed.

"I can understand that, from your point of view, anyway. There wasn't much to be jealous of. There wasn't any love between my parents, but I'm sure from the outside it looked a lot different."

"He tried to be a good man and do the right thing. I think he was caught between two hard places with no way to make either work," Hope says.

We talk until the restaurant closes and move to the bar. Hope runs a small not-for-profit organization that helps provide food and shelter for the local homeless. I tell her all about my sustainable community projects, which she already knew about from discussions with our father.

I discover we like the same sports teams and have similar taste in music. She and our dad even learned how to play guitar together. The more I talk to her, the more I realize the man I thought he was is not the version Hope had. It's painful to realize I missed the opportunity to understand him, but at least I'm getting a chance to know my sister and a side of him I wouldn't have known otherwise.

"Hey, I know this is probably a lot, but, uh, there's some stuff in Fred"—I clear my throat—"Dad's will that sort of involves you, and I figured I should tell you about it." I'm on my third scotch, and Hope is on her second. I'm buzzed enough to think this is a good time for this conversation. After everything went down with Gwendolyn, G-mom and I hired a private lawyer to review the will and discovered an interesting clause that could change the entire division of assets.

"What kind of stuff?"

"So the shares in the company are allocated a bunch of ways. My g-mom"—at her confused expression, I elaborate—"our grandmother has twenty-five percent. My mother had ten percent, but I bought her out. You'll love G-mom, by the way, she's badass."

"You call your grandmother G-mom?"

"We're pretty tight; she lets me get away with it. Anyway, ten percent of the shares are divided among the employees and the remaining fifty-five percent were divided between me and my brother equally. But there's a caveat in the will that stipulates all blood offspring have equal shares in the company and that would include you. Which means a little more than eighteen percent of Moorehead Media is yours, if you want it."

CHAPTER 27

MOOREHEAD LEGACY REVISED

WREN

It's amazing how goals and dreams can change in the blink of an eye. Okay, maybe it takes more than a blink. Maybe the impetus for change starts out as a scowly, grumpy, burly mountain man who transforms into a chin-dimpled, equally grumpy but incredibly devoted, amazing CEO of a company that was on a crash-and-burn trajectory less than six months ago.

Said CEO currently has me pressed up against his office door, wearing my favorite angry scowl. As much as I'd like to suck on that pouty bottom lip, we have a lot to do today, including a meeting that starts in less than fifteen minutes.

"I thought we talked about the lipstick," he growls.

If looks could kill, my lipstick would go up in flames. Also, it's absolutely ridiculous that he's referencing a conversation that happened months ago. I've never really understood why he hates it so much, other than he finds it distracting. "Correction." I slide a hand up his chest. "*You* talked about it."

"You agreed not to wear it anymore."

I scoff. "Right before we were about to have sex. Everyone knows that doesn't count."

His brows pull together. God, he's sexy when he's pissed off. But we really don't have time for an argument over my lipstick. In the months since discovering he has a half sister, Lincoln has fully embraced his role as CEO, and three months ago, he convinced Hope to come on board and help run the company with him. He also managed to persuade me to stay on as an independent consultant for their brand-new sustainable community outreach foundation. I still volunteer with my mother, but I've discovered a passion for this kind of work, where we get to help an entire community thrive. It's been hectic and amazing and exhausting. But I'm in love with this job and this man, so I can deal with any and all the bumps along the road. Even the kind that come in a sexy, glaring package.

His nostrils flare, and he dips down, surprising me when he captures my mouth. He pushes his tongue between my lips, stroking aggressively in a punishing kiss. He cups my chin, fingertips digging gently into my jaw, keeping me in place.

His thigh finds its way between my knees, and he punctuates every stroke of his tongue with a roll of his hips. I grab his shoulders, intent on reminding him of our meeting that starts very soon, but he tears his mouth from mine.

His eyes flare. "Holy shit."

I roll my eyes and smirk. I'm sure it looks maniacal, considering the mess he's made. "Seems like you got yourself worked up about nothing."

He rubs at his mouth with the back of his hand, and it comes away streaked with pinkish red. He releases my chin and pats his pockets, searching for a tissue. "Why didn't you warn me?" he grumbles.

"Because I didn't expect you to attack me with your mouth."

"Lie. Why would you wear red lipstick if you weren't trying to wind me up?" He abandons the mission to find a tissue and drops his mouth to mine again. I figure I can indulge him for a few more seconds before I push on his chest.

Which is the exact moment the door to his office opens. The knob hits my ass, and I stumble into Lincoln.

"Hey, are you—" Hope stops in the middle of the doorway, her expression shifting from confusion to annoyance. She plants a fist on her hip. "Seriously? You two live together! Can you not keep your mouths to yourselves for two hours? You look like a pair of demented clowns."

"I thought it was the lipstick that didn't come off." Lincoln goes back to searching for a tissue.

"He just attacked me." I manage to say it without laughing, which is pretty much a miracle.

Hope rolls her eyes. "Please. You could teach self-defense classes. That's the worst excuse ever. We have a board meeting in ten minutes, and I'm a little freaked out over here because you're leaving me in charge for two damn weeks. It'd be great if there was less pre-meeting making out and more sibling support happening here." She makes a face. "Wait. That sounds incredibly wrong. Can you clean up your mess of a face and talk me off the ledge, please?"

Lincoln rounds his desk and finds a couple of wet wipes. He tosses one to me and tears the other one open. "I don't understand what you're so worried about. G-mom is going to be here, and you've got a handle on things." He wipes his mouth and checks out the pink-streaked cloth. He looks to me. "Am I good yet?"

"Give it a couple more swipes and you should fine. What about me?"

"Same." He gives his sister his attention again. "Honestly, Hope, you're going to be fine. We're only a phone call or an email away if you need us. You have the emergency numbers in case our reception is bad, and most importantly, Armstrong actually listens to you and is semi-productive when you're around, so unless you parade a bunch of bikini-clad college girls through the office, you're in good shape."

Hope purses her lips and plants her fists back on her hips. I really like her, a lot. She and Lincoln are so much alike, it's uncanny, from their mannerisms, to their personalities, to their odd little quirks. "You know how unhelpful it is to make comments like that, especially when Armstrong's around to hear you. It feeds the behavior."

Lincoln taps his lips with his fingers. "Sorry. I'm trying. Old habits die hard."

"I know they do, but he's been great the past few weeks, so if you can make it through this meeting without goading him, I think the next two weeks will be that much smoother for me."

"Noted. I will not goad our brother during the meeting. But understand that I'm only doing this for you, because you asked."

"I'll accept that. For now. However, when you're back from your trip to Honduras, I've set up a dinner for the three of us, so we can spend some quality time together and commemorate Dad and the fact that we're all working together." She turns to me and smiles apologetically. "I hope you're okay with that."

I grin widely. "I'm perfectly okay with that, and I think it's a great idea."

Lincoln shoots me a glare, which he quickly schools when Hope beams at him. "Fantastic! It'll be a great bonding experience for the three of us."

I'm not sure exactly what Hope is looking to accomplish, but I think it's commendable that she's trying so hard with both of them.

At first, Armstrong was his usual asshole self when Hope came on board, but she took him aside and had some kind of closed-door discussion, and after that things changed. He's still a jerk a lot of the time, but with Hope, he's different. It's almost like an empathy switch has been flipped. It shorts out frequently, but it's clear he's trying to be less like his normal, awful self most of the time. At least with her. And that's progress no one else has made.

The meeting goes smoothly, with both Lincoln and Armstrong on their best behavior. Penelope and Hope have a way of forcing that out of them. It's mostly an overview of what's happening while Lincoln and I are in Honduras to initiate a new sustainable community outreach project.

In the months since Hope has joined the team, Moorehead has branched out and shifted gears. The focus has moved to real-world issues and stories that make a difference. The boost in ratings and profits are a testament to Lincoln's vision and dedication, but more than that, it's a legacy he can be proud of.

It's enthralling to watch Hope handle her brothers and their very different take on things. "While you're out there, can you look into what they need in terms of medical? I'd like a feature on that in the coming months. I think it fits well with the hospital fundraiser this fall."

"I wonder if we should look at the more obscure charities rather than just going with the most common," I suggest.

Hope points her pen at me. "I was thinking the exact same thing. Armstrong could organize a golf tournament before the end of the summer as a precursor. If that's something you would be interested in working on with me." Hope flashes a wide smile at her brother.

Armstrong blinks a few times and runs his hand over his tie. "We would work on it together?"

"If you'd like, sure. I mean, I'm sure you can handle it on your own, but it would be good experience for me, don't you think?"

His eyes flare with something like surprise, and a smile that doesn't look at all like a leer appears on his face. "Yes. Of course. It would definitely be good experience for you. I could work with you on it."

"Great. Well, that's settled, then." She looks around the table, and I, much like everyone else, try not to appear completely shocked by how easy that was or Armstrong's complete lack of bitching.

"I think we have some solid new initiatives to keep us busy while you two are in Honduras. Speaking of." She taps her phone until the screen flashes and gives Lincoln a syrupy smile. "You two have a plane to catch. Try not to hump each other in the bathroom."

Lincoln smirks. "Plane bathrooms are disgusting. That's what the ride to the airport is for."

"Linc!" I elbow him in the side. Over the months, there have been a number of occasions when the back seat of the car has functioned as a makeshift bed, especially when there's traffic. But Penelope doesn't need to know that.

He gives me a blank look. "What?"

"That's not funny." I kick him in the ankle and avert my gaze across the table, but he doesn't take the hint.

His lascivious grin grows wider. "Who says I'm joking?"

Penelope clears her throat. "I hope you're not using the company vehicles for purposes other than transportation."

Lincoln finally realizes he's been talking about screwing me in a car in front of his damn grandmother. "Absolutely not, G-mom. Totally talking smack."

"And embarrassing Wren. You're lucky she puts up with you."

"This is very true. I'm grateful that she tolerates my BS on a daily basis and hasn't threatened to laser my face in at least a week."

G-mom winks at me and pushes away from the conference table. "I have an appointment with my personal trainer, so I'm going to say my goodbyes now."

G-mom hugs me first and then Lincoln, whispering something that makes the tips of his ears turn red.

Once we're in the car on the way to the airport, I ask him what she said. He hits the button for the divider, cutting off our view of the driver.

"She told me I'm not the first person to christen the back of the company cars."

"Oh my God." My face heats with fresh embarrassment.

"She also said there was a reason the seats were leather."

I bark out a laugh that turns into a squeal when Lincoln

slams his thumb down on the release and does the same with his own seat belt.

"We have a six-hour flight ahead of us and likely a few days without running water or a shower, so I'm taking full advantage of the leather seats."

THIS BEAUTIFUL BEGINNING

WREN

Eight months later

I'm so hot. So, so hot and sweaty and very much on the verge of an orgasm. I grip Lincoln's hair with one hand and brace the other on the wall behind me. The one good thing about sleeping on a mattress on the floor is that nothing squeaks, except me when Lincoln uses his teeth.

He pauses on his quest to make me come to shush me.

"Don't bite me if you don't want me to make noise," I whisper and tug his hair.

So he bites me again, of course.

One of the hands currently gripping my ass relocates, and he presses his palm over my mouth to stifle my exuberance as he resumes his tongue torture. I bite his palm as I come—it's only fair considering all the biting he's been doing.

I'm barely cresting the orgasm when Lincoln stretches out over me, fits himself between my legs and pushes inside with a low groan.

"Shh," I half moan and pinch his ass.

He retaliates by biting my neck.

It's approaching six in the morning, the sun is barely cresting the horizon, but a dog barks somewhere close by, signaling the start of the day.

The sound of people milling around outside filters through the curtained, pane-less windows as Lincoln moves over me, pumping slow and steady, our panted breaths and occasional whispered admonishments and taunts the only sounds we make.

I want him to go faster, harder, but it's too quiet still, and sound carries here. Unless we want the entire crew and the lovely, sweet local volunteers to know exactly how much sex we have, we have to keep it quiet. And we have a lot of sex.

Thank God the fresh water well was the first thing we dug when arrived several weeks ago.

Somewhere close by a low buzz and ding starts up, it's a foreign sound here since reception is infrequent and spotty at best. Also, I'm orgasm high and looking for another hit, so I'm inclined to ignore it. Except Lincoln isn't as single-minded.

He pushes up on his forearms, brow furrowing. "What is that?"

"Dunno." I shift my hips to bring his attention back to more important things, like giving me another orgasm.

The buzz-ding happens again, and Lincoln's eyes flare. "Is that my phone?" He leans over to the nightstand and snatches it up. "Shit. It's Hope. I have to answer this."

He flips us over so I'm on top. I make a move to get off him, a little annoyed at the interruption, even though I understand the need to answer the call.

Lincoln grabs my hip. "Stay where you are."

"You can't answer a call from your sister while you're still inside me. That's wrong."

"It's not like she's going to know. Just hang on."

He answers the call on what I assume is speaker-phone, maintaining his hold on my hip to keep me in place. "Hey, sis, everything okay?"

"Hey! I wasn't sure if I'd get a hold of you or not. Sorry I'm calling so early on you, but I wanted to run something by you."

Usually we can only get reception when we're in the orphanage, and even there, it's not always reliable. Linc has daily chats with Hope, since she's back in NYC, keeping things running smoothly at Moorehead. Aside from Armstrong and his occasional douchebaggery, that is.

Hope has been extremely patient with him, and they seem to be developing some kind of oddly workable sib-ling relationship. He's still a pain in the ass, but he's less of one with her around.

"Sure, no problem, what's up?" Lincoln's voice is gravely.

"Are you sick? You look flushed. Wait, are you in bed? Oh my God! Why are you so sweaty?"

"Is that a FaceTime call?" I whisper.

"It's fine. I'm fine. It's hot here," Lincoln replies, half to me, half to Hope.

"Is that Wren? Where is she? Did you answer a call in the middle of sex? You know you can do that without the video component, you asshole!"

"I'm not in the middle of anything."

"You're such a liar! How many times have I knocked on your office door after you two have had one of your *private meetings*?" I can hear the italics in her voice at the last part. "I know your post-sex face, which is really disturbing, Linc. This is too much for a sister to handle. I'm hanging up."

"I thought you had a question?"

"It can wait. Finish servicing your fiancée and call me back. In the meantime, I'm going to call my therapist and bill you for the appointment."

"Sorry, Hope!" I call out.

"You could've tried to stop him!" She sounds more amused than angry. "I'm hanging up now!"

I slap Lincoln on the chest as he tosses the phone on the nightstand. "I can't believe you did that!"

"She's the one who FaceTimed me." He curves his hand around the back of my neck and pulls me down until our chests meet. Then he rolls us over, so he's back on top of me in a smooth, coordinated surge that makes every single one of his cut muscles flex.

My fiancé is hot as hell.

"Now, where were we?"

I clasp my hands behind his neck. "Trying to have some quiet sex, pretty sure your sister's shrieking has alerted everyone within a mile radius."

"Guess you don't need to be quiet anymore, do you?" He rolls his hips, hitting that spot inside that makes fireworks pop below the waist.

Lincoln's mouth covers mine, and his tongue sweeps inside in time to swallow up my soft moan. I wrap my arms and legs tightly around him, skin still slippery with sweat—his and mine. It doesn't take long to bring me back to the edge. My body shakes with the impending orgasm, and I fight against the urge to dig my nails into his back when the first waves hits.

Lincoln loves nothing more than wandering around

shirtless, showing off the crescent-shaped marks that last for hours afterwards.

He only disengages from the kiss when I stop shaking and then pushes up on his elbows, framing my face with his hands.

"I love you," he whispers against my lips.

"I love you." I hold onto his wrists as he pumps into me, watching his brows pull down as he gets closer to release.

"I'm going to come," he warns and pushes up, but I keep my legs wrapped tightly around his waist.

"In me."

"Wren." It's another warning. We ran out of·condoms a week ago, right after the supply run, and another isn't scheduled until next week. The condoms were less about contraception and meant more as a way to circumvent the potential mess. However, my pill prescription also lapsed last week, and I won't be able to get anymore until the next town run, or we get back to New York. We're only here for a few more weeks, then it's home for two months before we start another project.

On account of the aforementioned issues, Lincoln comes in one of two places—a tissue or my mouth. My mouth is obviously his preferred location.

He pushes up on his forearms, so he can look at me. His gaze is questioning, and under that inquisitive expression is tentative excitement. "You realize what you're asking for?"

I tip my chin to the side, where my tank lies discarded beside my head. "We can put that under me so the sheets aren't crunchy tonight."

He slows his movements. "Don't play with me right now, Wren. I'm right on the edge."

"I'm not playing." I stroke his cheek tenderly, pressing

my fingertip to the divot in his chin. "I want you to stay in me."

Lincoln rolls his hips. "I thought you said we'd have the baby talk after this project wrapped up."

I lift a shoulder. "It doesn't hurt to start trying now, does it?"

"I kind of planned to marry you before I knocked you up." Another grind of his hips, another low moan from me.

"We don't have to do it in any specific order, do we?"

"I guess not."

"Great, now stop talking and finish making love to me."

He drops his head, mouth covering mine, and we move with each other, a slow wave rolling in, building before it crashes down, pulling us both into the sweet, blissful undertow.

Afterward, he rolls us to the side and hitches my leg over his hip. "I can't believe you told me you want me to knock you up seconds before I was about to come. You can't say something like that; my brain isn't working properly when I'm in you like this."

"Better that you don't have a chance to overthink, don't you agree?"

He gives me a look. "If you get pregnant before the next project, we'll postpone it."

"Or we can send Hope. She's been dying to go." I run my fingers through his sweaty hair, pushing it off his forehead. "You're going to be the most amazing father."

"And you're going to be a kickass, sexy momma." He nuzzles my neck and then pulls back, expression suddenly serious. "You know, Wren, until you came along, I didn't think love like this was possible."

I smile up at him. "You just needed someone who could handle how amazing you are."

"You really are a miracle." He kisses me softly. "And I'm going to spend every day of our life together making sure you know that's the unequivocal truth."